Edited by:
Lura Lee Genz
Mia Manns
Rachel Weaver

Avenstar Productions
14717 Vine Street
Thornton, Co. 80602

verhab.12.11.13

ISBN: 978-0-9903314-0-7

www.markwaynemcginnis.com

HAB 12

A SCRAPYARD SHIP NOVEL

Written By

Mark Wayne McGinnis

Contents

Chapter 1

There were too many of them, and they were winning. At stake was not only the lives of the crew of *The Lilly*, but two others on board. The most important people in his life: Mollie, his eight-year-old daughter, and his ex-wife Nan.

He'd decided he'd rather destroy the ship than let the Craing take her. Now, perhaps, there was a glimmer of hope. In mere seconds, Jason went from reviewing *The Lilly*'s tediously slow self-destruct procedure to realizing he might yet find a way out of this mess. *The Lilly*'s systems had started to come back online. Slowly—not a second too soon.

Exhausted, Jason closed his eyes and massaged his eyelids. He blinked the ship's bridge back into focus. Crewmembers scurried from one station to another—necessary, given that they were undermanned and responsible for two or even three jobs. They were not out of the woods yet, but they had accomplished much. What was left of the Craing fleet, somewhere around two hundred and fifty warships, was now adrift in space. Even though their propulsion systems had been targeted, many of those vessels still had fully-functional weapons. Weapons that now bore down on *The Lilly*.

"Charging rail guns," Orion reported from tactical. "Both guns charged. AIs targeting and ... firing."

Jason felt the deck plates beneath his shoes begin to vibrate. *The Lilly*'s JIT rail munitions were being phase-shifted directly to each of the internal gun-ports. In a frenzied blur, both forward and aft gimbal-mounted guns acquired firing solutions. The meter-long projectiles—projectiles configured with unique antimatter characteristics—flared into space and devastated their targets with swift efficiency.

Craing warships had long dominated space—not because of their tactical or particularly advanced weaponry; their advantage lay in their shields. Typically the Craing decimated their adversaries—simply outlasted them. But even Craing warships were no match for the advanced weaponry of *The Lilly*. Jason and his bridge crew watched the display.

"Captain, Craing shields are failing," Orion, the ship's gunny, reported. "A Destroyer off our bow, and the two battle cruisers aft ... all three have hull breeches." The display went white with three consecutive flashes. Nothing remained of the enemy ships.

One by one, the Craing fleet was being ripped apart. But the question remained: was it happening fast enough?

"Multiple contacts, Captain!"

Jason spied smaller icons now filling the empty spaces between the Craing warships.

"Craing fighters, hundreds of them!" the gunny announced.

The XO, rushing back and forth between several stations, looked up and said, "They're all drones, sir. No live pilots."

"Gunny, deploy plasma cannons," Jason commanded.

The Lilly's AI spoke up for herself. "Captain, our four plasma cannons deployed as soon as that system came back online, and they are now targeting the enemy fighters."

Again, all eyes went to the display where vectors of crisscrossing yellow and blue firing solutions were constantly updating.

"Captain, The *Trickster* and The *Last Chance* have been engaged—both warships and fighters are concentrating their weapons, sir."

"Move to intercept—"

Only moments ago the four Craing battle cruisers had joined

the fight. Days before, Jason and his assault teams had boarded these same ships in Earth's higher orbit. Now, The *Trickster*, The *Last Chance*, The *Surprise* and The *Gordita* were the bulk of the newly formed Earth Outpost Allied fleet. Manned by inexperienced outpost personnel, the skeleton crews could barely maneuver these massive warships—let alone go into battle.

"The *Last Chance*'s shields are down to twenty ... now ten percent ... Their shields just went down, sir," Perkins said.

"Put us right in front of her—move!" Jason barked.

"Hull breech on The *Last Chance* ... casualties reported," Perkins yelled from comms.

"Tell them to get out of there—head back to Earth."

"They're trying, sir, but their drives are being targeted," Perkins replied.

The forward display segment zoomed in on The *Last Chance*. Multiple Craing warships, as well as numerous fighters, had concentrated their combined energy weapons on her. Within seconds, white flashes appeared and The *Last Chance* blew apart—first breaking into several large sections, then into smaller ones. The Craing fighters continued their onslaught. Anything larger than a few meters in diameter was targeted and destroyed. The Craing quickly shifted their combined arsenal onto The *Trickster*. Maybe it was because so many crewmembers had lost their lives, including those who'd fought to rescue these two ships away from the Craing in the first place, or maybe because Mollie had named them, but the flood of emotion Jason was experiencing was unexpected and debilitating. Forcefully clearing his mind, Jason brought his attention back to the present.

"Lilly, target the closest Craing vessels to The *Trickster*," Jason ordered.

The *Trickster* moved to escape, but the Craing fighters stayed in close pursuit. Jason watched the display. She was already in trouble.

"Her shields just went down, sir."

As with The *Last Chance*, the display flashed white as *The Trickster* blew apart. The Craing fighters relentlessly targeted the remaining remnants of the ship.

"Status, XO?" Jason asked.

"Both The *Last Chance* and The *Trickster* have been destroyed, no survivors. *The Lilly* has destroyed one hundred fifty enemy drone fighters, along with seventy-six Craing warships. Our own shields are down to sixty-eight percent and falling fast, sir," Lieutenant Commander Perkins reported. "Both The *Surprise* and *The Gordita* are now coming under attack," he continued.

"XO, get our own fighters out there," Jason commanded. He figured it was just a matter of time before both The *Surprise* and The *Gordita* would be lost as well, but he had to do something. "Helm, do we have phase-shift capability back online yet?"

Ensign McBride checked his console. "Just now. Yes, sir. All systems are operational—though shields are down to fifty percent."

Jason had come to rely on the phase-shift capability of *The Lilly*. A capability that allowed the ship to instantly move anywhere, even through solid matter, but it had its limitations as well—chiefly, a phase-shift radius of less than three miles.

Jason activated his NanoCom to his SEAL buddy, Billy Hernandez.

"Go for Billy, Cap."

"You and your team suited up?"

"Just need to put our helmets on. What's up?"

Jason was watching the display as he spoke. An odd-shaped cube, the Dreadnaught was measured in miles. A devastatingly powerful warship, but more importantly, the fleet's command ship. Taking that ship had been costly. Eventually, their emperor found his demise at the business end of a rhino warrior's hammer. Jason chastised himself; still on board were the Craing high priests—including High Priest Lom. Ruthless and powerful, Jason realized it had been a monumental mistake to leave any of them alive. No doubt, Lom had taken charge. Hell, he may have wielded more power than the emperor himself.

"Billy, get down to the flight deck—I want you and your men back on that Dreadnaught. Bring back Lom and the rest of the priests."

"Seems like a Hail Mary, Cap."

"Right now, it's all we got."

"Captain, our fighters are directly engaging the Craing fighters. We're outnumbered fifty to one, sir," the XO reported.

"Tell our pilots to either phase-shift back to *The Lilly* or into Craing holds as necessary."

"Shuttle #2 is on the Dreadnaught," both Orion and Perkins reported simultaneously. That was Billy's team — they had phase-shifted into the Dreadnaught, just as planned.

Jason answered an incoming hail. "Go for Cap—what's your status, Billy?"

"We're at the drop zone. Looks like the Craing have already taken back control of the Dreadnaught," Billy replied from the shuttle.

"Damn!" Jason shouted, losing his cool. What he needed was real-time visuals. He looked up to see Ricket staring back at him. It was uncanny how he tended to show up like that— always at just the right moment. He was originally Craing. Three and a half feet tall, and a strange amalgamation of mechanical and biotic alien body, *The Lilly's* Science Officer patiently stood there. Jason pointed to the display. "Can you display Billy's and his team's helmet-cam feeds?"

Ricket simply nodded.

Within seconds, the wrap-around display segmented into six new helmet-cam views. Billy and his team were on board the huge Craing Dreadnaught, and each one was staring in the same direction. Jason recognized the familiar surroundings; a smoky haze hung stagnant in the air. The shuttle had set down on the concourse in front of the Grand Sacellum—the Craing's religious center and home to their high priests. Jason sat forward and frowned.

"Billy, what's that approaching in the distance?" he asked.

Even before Billy replied, Jason knew.

"Security hover drones, Cap," Billy replied. "Hundreds of them headed our way from both directions. Craing bridge must have reactivated them."

Jason had come up against these drones before. They were white, cylindrical in shape and about three feet in length. Not only could they hover and spin in any direction, they could target and fire from their two separate mini-pulse cannons simultaneously, making it nearly impossible to get a clear shot.

"Captain, there's no way—"

"Hold on, Billy; I have an idea." Jason hailed the Pacesetter fighter pilot.

"Go for Wilson."

"Need you to phase-shift your Pacesetter to the main inside corridor of that Dreadnaught."

"I'm on it, sir." An instant later, the Pacesetter's icon disappeared from the overall battle logistics feed. A new segment displayed the Pacesetter's POV within the Dreadnaught's massive main corridor. Over one hundred security hover drones were approaching ahead. The screen blurred as the Pacesetter rapidly accelerated to intersect. Jason felt a momentary pang of envy, wishing he were at the stick himself. Energy pulses erupted from the oncoming security drones. A moment later the Pacesetter's forward plasma cannon deployed, with a significantly more powerful barrage of plasma fire of its own. The security hover drones had little in the way of shielding and, one by one, were quickly turned to smoldering slag—falling to the Dreadnaught's deck plating below. The Pacesetter did a quick end-over maneuver to intersect with the secondary group of drones coming from the other end of the corridor. It seemed Wilson had the security drones well in hand, so Jason brought his attention back to Billy and his men. With the arrival of the Pacesetter, Billy and his team of SEALs were free to complete their own mission.

"Ricket, best you head on down to the flight deck to be ready. You know what to do?" Jason asked.

"Yes, I believe so, Captain," Ricket replied, hesitating a few seconds before he left the bridge.

Billy's team was now inside the main room of the Grand Sacellum. Just hours before, the room had been in a disarrayed mess: tables, chairs, and grilling caldrons strewn about the floor. Now everything was back in place, as if nothing had happened. Fires blazed again in vessels at the center of each table. Billy and his SEAL team quickly made their way from the rear of the room to the small stairway that led to the upper levels. The assault team moved up the winding staircase towards the third floor.

"Captain, both *The Gordita* and *The Surprise* have left the fight—both have taken heavy damage, and they're attempting to limp back to Earth. Fighters are taking a beating. One has shifted back to *The Lilly*. Repair drones are standing by," Perkins reported.

"Captain, our shields are down to thirty percent," Orion piped in, now clearly concerned.

Putting his attention back on the display feeds and the assault team, Jason saw they had entered the third floor vestibule and were heading for the congressional prayer room.

Move it, guys, we're running out of time here, Jason said to himself.

"Cap, looks like there's a barricade. It's some kind of rock or marble. This could take a while," Billy said apologetically.

"We don't have a while—"

"Wait a minute, Ricket just sent me the access code—hold on."

Jason watched as one of the SEALs entered something at the access node off to the right of the entrance. He must have entered the keys incorrectly; he shook his head and started over. Jason caught himself holding his breath. The barricade silently slid open. The assault team rushed in.

Once inside, it took a moment for their helmet cam optics to adjust. Tall, thick candles flickered in the dimly lit room. Here again, the room had been transformed. All furnishings had been removed, with the exception of what appeared to be a marble platform of sorts. The familiar six high priests, in long silk robes and peculiar cone-shaped headdresses, knelt around the platform in prayer. The top of the platform held the remains of their late Emperor Quorp.

Jason wondered how Billy was going to handle the situation. He watched as the SEAL team took up posts around the room while Billy approached the platform. The first to rise was High Priest Overlord Lom.

"How dare you interrupt our sacred solicitation," Priest Lom said, angry contempt in his voice.

Without any preamble, Billy simply scooped up Emperor Quorp's remains, threw the lifeless body over his shoulder, and headed back out of the room. Jason held back a chuckle.

Well, that's one way to do it, he thought. Billy quickly moved back into the vestibule and down the stairs. No one left the room empty handed. Each SEAL team member snatched up one of the high priests, who kicked and fought them every step of the way. Within minutes, they were all secured in the shuttle and had shifted back to *The Lilly's* flight deck. Jason arrived as the shuttle's rear gangway door lowered to the deck. Standing at the rear of the shuttle were Billy and the other SEALs—each still wrestling with a Craing high priest. Jason took a breath, realizing he needed to play things just right. High Priest Lom was the first to notice him and stopped fighting. The others followed suit.

"How dare you treat us like this? Your death will be slow and painful."

Jason simply nodded. He was being hailed. "Go for Captain."

Orion's voice was strained. "Captain, our shields are down to ten percent. All but one of our fighters have returned. The Pacesetter is back in open space, but her shields are failing as well."

"Thank you, Gunny. Have Wilson phase-shift out of there." Jason brought his attention back to High Priest Lom.

"I don't have a second to waste here. To prove that, I'm going to make my point. One of you will die within the next twenty seconds. It will be up to you to decide who."

Slowly and deliberately, Jason removed his sidearm. The barrel of his energy pistol moved across the group at head level. Jason looked into each high priest's eyes. He saw their fear. They believed his threat. "Five seconds, who will it be?" Jason calmly asked.

The priests looked to one another, then back at Jason. "There is no need to kill any one of us, Captain," Lom said, a slight quiver in his voice. "You are truly barbaric, but we will do as you ask."

"Fine. You will instruct your people, your fleet commanders—that Emperor Quorp is dead. Everyone is to follow the wishes of Emperor Reechet." Jason continued to point his weapon directly toward Lom's head.

"Yes, yes ... agreed—we all agree! Put away your weapon," Lom pleaded, and nodded in the direction of the others to also obey.

Jason moved quickly. First, he grabbed one of the priests by the elbow, separating him from the group.

"Take off your robe and hand it to Emperor Reechet," Jason commanded. The priest stood immobile, an incredulous expression on his face. "Come on, move it or I'll strip you down myself." The priest looked to the others for help, but received only blank stares in return. Reluctantly, he removed his robe and headdress and placed them in Ricket's outstretched arms, leaving the priest looking most uncomfortable standing solely in what was not significantly different from a woman's long slip. Jason helped Ricket into the robe and swapped his baseball cap for the new headdress. He then took the lifeless body of Emperor Quorp and placed it unceremoniously on the floor in a seated position. Ricket stood to the side of the emperor's body.

"Lilly, please record visuals and audio of Ricket standing alongside Emperor Quorp's body. Ensure this is broadcasted to the bridge of every Craing vessel," Jason emphasized.

"Recording has begun, sir," the AI replied.

Ricket, standing in his newly-adorned robe, looked more regal than Jason had thought possible. He started talking immediately. "I am Emperor Reechet. Once again, I am your sole Emperor. Quorp has passed and stands among the other fallen emperors and is now one with our noble ancestry. Now look upon the body of Emperor Quorp and see for yourselves, he is no longer of this world. Look upon the faces of your high priest overlords." On cue, the high priests filed in around Ricket and stood at the bulkhead. With their heads bowed, each in turn looked up and nodded his head. "You, those of the Craing fleet, I order you to stop this battle. Stop fighting now and prepare your ships to be boarded. And pray you are not the one to be selected for the caldrons—*to be consumed by your conquerors.*"

Jason subsequently received two hails in quick succession. He addressed them one at a time.

"What do you have for me, Gunny?"

"They've stopped, Captain," Orion said, astounded. "The Craing fleet—all of their warships—they've all stopped firing!"

"Go ahead, XO"

"Captain, the fleet is surrendering. We're being hailed by each of the Craing warships. They want to know Emperor Reechet's wishes."

"Instruct them all to drop their shields and prepare to be boarded," Jason replied. He took a long breath and let it out slowly. Although done unconventionally, the battle had been won.

Chapter 2

Three weeks later.

"No, not that one—how many times do I have to tell you? The 9/16th. What am I supposed to do with a ½ inch?"

Jason, biting his tongue, fingered through old Gus' ancient metal toolbox until he found what he was looking for. He handed his father the 9/16th socket. His father, Admiral Perry Reynolds, took the socket, snapped it onto the wrench and was back, elbows deep, into the Ford's flat head V8.

Jason went back up to the porch and sat down. "Dad, I thought you were going to spend some time relaxing. You'd think after fifteen years of fighting the Craing, there'd be something better you could do with your free time—something other than fighting with that clunker." Upon returning to San Bernardino, Jason watched as his father quickly immersed himself into rebuilding the 1949 F1 pickup truck. Obviously escaping. And why shouldn't he? A warrior had come home, yet he'd been defeated in battle. He was their leader and so many thousands had died. Would he find the answers he was looking for under the hood of that beat up old truck? Had he given up? Jason didn't know.

An early autumn breeze made its way into the scrapyard, making San Bernardino's hot climate almost bearable. Jason, feet up and a six-pack at his side, made a few more additions to his report before closing down his virtual tablet. *The Lilly* had returned a battered mess—barely able to make it back to Earth before shutting down completely. For three weeks Jason, a handful of repair drones, and what remained of the crew worked tirelessly to bring the vessel back to an operational level again. Jason had stayed in touch with the outpost, but being away for such an extended period of time created its own issues. Even though he'd felt comfortable with Admiral Cramer heading up the Earth Outpost for the United Planetary Alliance—the EOUPA—something was up. Communications had become sparse and incomplete. And that was another issue. Jason had been clear, Admiral Cramer would report back to him. But what now? His father, in actuality, was the true Allied Commanding Officer. Would his father even want that responsibility again?

Near the tool shed, more swearing erupted from under the truck's hood. From Jason's experience, no one could out-swear a sailor—and that went double for an admiral. He took another long slug of his beer and surveyed the yard. Added to the hundreds of junked automobiles, trucks, vans, and buses, and miscellaneous auto parts, was the newer addition of two stripped-down F-22 fighter jets. After three weeks, they too had begun to blend in—becoming one with the acres and acres of scrap metal.

Jason heard the familiar ping in his ear; his NanoCom had been activated. He was being hailed.

"Go ahead, XO."

"Captain, we're receiving FTL markers—a transmission from deep space to your attention."

"Give me ten minutes. Actually, make that fifteen," Jason replied, getting to his feet. He grabbed up the empty beer bottles and disappeared into the back of the house.

Ten minutes later, he'd showered, put on his officer's jumpsuit, and was halfway into the scrapyard. Walking along the concrete pathway, as he had every morning over the past few weeks, were the same, now faint, brown footprints. His own bloody footprints. He had been running barefoot the night everything changed—the night he chased what appeared to be a small man down this very path. Later he discovered it wasn't a small man, but the mechanical alien called Ricket. The same alien who later mistakenly shot and killed his eight-year-old daughter, Mollie. Inexplicably, Mollie was saved, brought back from the clutches of death. That same strange being, Ricket, had rushed them to an advanced alien spacecraft hundreds of feet below the same ground he now trod.

One of the first orders of business once Jason returned home was to modify access to the underground aquifer. The old red Caddy, cramped and just barely accessible to climb in and out of, had been removed. A bright yellow, albeit ancient, school bus now sat in its place.

Pressing a hidden button beneath the front right fender caused the bus door to swing open. Just like the old Caddy, the bus had been gutted and only served as an entryway to the lift system that took Jason down a hidden shaft to the dried-up aquifer hundreds of feet below.

Once below, and turning the last bend, the tunnel opened up into a massive cavern. There sat *The Lilly*, black and curvaceous— her gracefully sweeping aerodynamic lines never ceased to make Jason's heart skip a beat. He scurried up the gangway and disappeared into the stern of the spaceship.

"Captain on deck," announced Jason's arrival to the bridge by *The Lilly* AI. He moved directly to the command chair and sat down.

"What do we have, XO?" Jason asked.

"It's the Craing, sir. Actually, it's the Craing representative."

Jason knew who it was before Perkins replied.

"It's Brian, your brother. He's been awaiting your arrival."

Jason was still grappling with his mixed feelings, and even suspicions, towards his brother. Although claiming to have a wife and small child on a Craing controlled planet, with their safety constantly threatened, something didn't add up for Jason. He wasn't sure what Brian's true motivations were. Who was it he was actually working for within the Craing Empire?

"Go ahead and make the connection, XO," Jason said.

The forward section of the large wrap-around display came alive, and the face of Jason's brother filled the screen. "Hello, Jason. Good to see you again."

"Good to see you too, Brian. I see you're still doing the Craing's bidding."

"As I told you before, everything I do is for Earth as well."

Not wanting to get into another debate with his older brother, he let that pass and simply nodded his head with a less than sincere smile. "So how can I help you? I take it you received our package?" Jason queried him.

"Oh, you mean the return of a few Craing crewmembers?"

"That and fifty of their warships—more than a few. I thought that was quite generous on our part."

"Well, they would have preferred to have all five hundred of their ships returned and every last one of their crewmembers. The rest of the Craing crewmembers you're still holding will need to be returned. But yes, the gesture hasn't gone unnoticed. But that's not why I've been instructed to contact you."

"Let me guess. The Craing find themselves suddenly without an emperor—and it just so happens that Emperor Reechet still lives and breathes right here among the Alliance. Something along those lines, huh?" Jason asked with a smile.

"Make light of it all you want, but the Craing take few things as seriously as they do their aristocracy."

"Why can't they make someone like High Priest Overlord

Lom their next emperor? I bet he'd jump at the chance—"

Brian cut him off mid-sentence. "Go ahead and be smug, but this is quite serious. When you sent the remnants of the Craing fleet back to their home worlds, you inadvertently sparked a Craing uprising. Not only did they receive the mangled body of their late Emperor Quorp, they received news that Emperor Reechet still lives. And there has never been a time when—"

This time it was Jason's turn to interrupt: "—they have been without a living emperor. Yeah, yeah, I've heard it all before, and I don't give a rat's ass what upsets the Craing populace. They are a cowardly, murderous people," Jason replied, feeling his temper rise.

"Just let me finish because this is important, Jason."

"Well, go on, then—finish what you have to say."

"What if the Sol system, Earth, could be free from Craing hostilities—forever? All they ask is the return of their emperor."

"You can't be serious. Even if I was open to that, which I'm not—we're supposed to believe them? You do realize these are the same barbarians who make a habit of dining on human flesh. The same people who've terrorized hundreds of worlds of the Alliance, not to mention the rest of the universe. We're supposed to save ourselves while the rest of our allies continue fighting? No,

I'm not giving up Ricket, or anyone else. And tell your friends that their dynasty is quickly coming to an end."

"The resources of the Craing are almost incomprehensible. The few hundred ships you've absconded with are but a fraction of their total capacity."

"I don't care," Jason said, indignation rising.

"We're talking tens of thousands of warships. Do you really want a force of that magnitude barreling down on Earth? And there's something else: three ships discovered hundreds of years ago by the Craing—ships of a technology so advanced no one figured out how to power them on, let alone fly them. They've been stored beneath the ground, mothballed, collecting dust. Something's changed. The ships came alive. Suddenly became operational. They are in orbit around Terplin as we speak, and from the reports I've heard, their capabilities are nothing short of amazing. Capabilities that aren't dissimilar to that new ship of yours. With little doubt they're of the same technology, and I'm betting have the same Caldurian origins. Anyway, the Craing are learning to fly the things, even calling them the Emperor's Guard. My guess is they're coming for their emperor or to destroy that ship of yours—perhaps both. I'd be proactive here. Hand over that old robot and be done with it. Do it now.

"That's not going to happen," Jason said flatly.

"They will not hesitate to unleash a hell storm on Earth. I've seen them do it time and time again. This time it would be Earth that would be uninhabitable for a thousand years, maybe more. Their newly appointed high priests have given them eight days to learn how to fly these ships, get familiar with their weapons systems."

"Why don't they just send the rest of their fleet, a few more dreadnaughts?" Jason asked.

"They still don't understand how that ship of yours destroyed or incapacitated five hundred of their fleet ships. It's an embarrassment they don't want to repeat. No, better to send these three ships. Ships with comparable technology."

"You mentioned the high priests. So they're giving the orders now?" Jason asked.

Brian smirked. "High Priest Overlord Lom had always been in charge. Sure, the emperor is a living symbol to the people, but it's the high priests that make the decisions. And unlike the emperor, they can be replaced. What happened with that robot of yours acting as Emperor Reechet won't be allowed to happen again. Yes, they want to have him back, prop him up as a figurehead, but they certainly won't let their masses blindly follow him."

"It's not up for discussion," Jason repeated.

"You have eight days before those three ships, their new Emperor's Guard, leave Craing space. I'm going out on a limb here even telling you this."

"Careful, Brian. I certainly wouldn't want to get in the way of your cozy relationship with the Craing."

"This is bigger than just you and me, Jason. You need to bring this to the attention of the right people: Washington, other world governments. You need to prepare. Please make the right decision." The screen went black and the bridge went quiet.

"XO, what's the earliest *The Lilly* will be ready for flight?"

"Early tomorrow morning, Captain. Where to?"

"The Chihuahuan desert. The Alliance outpost."

* * *

Back up top, it was Jason's turn to make dinner—spaghetti and meatballs. Smoke filled the kitchen from the first batch of garlic bread scorching in the oven. As Jason ran around opening windows and flapping a dish towel, he thought about his father. Admiral Perry had become even quieter, more reclusive. In fact, Jason couldn't remember him saying more than three or four words in days. Jason had hoped that some downtime revisiting the scrapyard, his old stomping grounds, would provide Admiral Perry the necessary time to heal his inner conflict. But there was something else disturbing the admiral. Perhaps, in his view, he had failed the Alliance. On top of that, Jason was able to accomplish what his father could not: defeat the Craing in open space. But the admiral wasn't taking into account that it wasn't so much Jason's extraordinary skills as a commander as it was his taking advantage of the resources around him—namely *The Lilly*. Where the admiral had kept the ship hidden and protected, Jason had exploited its phenomenal resources.

As the smoke cleared, he opened the oven door and checked his second batch of bread. What his father didn't get was that the Alliance would soon fall apart without the admiral's strong presence. Fifteen years of work. One by one, Admiral Perry Reynolds had made planetary alliances across multiple sectors, committing even the most reclusive of planets to come together to unify against the Craing. What his father wasn't considering was that, without himself at the helm, the Alliance's chances of defeating the Craing were nil.

* * *

Their evening ritual was sitting on the porch, plates on laps, and a six-pack shared between them.

"Progress with the rebuild?" Jason asked, passing his father the basket of garlic bread and expecting a one or two word answer.

Admiral Reynolds took the basket and placed several pieces at the side of his plate. He thought for a moment and shrugged.

"Got it to turn over."

"Seriously? That's something," Jason commented.

"Timing's still shot to shit, but ... yeah."

"So, a few more days under the hood?"

"Need to scrounge a few more old parts from the yard. There's another old F1 pickup out there somewhere—think it's a '48er, though," his father replied.

Jason nodded and said, "Northeast corner of the yard. Look

for the old blue Econovan. You'll see it." Jason took another slurp of spaghetti before continuing: "I'm headed back to the outpost tomorrow. You okay here by yourself for a while?"

His father didn't answer right away. "Hmm ... I don't know. I mean, after sixty years of wiping my own ass, I might need your help."

"I just meant—"

"I know what you meant. Go. I'm fine."

Somewhere, not so far away, a dog barked—then two others barked back. A woman's voice yelled *"Dinner!"* farther off in the distance.

"I talked to Brian this morning," Jason said. He noticed his father looked up from his plate for the first time.

"What the hell did he have to say?"

"Just that Earth will be free of the Craing forever. All they want is their emperor back."

"Emperor being Ricket...?"

"Yep."

"Your mother, God rest her soul, must have been screwing the milkman, because there's no way I share the same DNA with that boy," his father said with a smirk and a shake of his head.

"He honestly believes in what he's doing," Jason replied, encouraged by his father's unexpected chattiness.

"He's thinking from a flawed perspective. He's thinking with his head up his own ass."

Jason thought about that for a moment and started to laugh. Then so did his father. They sat together laughing a little while longer as the sun dipped behind the San Bernardino foothills.

Chapter 3

Jason awoke early the next morning. He'd started sleeping in his childhood bedroom again and wondered why he had been so reluctant to do so. While it was still dark out, he stumbled his way to the hall bathroom and got the shower going. The old water heater had seen its best days, taking longer and longer each morning to come back alive. It would be easier to just stay on board *The Lilly*, but he wanted to provide Mollie with some semblance of a normal home life when she stayed with him. Both Mollie and his ex-wife Nan were returning from a prolonged trip to Washington later tonight. Part summer vacation for Mollie, part work for Nan. Reluctantly, she had agreed to become the legal envoy between the Earth Outpost for the United Planetary Alliance and various allied governments around the world, but mostly from Washington's directive.

As Jason stood beneath the now steady stream of hot water, he noticed several inches of water accumulating at his feet. *Terrific, roots!* They'd begun to invade the old pipes under the house years ago, but lately the problem had worsened. Just one more thing needing fixing around here. Maybe he should rebuild the house. He'd think about it when things got back to normal. If things got back to normal.

To Jason's surprise, his father, dressed in his admiral spacer's jumpsuit, was sitting at the kitchen table.

"Here, I made you a cup of coffee," his father said, sliding the still steaming cup across the table.

"Thanks." Jason, standing, took a long sip. Eyeing his father's uniform, he asked, "So, had enough of the old '49?"

"For now. It'll still be here after we crush the Craing."

21

"Yes, it will ... Hell, I may even help you with it."

* * *

All eyes were on them as Jason and the admiral entered the bridge together.

A bosun's whistle blew and The Lilly AI announced, "Captain on deck."

Jason took the command chair while Admiral Reynolds sat to his right and slightly behind him. Ensign McBride, XO Lieutenant Commander Perkins, and Ricket were seated at their stations and awaiting instructions. With the exception of engineering—Chief Horris and a skeleton crew scattered around the ship these past few weeks—everyone else had been deployed to the Alliance outpost to provide training and support for the newly acquired Craing ships. Jason, like his father, kept within close proximity to The Lilly. With their latest exploits in space and victories against the Craing fleet, word had gotten out.

Governments and militaries from virtually every nation, as well as the world's largest science and technology companies, were all applying what political juice they had to pressure Washington and the Alliance for more access to the newly acquired Craing fleet, but more so to The Lilly. That may well happen with the Craing fleet. But not The Lilly. It was obvious to Jason that no one nation could control this technology, especially the phase-shift capabilities, without causing a total imbalance. Even the Alliance outpost, which was a self-contained entity separate from any of the U.S. military branches, had become more and more politically inclined, and having several hundred Craing warships in its arsenal, it had quickly become the most powerful military force on the planet. Jason had insisted that Admiral Cramer break all ties to her Navy commission before being placed in charge of the outpost. But Jason knew she still had a lifetime of prior loyalties—loyalties that would be hard to ignore. For the most part he trusted her, but he wasn't stupid. Jason and his father agreed: *The Lilly* needed to be kept under wraps—hidden underground here in the aquifer or at other secret locations around the country.

"Status, XO?" Jason asked, pulling up his virtual tablet and reviewing the ship's daily systems report and crew roster.

"All systems are operational. Last of the hull repairs were completed yesterday. As requested, Ricket and I found another potential subterranean drop location."

"Dry? Big enough for *The Lilly's* wide keel?"

"All the above, sir."

"Distance from the outpost?" Jason asked.

"Just under three miles. Actually, closer to two," Perkins replied.

"That should work." Jason closed down his tablet and looked up towards the large wraparound display.

"One other thing, Captain. It may be a systems glitch, and Ricket is checking on that, but we've been out of NanoCom contact with any of *The Lilly's* crew since last night."

"I've been using my NanoCom all morning," Jason said, shrugging.

"The problem seems to be with those at the outpost or still in orbit. Their vitals are normal, we just can't communicate with them."

"Keep me appraised—I don't like being out of touch with our people."

"Aye, sir. There's something else."

"What is it?"

"The military, all branches, are on high alert. Something's up with the outpost."

"Let's find out. Secure the gangway and disconnect umbilicals. Helm, once you've determined that things are clear above—go ahead and phase-shift."

Within several moments, *The Lilly* was less than a hundred feet above the scrapyard. "Take us into the stratosphere, Ensign."

The scrapyard disappeared in a blur and *The Lilly* reached for the sky. Jason felt the internal dampeners engage as G-forces increased. He noticed the admiral had gotten to his feet, turned, and was watching as their home disappeared behind them. Bright blue skies transitioned to grey and then to the blackness of space. The ship leveled off for several moments and began its descent back towards Earth.

The familiar landscape of the Chihuahuan desert came into view. Jason had ordered McBride to approach the outpost from the east. At fifty miles out, they were skimming thirty feet above the desert floor. Jason wanted to keep their visit unannounced. Fortunately, unless you were looking right at her, *The Lilly* was virtually impossible to detect with any technology currently available on Earth, or anywhere else for that matter. The ship slowed and then came to a complete mid-air stop. Hovering two miles from the outpost, Perkins said, "We're right above the subterranean cavern, sir."

Ricket scurried over to another station, entered something on a keypad, and the wrap-around display changed to a virtual below the ground landscape.

"Captain, what you're looking at is a best-guess representation of what lies approximately one mile below us," Ricket explained. "The cavern walls are solid granite. The floor of the cavern isn't quite level, but we believe this area here to be no more than a three or four percent grade." Ricket pointed to an area of the cavern highlighted by a red circle.

"A mile down, solid granite." Jason stared at the display for several more moments. "How do we know this doesn't push the limits of *The Lilly*'s phase-shift capabilities? Hell, we could get marooned down there."

Ricket removed his LA Dodgers baseball cap and placed it onto the console. "If our calculations are correct, we have adequate leeway for three to four times that distance—even into solid rock."

Jason shook his head. "I don't like it. I'm not willing to risk ship and crew on a good guess. Don't forget how old Gus initially found *The Lilly*, partially buried underground fifteen years ago. Can you imagine? This would be a hell of a place to get stuck."

Admiral Reynolds shrugged. "Why don't you phase-shift one of the fighters down there first—check it out and shift back."

"I like it. Who do we have ..."

"Sorry, Captain, all of our fighter pilots are currently in orbit—training the new pilots," Perkins replied.

Jason looked concerned, but no one was buying his act. Jason's newly acquired love of flying the Pacesetter was no secret. "Well, I guess I'll just have to go myself."

* * *

Entering the flight deck, Jason was accosted by the stillness and utter silence. With the exception of several small maintenance drones, he was all alone. Two large shuttles sat idle at one end of the deck, while six sleek red fighters were secured and kept under wraps along the back bulkhead. Even before he'd settled into the cockpit of the Pacesetter fighter, Jason felt his heart rate start to increase. Like a kid with a new toy, Jason had a hard time keeping a silly grin off his face. He brought the fighter to life and maneuvered it onto the middle of the flight deck. Jason double-checked the phase-shift coordinates and ran through his standard pilot's checklist. He was ready. He hailed the bridge.

"Go for XO," Perkins replied.

"If I'm not back in fifteen minutes, or if you haven't heard from me—you can pretty much assume I'm stuck down there. It will be up to you to figure out how the hell to get me out."

"Aye, Captain. Rest assured, we'll be tracking your every move," Perkins replied.

With that, Jason phase-shifted the Pacesetter to the underground coordinates. He was surrounded by total and absolute blackness. It was only the soft amber glow of his HUD readout and dash backlighting that provided any semblance of connection to the living. *Where are the lights on this thing?* After several long moments of fumbling around in the dark, he had it. With the flick of one switch, the Pacesetter's running lights somewhat illuminated the darkness. *Better, but not great.* He found the other switch for the big forward spotlight. The cavern came alive. Reflected light bounced off pristine white granite walls. Minute flecks of mica and other reflective compounds twinkled like a million tiny stars. Spellbound by an ethereal world no man had ever witnessed, Jason sat quietly for a long time. Slowly, Jason brought the Pacesetter several meters off the ground and cruised the inner perimeter of the cavern. From what he could see, just as Ricket had indicated, the center of the cavern was the flattest and best location for *The Lilly*. He hailed Lieutenant Commander Perkins.

"Go for XO—I can hear you loud and clear, Cap," Perkins said.

"Good to know. I'll be ready to phase-shift back in a few moments—just checking in."

His HUD indicated breathable air here, although the temperature was a chilly 38 degrees. Coming to a narrower end of the underground space, there appeared to be an adjacent cavern, almost as large as this one—but someone would need to be on foot to access it. As far as he could ascertain, this cavern would work just fine. He set the return coordinates and entered the command to phase-shift.

Nothing. He rechecked his coordinates—double-checked them. He could feel beads of sweat forming on his brow. He tried it again ... Still nothing. Jason looked around at the pristine landscape. *This wouldn't be the worst place to end up.* He hailed Ricket.

"Go for Ricket."

"Ricket, I can't seem to phase-shift out of here. Am I doing something wrong?" Jason asked, hearing his own nervousness.

"You won't be able to phase-shift—"

Jason could not believe what he was hearing. "What do you mean I won't be able to phase-shift?"

"As I was saying, Captain, you won't be able to phase-shift for several more minutes. As you'll recall, the fighters with their limited power supplies need more time to recharge. You're coming up on the twelve-minute mark soon; try again then."

He watched the small digital mission-elapse timer on his HUD. He still had several more minutes. Looking at the surrounding terrain, something caught Jason's eye. Actually, two things caught his attention. First, even the small amount of light from the fighter's spotlight, which cast some illumination into the area ahead, showed the adjacent cavern looked nothing like the one he was in. The rock walls were not the same sparkling white granite. There seemed to be splashes of color on the walls. And second, Jason could swear there was something carved into the far elevation of the second space. Perfectly straight lines and ninety-degree angles do not typically form in nature. What he was peering at, he thought, were stairs hewn into the rock face.

Intrigued as he was, the cavern's exploration would have to wait. Once the full twelve minutes had elapsed, he tried again. It worked. He was back aboard *The Lilly*. Taking a deep breath, Jason guided the Pacesetter back to its mooring position next to the other fighters. Within a few moments, Jason headed off the flight deck.

Chapter 4

Entering the bridge, Jason walked into a flurry of activity.

"What's going on, XO?" Jason asked, looking up at the display and seeing multiple Allied Craing warships.

"We've got five Alliance Craing battle cruisers maintaining a slow perimeter around the outpost, sir. Multiple hails have been ignored. Totally unresponsive with the exception of a repeating message. They're providing *The Lilly* with heading and specific landing instructions."

Jason watched the distant warships and wondered who was manning them. He had his flight crews in orbit conducting training, but they wouldn't have been ready for this. *Perhaps the prisoners, the Craing crewmembers?* But he hadn't authorized their use, at least not here at the outpost.

"Captain, I believe the outpost has been compromised," the XO said, "Communications to the rest of the world has completely gone dark. There's definitely something going on."

* * *

Fifteen minutes later, Jason was back in the cockpit of the Pacesetter and skimming across the desert floor at close to three hundred miles an hour.

"For God's sake, why so fast? And why so close to the ground?" Admiral Reynolds asked from the second pilot's seat behind Jason's.

Just what I need, Jason thought, *a backseat driver*. "I want to come at the outpost from a completely different direction than from *The Lilly*'s underground position. Probably being overly cautious, but—"

"That doesn't explain your flying like a lunatic," the admiral shot back.

Jason didn't respond. Truth was, he was worried. Ultimately, the outpost was his responsibility—the outpost was his idea, he had set it up, and he had put Cramer in charge. Coming within a mile of the outpost, Jason pulled back on the stick to gain some elevation. If he hadn't known better, he'd think he had the wrong coordinates. The outpost he visited three weeks ago, with its ragtag collection of tents and hastily constructed structures, had been replaced by what looked like a sprawling, modern military compound. Multi-level buildings, three runways, several large hangars, ten Apache helicopters, and the remainder of the massive Allied Craing warship fleet, hundreds of them all lined up in perfect rows disappearing off in the distance well beyond the confines of the original base. Fifteen-foot fencing, topped with razor concertina wire, outlined the distant perimeter. Separate and to the east, also surrounded by fencing and more concertina wire, hundreds of small tents were clustered together. Commonly referred to as *Craing City,* they hadn't finished erecting this area three weeks ago. More like a prison, this is where the enemy crewmembers and overlords were being held. Jason took in the view of the outpost below. *Strange,* Jason thought. *No activity—not a soul in sight.* He wasn't going to get any answers hovering up here in the air. Jason looked for a suitable place to set down.

"Aren't you going to request permission to land?" the admiral asked.

"I've already left word with Admiral Cramer. Seems to be a real hotbed of activity down there—I think we can find a place to land," Jason replied sarcastically. Like *The Lilly,* the Pacesetter was undetectable to sensors, although visible to the naked eye. He scoped out the landscape ahead, entered new coordinates, and phase-shifted from a mile out. An instant later, the Pacesetter was stationary—thirty yards from the entrance into the compound's largest building.

* * *

They had been ready for them. Even before the cockpit canopy had time to fully open, assault teams were filing out from multiple buildings—easily one hundred men wearing dark grey uniforms and holding automatic weapons were surrounding the Pacesetter. Jason didn't recognize any of these men; they were definitely from another unit. Some had long hair. Others wore beards. Suddenly, the five Craing battle cruisers dropped from the sky in unison and held position at several hundred feet above the ground. New trainee pilots couldn't have made that maneuver.

"Shit, Jason—what the hell were you thinking?"

"Oh, come on, Dad ... It's good to be unpredictable sometimes. I'm sure it's fine." An alarm claxon started howling from all ends of the compound. "But to be safe, don't make any sudden movements," Jason said warily.

"You think?"

They both slowly emerged from the fighter, one following the other. Once down, they stood with their hands raised. No one spoke, no orders were issued. That's when Jason noticed the flag. Why would the stars and stripes be flying here—and something else. Something was different about the flag.

More armed, grey-uniformed soldiers emerged from the nearest building. It was her bright patch of red hair that caught Jason's attention. Admiral Malinda Cramer, an air of authority in her hurried gate, was leading a small armed contingent headed in their direction.

"She doesn't look happy."

"That's right. You haven't had the pleasure yet," Jason replied.

"I'm not sure if I should be intimidated or strangely aroused. That woman projects one hell of a presence," the admiral said.

Admiral Cramer halted ten feet in front of Jason and his father.

"Good morning, Admiral. I'd like to introduce you to—"

"Be quiet. Don't speak unless spoken to, Captain Reynolds," Admiral Cramer commanded. Her eyes flickered towards Admiral Reynolds and then back to Jason. "Where is *The Lilly*?"

"She's safe."

"Don't play games with me. I'm the last person you want to fuck around with right now."

"Actually, you'd be the last person I'd want to fuck around with—ever, Admiral. Are you sure you want to play things this way?" Jason replied, his own temper rising. "Have you forgotten to whom you report, Admiral?"

Steely-eyed, she looked at him for a long moment before she signaled her team. "Lock them up." As quickly as she'd arrived, she was strutting back in the direction she had come.

"Just so you know ... Seven days, Admiral," Jason yelled after her. She slowed but didn't stop.

"Three highly-advanced warships. They make up the new Emperor's Guard. They'll be here in seven days," Jason shouted, wincing as *PlastiCuffs* were tightly secured around his wrists. He felt a pang of guilt seeing his father, also secured, needlessly shoved towards a row of buildings off to their left. He should have left him working on his old '49 pickup or, better yet, remain safely aboard *The Lilly*. They pushed Jason to follow in the direction of his father.

* * *

They were held several floors underground in a holding cell of sorts. No metal bars, but a cell just the same. Jason and his father sat on a long metal bench that was bolted to the floor. Across the room, three guards stood with M-16 rifles pointed at Jason's and Admiral Perry's heads. Jason, getting the younger of the three soldiers' attention, started to speak. Angered, the soldier flipped his rifle around and jabbed the butt into Jason's left cheek, sending him sprawling to the floor. He felt the flesh of his cheek hanging loosely beneath his eye. The bleeding stopped almost immediately. Feeling the familiar tingle, the open wound was quickly being repaired by thousands, if not millions, of internal nanites.

What did this harsh treatment mean? Had Admiral Cramer's commitment to a separate United Planetary Alliance Outpost on Earth been nothing more than a greedy power play? A ruse to obtain *The Lilly*'s advanced technology? Each question triggered a new one. How high up did this go? Jason found it hard to believe that Secretary of Defense Ben Walker, who seemed a man of integrity, would be a part of this. And what about the president? Perhaps Craing hybrids had made new inroads into the government?

Jason sat quietly on the bench for over an hour. He opened a NanoCom channel to *The Lilly*. It had taken a while to figure out the *advanced options* for the NanoCom menu system and the specific area that allowed for nonverbal communications. After mentally scrolling through several sub-menus, he found the option he was looking for: NanoText Off/On. Once activated, the process involved optically selecting letters and whole word suggestions, not so different from cellphone texting—something

Jason rarely did. Alphanumeric characters appeared optically, appearing to float in space before his eyes. Characters were in turn selected, simply by placing prolonged attention on them. It took some practice, but he was getting the hang of it. On the positive side, no one other than *The Lilly*'s crew and SEAL teams had been configured with these unique internal nano-devices.

He had just updated Ricket when their cell door clanged open. Still bound with their hands behind their backs, they were not so gently ushered into the hallway and marched back upstairs to a large conference room. Once their restraints were removed, they were told where to sit. The conference table could easily sit twenty people, although a mere handful of officers occupied the other seats. Large flat screen displays were situated on three walls. At the head of the table sat Admiral Cramer. To her left and right were other officers Jason didn't recognize. Behind Cramer, the stars and stripes hung. Although the rows of fifty stars on the navy blue field were now aligned in a circular pattern and an added, larger, fifty-first star sat at its very center. The flag took up most of the wall and hung from a brass rod at the ceiling. A banner at the top of the wall read *Licentia vel nex*. Jason looked at the banner and then to back to Cramer.

"My Latin is a little rusty. Let's see ... *Freedom or Die?*"

"Freedom or Death," she corrected.

"Whatever. What the hell is this all about, Admiral?"

"It's about doing the right thing. It's about the beginnings of a new nation. And it's about taking advantage of opportunities."

"Where are the men and women who were manning this base?" Jason asked, fighting to stay calm. "There must be hundreds of them—what the hell have you done?"

"I did what had to be done to ensure the longevity of this great country."

"What does that even mean? I want those people released."

"We'll get right on that, Captain," she said sarcastically.

"So all along you were lying to me. A ploy to make a power play?" Jason asked, more of a statement than a question.

The admiral shrugged, then looked to her fellow officers with a smirk. "Are you really so naive, Captain?"

Jason didn't answer.

"You were a convenience. Please, don't get me wrong; you've proven yourself to be immensely resourceful. Undoubtedly, the American people—the world—owe you their eternal gratitude. You helped save our planet from a horrible fate. But don't mistake my gratitude for stupidity." Jason was about to respond when a display on the wall at the end of the table flickered to life. On view was CNN Breaking News, an aerial view of Washington D.C. Two Craing Battle Cruisers hovered in the air—one directly above the Pentagon, and the other above the Capitol building. The feed changed and a third warship was shown parked in front of the White House.

"As you can see," the admiral said, enjoying the theatrics, "we've adopted some of your unconventional tactics, Captain."

Dark smoke rose from several locations—the most notable being the Jefferson Memorial. It had been obliterated.

"Close proximity military bases, including Fort Myer and Fort McNair, were also destroyed." She stood and walked to the display. "Everything is coming together. You may not see it—you may not understand it—but we're patriots, Captain. Understand, we're not out to destroy America. We're out to make this country great again. Now, with our fleet of Craing warships, real change can take place. I hope you can see that."

"I know crazy when I see it, and you're certifiable," Jason replied, finding it hard to take his eyes from the screen.

"You'll come around."

"Not likely."

Admiral Cramer waved him off with her hand and said, "I'll be leaving this evening to speak with the president and Joint Chiefs. Talk about ideas for real change. But who knows? They may not be the right people for the job."

"I think you're fucking crazy," Admiral Reynolds piped in.

Admiral Cramer ignored the remark. Another display came alive. "I think you recognize the emissary for the Craing Empire?" Admiral Cramer smirked.

Jason looked up to see his brother. His father looked disappointed.

"Hello, Jason ... Dad," Brian said. "I'm sorry. This is not the way I wanted things to go down."

"Your deceit and treachery seem to have no bounds."

"On the contrary, Dad, I'm ensuring Earth's long-term survival. Why can't you get that through your head? At least now, with the help of Admiral Cramer and others, the Craing Empire will no longer be a threat to Earth."

"Then you're a bigger fool than I thought you were, Brian. All you've done is hand the Craing our planet on a silver platter. For fifteen years, I've experienced their lying, their deceit," Admiral Reynolds spat. There was a renewed fire in his eyes, one that Jason hadn't seen for weeks.

"Enough!" Admiral Cramer was seated again at the head of the table. "Here's what's going to happen. We will graciously accept the Craing Empire's offer. We will return to them their damn robot, Emperor Reechet. Second, they have agreed to share their advanced technology—and we'll provide limited access to *The Lilly*. Together, our two civilizations will build a long-term mutually beneficial relationship. In the process, we will become strong again here on Earth and as we venture into deep space."

There was something missing here. Jason didn't get it. Considering both Ricket and *The Lilly* were far out of reach from

Admiral Cramer's grasp, what made her think she could pull any of this off? She must have been reading his thoughts. Leaning back in her chair with an all-knowing smile, another display went active. The last person Jason expected to see on the screen was his eight-year-old daughter, Mollie. Eyes wide and obviously scared, she stared blankly into the camera. The screen changed perspectives and a wider shot of both Mollie and her mother, his ex-wife Nan, came into view. Although Mollie looked fine, Nan was not. Several purple bruises and a scrape across her forehead made it clear she had been mistreated. All eyes turned to Admiral Cramer. Even Brian looked shocked. She returned Jason's glare, then looked away.

"Mark my words. Before this is over, I'll have both my hands wrapped around your neck." Jason's words hung in the air.

"You will comply with everything we ask. This is a revolution. People have already died; we have already killed for our cause. Do not doubt our resolve here, Captain. If you want your wife and child to live, do as we ask—it's really that simple," Admiral Cramer said, regaining her composure.

Jason looked back to the screen. Knowing Mollie couldn't see him, he still wished he could reassure her. Then she did something unusual. Mollie casually touched her ear—strange— she touched her ear with two fingers.

"You have one hour, Captain." The admiral signaled to one of the guards. Both Jason and his father were pulled out of their chairs. Before they were ushered out of the room, Admiral Cramer spoke again. "I want *The Lilly* and that robot delivered to the outpost today. Make no mistake about my resolve here, Captain. Do as I say, or witness the deaths of your daughter and ex-wife." The guards manhandled them out of the room and into the hall.

Chapter 5

Back in their cell and still at gunpoint, Admiral Reynolds wanted to talk. After three weeks of brooding silence, he'd picked this time to come alive. What Jason needed was quiet. Multiple conversations were going on in his head via what he'd recently determined was referred to as *NanoTexting*. Earlier, Jason had tried to communicate to his father this way, but apparently he hadn't activated that NanoCom option. Jason couldn't fault him; until several minutes ago, he too had no idea the option even existed.

Jason turned to his father and held up a hand. "Dad, please! Just give me a few minutes to think. I'm doing some ... internal processing here, do you understand?" The admiral sat back in a huff; his frustration seemed to be rising by the minute. Jason closed his eyes and returned to his in-process NanoText conversation with Ricket.

Capt. Jason Reynolds:
... No, Ricket, I saw her. It was like a signal. She held two fingers up to her ear, just as we do when communicating in public via NanoCom. What I'm asking you is this: was she nanotized like the rest of us—-perhaps back when she was injured? I need to know if, like the crew, she has the same NanoCom tech in her head.

Science Officer Ricket:
Yes, she was nanotized, but restrictions were placed on her devices. She cannot initiate conversations—only respond to those of others—and only from those at officer level.

Capt. Jason Reynolds:
So she would know that she has those capabilities. She was

telling me to contact her.

Science Officer Ricket:
That seems like a logical assumption, Captain.

Capt. Jason Reynolds:
Can you do that now? Go ahead and remotely configure her NanoCom? And configure NanoText for her as well?

Science Officer Ricket:
Yes, done.

Capt. Jason Reynolds:
And what about Admiral Reynolds? Can you configure his as well?

Science Officer Ricket:
Yes, done.

Capt. Jason Reynolds:
Also, is there a way for you to access the Pacesetter remotely?

Science Officer Ricket:
Yes, Captain.

Capt. Jason Reynolds:
Is she located at the same coordinates here at the outpost where I left her?

Science Officer Ricket:
Yes, sir. Although several unsuccessful attempts have been made to enter her cockpit.

Capt. Jason Reynolds:
Thank you. I'll be back to you shortly.

Disconnect NanoText Command: Science Officer Ricket

Establish outbound NanoText hail: Crew Member Mollie Reynolds:

Crew Mollie Reynolds:
OMG, Dad, what took you so long?

Capt. Jason Reynolds:

For one thing, I can't text as quickly as an 8-yr-old can. How are you? How is your mother?

Crew Mollie Reynolds:

I'm fine. Mom's OK too. She punched a man in the face and he pushed her to the ground really hard. They did that twice.

Capt. Jason Reynolds:

Are you alone? Is someone there watching you now?

Crew Mollie Reynolds:

No, we are alone.

Capt. Jason Reynolds:

I want you to tell your mother I'm coming for you. Tell her to hang on. Also, do you know where you are? Where you're being held?

Crew Mollie Reynolds:

Yes. We are on The *Gordita* in the cages. It's really gross and it smells bad. Mom and I are in the same cage together. All the crew people from *The Lilly* are in cages too. Mom says they gassed us last night while we slept and then moved us here.

Capt. Jason Reynolds:

How about Billy and the rest of the SEALs? Where are they?

Crew Mollie Reynolds:

Here too. They are mad. Billy keeps yelling bad words I can't repeat.

Capt. Jason Reynolds:

One last question: Do you know where The *Gordita* is? Still in Washington? In space?

Crew Mollie Reynolds:

I don't know. I'm scared, Dad! Please hurry!

Capt. Jason Reynolds:

Hang on just a little longer, kiddo. I'm proud of you and I'm on my way!

Disconnect NanoText Command: Crew Member Mollie Reynolds

The whole texting process left Jason mentally exhausted. *How the hell do kids do it all day long?* And since Ricket had also reconfigured each of the crew's NanoText settings, he was far from finished.

Within the hour, the cell door clanged opened and they were marched back to the conference room. The feed from Mollie and Nan's cage was back on the screen.

"Well?" said Admiral Cramer. "I have an unscheduled appointment at the White House. You're going to do as I've asked. Right now ... or you will witness first the death of your former wife, and then that of your daughter." Two soldiers had entered Mollie and Nan's cell, rifle barrels held mere inches from their heads.

"So, what's it going to be, Captain?" Admiral Cramer asked.

She'd always borne an irritating air of superiority, but now her smug tone carried it to a whole new level.

Jason and his father looked at the screen, seemingly weighing their alternatives. Mollie was trying to hold it together, but was starting to lose her composure. Scowling, Jason shook his head toward the display. It started with a smile. Then Mollie was holding back a giggle. Then Nan was holding back a smile and then a giggle as well.

"What the hell's wrong with those two?" Admiral Cramer barked, looking back and forth from the display to Jason and his father. "I don't think you understand the seriousness of—" She abruptly went silent with the appearance of two different soldiers who'd moved into camera view and taken seats next to Mollie and Nan. Billy Hernandez smiled and waved up to the camera.

Jason slowly stood and walked to the front of the room and sat down next to Admiral Cramer. "Let me tell you where your plan fell apart, Admiral ..."

There was new activity from the display with the CNN news feed. High above, perhaps from a news helicopter, the scene was of Washington D.C. Both Craing Battle Cruisers hung in the air, big and ominous-looking, and were firing their energy weapons from multiple guns. Difficult to see at first, the dark-red Pacesetter fighter came into view maneuvering at incredible speeds. Astonishingly, it was avoiding plasma bursts from the Craing warships. The Pacesetter then took a direct hit to her aft shields. Seemingly undamaged, the small fighter returned fire. Jason wasn't sure who on *The Lilly* was remotely piloting the fighter, but his or her skill level was impressive. Obviously the fighter was using the latest highly-effective type of munitions. First one and then the second Craing warship ceased firing. Drifting, they'd taken damage to their drives. Slowly at first, then picking up speed, the mammoth vessels fell from the sky.

A mile apart from each other, the two warships billowed dark smoke into the air—miraculously avoiding the populace below, each crashed onto opposite banks of the Potomac River.

Admiral Cramer sat back in her chair, realization of the situation coming to bear.

The news feed changed again, this time to the third Craing cruiser, still sitting on the White House lawn. Seeing the spaceship, Admiral Cramer's confidence returned.

"One Craing Battle Cruiser is more than enough to bring Washington to its knees, Captain," she said with contempt.

"Don't get your hopes up, ma'am," Jason said, pointing to the display. "See those markings—there towards the stern? I memorized those marks—saw them when that ship landed in San Bernardino and took my ex-wife captive. Ironically, my daughter had named that very same vessel. She called it *The Gordita.*" Jason pointed to the other display and the now empty cage. "You forget, Admiral, just like the Pacesetter, *The Gordita* has been configured for remote access. All her onboard systems can be controlled by *The Lilly*—weapons systems, navigation systems, even the ability to open prisoner cage doors. Billy Hernandez and his SEAL team took back control of *The Gordita* several minutes ago." The admiral watched as her one last hope lifted off from the White House lawn and quickly flew out of the camera's view. "*The Gordita* is currently on her way back to the outpost," Jason said.

Chapter 6

The Lilly phase-shifted to several hundred feet above the outpost, hoping to surprise each of the five Craing warship's bridge crews. With her two rail guns deployed, she immediately went to work on the closest ship. *The Lilly*'s weaponry, especially her unique antimatter munitions, had become infamous throughout the fleet. One look at the distant ridge-line only reinforced the magnitude of destruction they were capable of. At that moment, these same munitions were ripping through the Craing ship's shielding and decimating her drives. The warship fell from the sky like a rock and crashed into the desert below. The other four warships showed no interest in continuing the battle. One by one, they hailed *The Lilly*, surrendered, and landed at the outpost. Within minutes, U.S. armed forces were approaching the outpost from land and air.

Cramer's militia fought on in earnest for several hours, but eventually, without the support from the Craing fleet of ships, gave up and laid down their weapons without further incident. Some chose to escape into the desert and take their chances against the elements, while others stayed to face the music. Jason's first priority was to locate the missing base personnel. Tight-lipped, Admiral Cramer was no help. She had requested legal representation and said nothing more to anyone. Her militia second in command, a Montana hometown cousin, Ronald Billings, was eager to lead Jason and his father—first to one and then to the second of the two massive aircraft hangars.

All entrances had been chained and padlocked. Of course, nobody had keys. Valuable time was lost looking for an adequate-sized bolt cutter. Jason, his father, and two of Admiral Cramer's now-quite-helpful militiamen entered the first of the two hangars. All four men retched. Ventilation had been turned off, making the corrugated steel building nothing less than a hotbox.

"It must be a hundred and twenty degrees in here," Admiral Reynolds angrily said, squinting into the darkness. Reflexively, each of them brought their hands up to cover mouths and noses against the overwhelming smell. As Jason's eyes adjusted to the darkness, he saw what looked like bundles on the floor. A breaker was closed and the overhead lights came on. They'd discovered the missing outpost personnel. Nearly two hundred bodies here in this structure alone. Each body was tightly wrapped in duct tape and placed side-by-side, mummy-like, on the floor—unable to move, deprived of water, and lying in their own excrement for God only knew how many hours. *Were any of his* Lilly *crewmembers amongst these bodies?*

Jason was barking orders and moving fast. "Get the air circulating in here and we need water—go!"

Some had survived. Most had not. Heat and dehydration had taken its toll. Those that did survive were confused and slow to recover from the effects of the odorless and invisible halogenated ether. The captives' accounts told the same story. No one had expected an attack from within their own ranks. Well planned and executed, base personnel had been taken completely off guard. Apparently, Crawford's militia had taken little care with their measurements. Once the best-guess oxygen and nitrous oxide formula had been mixed, and wearing gas masks, the militia introduced the *sleeping gas* concoction into ventilation systems throughout the outpost's barracks. The few soldiers on guard duty were easily dealt with. A similar process was repeated for the Allied ships in orbit.

* * *

The shit hit the fan. Washington politicians and military brass alike converged onto the base like bees to honey. Troops from each of the service branches were deployed—the Army especially. They had recently gone above and beyond to filter out any Craing mutants from their ranks. Admiral Cramer's rebellious grab for power had been quickly squashed. Her Alliance takeover plan was a shaky house of cards at best. To her credit, she'd managed to pull together several hundred devout followers—many of them Montana militia wackos and extremists. Her advantage had been the unhindered control over the remaining Craing fleet of two hundred and thirty-five vessels. She also had access to the Craing captives—prisoners— convincing enough of them to resume their previous posts as pilots and crew on eight of the battle cruisers. If she had been able to crew more of the warships, the outcome most definitely would have been different.

It would be years before government investigations, review boards, and tribunals had run their course. For now, Jason and his father sat in the largest of the outpost's conference rooms, waiting for the hammer to come down on their heads.

Not officially under arrest, the two knew they were in deep trouble. Jason had fought for how the outpost would be managed and run—exclusion of the U.S. military being the hardest pill for the government to swallow. Now, with hundreds dead, not to mention embarrassment around the world, Jason knew things here would have to change.

No less than ten executive-level officers accompanied the Secretary of Defense. They piled into the conference room, stern-faced and arrogant. Jason and Admiral Reynolds stood and waited for all to be seated before sitting back down themselves.

"Jason, Perry. We have a lot to discuss, shall we get started?"

"Yes, sir," they both replied.

"The failings of this outpost have been nothing short of stellar. What a clusterfuck."

"Yes, sir."

"As of today, all the Craing vessels here are the property of the U.S. government."

"Yes, sir."

"*The Lilly* is the property of the U.S. government."

"No, sir."

Ben Walker eyed Jason and his father warily. "I could hold you, throw you both in a hole you'd never crawl out of."

Jason was about to speak up when his father got there first.

"Ben, you want to blame the actions of a right-wing separatist wacko, one who should not have passed muster in your military in the first place, then fine. I'll gladly take that on. But let's not pretend you are carrying the big stick here, okay?" Admiral Reynolds said with a wry smile.

Walker's face was turning red, "This isn't a game. The president made it perfectly clear that this is not to be a negotiation. Who the hell do you think you are?"

Again, it was the admiral who spoke up. "Who am I, you ask? I am the only person on this planet who has experience leading military forces in deep space. I am the only person on this planet who has the foggiest idea about the enemy. For fifteen years, I have witnessed their cunning first hand, their brutality. I know how they think. And if that's not enough, I am the only person on this planet who has strong, personal relationships with the leaders of the other worlds that make up the Alliance. Close to one hundred billion people. Bluster all you want, Ben, but when it comes down to *who I think I am*, I'm the United Planetary Alliance Commander for those worlds, and as far as they are concerned, I outrank the president, and I certainly outrank you. There is only one way in which you can take charge of any allied vessel, and that is if I allow it."

Jason was having a hard time staying in his chair. In fact, he wanted to stand up and cheer. But Jason's expression didn't deviate, not even a smile crossed his lips. What made Jason really want to high-five someone, anyone, was seeing how his father had recaptured his spirit. The fight was back in his eyes. This was the man warriors across the universe wanted to follow into battle. He was back.

In the end, Admiral Perry Reynolds was appointed the interim Alliance Outpost Commander. The general consensus was his loyalty, experience, and commitment to the Alliance was beyond reproach.

Jason had learned a few lessons the hard way. He needed to better oversee to the care of his family, as well as *The Lilly* and her crew. He'd lost five crewmembers in those hangars.

* * *

It was close to midnight. Jason, Billy and Ricket approached the outpost's subjugated Craing City from the south. Countless fires burned throughout the camp. The air smelled of soot and burning meat. Groups huddled close together for warmth against the brisk night air. There was an almost carnival atmosphere to the place; sounds of laughter and spirited conversations could be heard in the distance. Alliance soldiers patrolled the outer perimeters from outside the high metal fences. Only moments before, radios alerted sentries of Jason's approach. At the gate, two soldiers looked up as the three figures stepped out from the darkness.

"Sergeants," Jason said, as they came to a stop several paces in front of them.

"Good evening, Captain, Lieutenant ... Um, I apologize,

I'm not sure how to address you now, sir," the sergeant said, his eyes darting from Ricket to the others and then back to Ricket.

"You can refer to me as Ricket—same as always."

"Yes, sir—I mean Ricket."

"How about opening the gate, Sergeant," Jason prompted. "We won't be here long."

"Yes, sir." The second sentry used a key to unlock a large padlock and swung the double gates wide enough for the three to pass through.

Once inside the compound, Ricket took up the lead, with the others following close behind. They headed off into the hordes of the three- to four-foot tall populace—all surviving prisoners leftover from the Craing fleet.

Heads turned and eyes narrowed as they moved past. The sight of Ricket within their compound created a commotion. Conversations abruptly stopped—small alien beings squared their shoulders and stood up tall. Open tent flaps revealed secluded card games in progress or individuals eating their dinners in solitude.

A group of excited Craing fell in behind them, a procession of sorts—all heading towards the back of the camp. Ricket slowed and came to a stop. A bonfire blazed. Three Craing sat on five-gallon buckets; the camp had gone quiet and a circle was forming around them. A Craing, seated on the middle bucket, rose to his feet and the two others also stood up. The center alien was surprisingly tall—close to four-and-a-half feet. Typically naked, or nearly naked, these Craing, and others seen around the camp, were wearing green army jumpsuits. Three more buckets were added around the fire. Jason took in the scene. These three Craing, especially the taller one, were obviously the leaders here.

"Pronunciation would be difficult, so you may call me, uh—Glenn—this is Rob and that's, uh, Carl. You honor us with your presence." The taller Craing bowed slightly and gestured for them to join them. They sat down in unison. The leader, Glenn, watched as something black and large was pulled from the open fire and placed upon a nearby table. Off to the side, two young Craing worked feverishly in the silence. Long knives moved quickly and with precision.

One by one, wood platters were delivered; first to the three visitors and then to the three Craing leaders. Smoke drifted into the air from charred meat. Jason's mind flashed back to the flaming caldrons in the Craing Grand Sacellum—human flesh popping and sizzling upon their metal grills. Jason received a one word NanoText message. *Lamb.* Jason looked over to Ricket, giving him a subtle nod. They ate in silence.

Billy was licking his fingers and making appreciative sounds of mmm's and ahhh's. "Amazing. Not sure what the hell I just ate, but wow."

The taller Craing bowed his head and smiled.

Jason said, "Glenn, thank you again for sharing your meal with us. Ricket, *Emperor Reechet*, tells me you, as the leader here and overlord, wish to discuss something—"

"Yes, something of great importance, Captain. Although another matter presents itself which must be discussed first," Glenn responded.

Jason nodded for him to continue.

"Our situation here. We would like to inquire about your plans for us."

Several hundred Craing had encircled their group. They hadn't made a sound.

"As you know," Jason replied, "we've already returned many of your citizens to your home worlds. We have every intention of returning the rest. I apologize for these conditions—"

"You misunderstand, Captain. The Craing here do not wish

to return to our home worlds. No, they would like you to help them migrate."

Jason started to reply, but realized he didn't know how to respond. "We fought against each other in battle. We're enemies."

"There is a small Craing settlement no more than three FTL days' travel. We wish for that settlement to give us asylum. With your help, they can grant us asylum."

The crowd around them stirred. Soft murmurs, then louder, "Asylum, asylum, asylum ..."

"Our people, the crewmembers you have returned to the Craing Empire... They returned in disgrace. Without exception, each will come before a warrior's claxon sword. Their heads an offering—their flesh to be consumed by their masters."

"I didn't know," Jason said.

"It is our way."

"Glenn, there is small Craing fleet, although possibly more powerful than the last one, leaving Craing space and headed for Earth in seven days. At least that is what we've been told. Perhaps you've heard of the Emperor's Guard?" The three Craing sat still, eyes wide. Murmurs erupted from those encircling them.

"There is a good chance they will use nuclear or fusion missiles or some other advanced technology to destroy life on this planet. This might not be the best time to discuss this asylum thing," Jason said with a shrug.

"Then this brings up the second thing we must discuss."

Jason was getting restless; he wanted these people to cut to the chase. "What is this really all about?"

Glenn's eyes darted to Ricket. He then stood and addressed the crowd. "Leave us now. Please. Let us talk in private." The onlookers shuffled off. The two workers skilled with carving knives also left.

Glenn returned to his bucket and spoke quietly. "Are you

familiar with Craing society?"

"No. Not really," Jason replied.

"Two hundred years ago, the Craing Empire had few similarities to the one that plagues the universe today. We were a people of honor who kept to ourselves. Yes, we had our enemies. Yes, we went to war. But we had little interest in conquests."

"What changed?"

"What I'm about to tell you is among the most guarded of all Craing secrets. In fact, I'm sure with this knowledge you could stop the Emperor's Guard from reaching Earth. Understand, I do not wish for anything but the best for my people, but their hunger for conquest must stop. Things must return to the old ways. Honor must be restored."

"I'm listening," Jason said.

"You must agree to my terms, Captain. First, you will transport the three of us to the Craing settlement so we may speak face-to-face with our brethren. Second, if they agree and grant our people asylum, you will transport the remaining Craing here on Earth to the settlement."

"I still don't see why this is in our best interest."

"Because what I'm about to tell you will alter the balance of power with the Craing. It won't be easy. And you may decide you're not up to the task. That will be up to you."

Jason didn't respond, but looked to Ricket. He'd learned to trust the mechanical being more than he'd thought possible. If what this overlord was saying was true, war could be averted. Earth could be saved. Jason and Ricket exchanged glances. As if reading his thoughts, Ricket nodded.

"We'll trust you for now, Glenn. Cross us and you'll be the first to die. Understood?"

"I will not cross you, Captain. You are making a wise decision."

"Tell us this secret," Jason said. "Tell us how to level the playing field with the Craing."

Ricket interjected, "Here is what I've learned from Glenn and the overlords. The Craing worlds are a star system unique in the universe. The location of their home worlds are many thousands of light years travel from Earth. Even with FTL, it would take many lifetimes to traverse that distance. This kept the Alliance always on the defensive—never able to attack.

"How is that possible?" Jason asked.

Ricket continued on: "The Craing worlds—eight class M planets revolving around a single red giant sun. What is unique is that each of these planets shares the same orbit, and each of the planets is the same distance from their sun. Over many millennia, hundreds of black holes had formed. The gravitational anomalies that this created made space travel for the Craing precarious at best. Subsequently, many lives were lost attempting to leave their orbits. Needless to say, the Craing Empire was slow venturing into deep space."

"So what happened?"

"The same anomaly that kept the Craing Empire close to home eventually became that which allowed for unparalleled travels to far-out reaches of the universe. Two hundred years ago a Craing scientist proposed a revolutionary, albeit controversial, idea. His plan was to instigate an artificial black hole—one powerful enough to negate the gravitational properties of the smaller black holes. Limited experiments were approved. Powerful lasers were constructed and positioned, one on the southern-most pole of each of the eight Craing home worlds. Then, corresponding mirror arrays were placed in space. For the experiment to be successful, the lasers needed to be perfectly aligned—toward a specific point thousands of miles out into space, and each needed to be energized at precisely the same instant."

Glenn explained, "In one regard, the experiment didn't work. It wasn't a unifying black hole that was created, but a massive wormhole instead.

Jason saw where this was going. "Let me guess, they now had access to a wormhole that literally allowed them travel across the universe. To star systems hundreds, if not thousands, of light years away?"

"Yes. And by changing the power level, even minutely, of any one of the eight lasers, they found that properties of the wormhole also changed," Ricket added. "Change the properties of the wormhole, change the outpoint. It's taken time, hundreds of years, to map these outpoints. That is why the Loop is the Craing Empire's most-guarded secret. With the destruction of one or maybe two of their home-world lasers, the imbalance would be sufficient enough to collapse the wormhole, the Loop itself, and send the Craing back into spatial isolation, and very far from Earth."

Jason took in the information. If what Glenn was saying was true, this most certainly could be a game changer.

"We hope this information will be of use to you, Captain. With the exception of the Craing high priests and a select few scientists and overlords, few know the technical aspects of the Loop—and how easily it could be disrupted. Captain, if what you say is true, and this Emperor's Guard, those three highly advanced alien ships, are in fact making preparations to come to Earth, you have little time to take action. I am not sure how you could reach the Craing worlds in time."

"Who knows where these lasers are physically located?"

"The lasers are huge, out in the open. As far as the populous is concerned, their prime function is for inter-world communications," Glenn replied. "Their connection to the Loop, that is a tightly held secret."

"So what do you need?" Jason asked.

"I'll need access, right now, tonight, to a Craing ship to initiate an FTL communication to the Craing worlds," Glenn said.

"Why?"

"Once on Halimar, you'll need help. Revolution is brewing. There is much dissent among the Craing—especially among the youth. I'll set up a rendezvous with my people there—with luck they'll have a ship available. I'll tell you how to contact them, how to provide them your landing coordinates. It will take me a few days to hear back. We'll need to talk again, Captain. At that point I can give you more specifics."

* * *

"Twice! I've been thrown in those disgusting damn cages twice now! And don't get me started on the jeopardy Mollie was placed in. Who the hell lives like this?" Nan stopped yelling when she realized she wasn't getting any argument from Jason. He let her get it all out. Hell, he didn't blame her.

They were back in her suite on *The Lilly*, Mollie put to bed an hour earlier, as Jason sat next to her on the edge of her bed. She'd showered and had her hair wrapped-up in a towel the way women do.

"I'm sorry. It's my fault. If you knew how terrified I was when I saw you and Mollie sitting there at gunpoint ..."

"Oh, just shut up," Nan replied, rolling her eyes. "I'm venting. So you really don't need to say anything. Actually, it's probably best if you don't. And yes, I signed up for the outpost's damn Envoy position—what was I thinking? And yes, I remember you tried to talk me out of it."

This was classic Nan. Same as when they'd been married—she would get upset and Jason would back off. With her innate ability to debate just about anything, law school had been the perfect choice. And later, as a defense attorney, she rarely, if ever, lost a case. Jason also knew Nan would continue to argue aloud both sides until she came to some kind of resolution. That was her process of dealing with things. Jason smiled inwardly; he didn't mind her chatter one bit.

She now looked at him with brows raised. "Are you even listening to me?" She shook her head in disbelief.

"Yes. Well, actually ... no, not really. I was thinking how familiar this seems, what we're doing, to when we were married."

She looked at him for a while. Eventually the anger or frustration fell away and she smiled.

"Yeah, I guess it is." She pulled the towel away from around her head and let her long hair fall free. She looked into his eyes and then slowly pulled him closer. They kissed. Eventually, she pulled away and took a breath.

"You better go before I do something I might regret." Jason kissed her cheek and reluctantly stood up. As he turned to leave, she grabbed his hand.

"Oh, and if I ever get thrown in one of those damn cages again I will hunt you down and ... well, you don't want to know what I'll do to you."

* * *

Jason, aware that time was of the essence, called for an immediate emergency meeting. The captain's ready room was filled to capacity. Those who couldn't find a seat found an open area on the bulkhead to lean against. Jason stood and let Mollie have his seat at the head of the table, bringing smiles from around the room.

"We're right back where we were a month ago, with Craing warships en route to Earth. Even if we could repair the Craing vessels that are in our possession and even if we had enough trained pilots—"

"We could still lose," Ricket interjected.

Jason nodded, letting the point sink in. All eyes turned towards the small alien cyborg.

Jason continued. "We need time to ready our fleet—bolster Earth's defenses. Hell, we need a year, maybe two."

"So this plan the Craing overlord is proposing, can we believe it?" Nan asked. "Sounds a little self-serving, if you ask me. I mean, I'm certainly no military tactician like you guys, but it seems like we'd be putting a lot of faith, not to mention resources, hinged on one Craing's obscure promises."

"Maybe. But if what he says *is* true, and we can—if not bring down, at least greatly hinder—the Craing's ability to traverse the universe, maybe we need to risk it."

"You really think there's a way—?" the XO started to ask.

Chief Horris interjected: "First of all, even with *The Lilly's* advanced FTL drives, there's no way we could make it to the Craing worlds days or even hours before the Emperor's Guard gets under way."

XO Perkins shrugged. "So that still leaves the problem of getting there under seven days. And do we even know where these Craing worlds are located?"

"We have a good idea where Terplin, their home planet, is located. Unfortunately, no one in the Alliance, perhaps other than my son, Brian, has ever been there," the admiral replied.

"That brings me to the second issue," Jason said. "Somewhere along the line I've heard both Mollie and Jack talk about a habitat in the Zoo—something about one with Serapin-Terplins—did you bring the information I asked for?" Jason looked toward Jack, the Zoo caretaker.

"Yes, Captain. That would be HAB 12." Jack had handwritten some notes on several small index cards. "The Serapin-Terplins—*weird*, the Craing use the word Terplins a lot throughout their language—inhabit a world called Halimar. Halimar is within the Craing eight-world solar system. According to the meta-data information tied to that habitat, both the Terplin and Halimar planets are in a shared orbit around a shared sun—which is a red supergiant."

Jason turned his attention back towards Ricket. "Would it be possible to access Halimar via HAB 12?"

Ricket looked uncomfortable with the question. "First of all, you need to understand that habitats, such as HAB 12, do in fact reside on other planets, such as Halimar—not here on board *The Lilly*. They can be hundreds of square miles in size. Also note that habitats exist in a completely different reality—one that is slightly *out of phase* with our perspective. For instance, if you were to travel to Halimar, you would not see the animals and terrain of HAB 12 ...although they are there, occupying time and space, it's a time and space slightly *out of phase* with our own."

"And accessing those habitats could be accomplished via the same technology we utilize with our DeckPorts and phase-shift capabilities, correct?" Jason asked.

"Theoretically, that is correct," Ricket replied.

"And just as we have port access to each of the habitats via *The Lilly's* Zoo, it makes sense that there would be a secondary port, within the habitats themselves, to access these corresponding planets, yes?" Jason asked, now looking around the room to make sure everyone was following along.

"Yes, each habitat has a minimum of one, often more than one, portal to their originating home world reality. This information is already provided within the accompanying habitat meta data—although not the exact locations," Ricket explained. "The Caldurians, original designers of the Zoo and habitats system, not to mention *The Lilly* itself, built in security safeguards for this very reason. The habitats were never intended for subversive use, for the very same reason we wouldn't want inhabitants of other planets infiltrating *The Lilly's* Zoo."

"I'm sure you already know what my next question will be," Jason said.

"You want to know if I can bypass the safeguards," Ricket replied flatly.

"Yes. Jailbreak the thing—not only get us into HAB 12 but eventually onto Halimar itself."

"Whoa, whoa ... hold your horses, everybody," Jack exclaimed, wide-eyed and looking around the room. "HAB 12 is one of the most dangerous, if not *THE* most dangerous habitat. It's an environment that makes Earth's own Jurassic period look like a trip to Disneyland in comparison. Not just carnivores inhabit the place—we're talking killing and eating machines. Feeding drones are never idle—meat supplies never stop. Hell, I've seen Serapins even try to eat the drones."

Fidgety, Admiral Reynolds got to his feet. He gestured for Nan to sit. "Even if Ricket can get us access to HAB 12, and we deal with the environment and wildlife situation, and, let's suppose, we also navigate to where the alternate portals are located, and after we do all those *impossible* things, what then? What's the end game?" the admiral asked, looking at Jason.

"Simple. We locate and destroy the Craing's ability to move about the universe. Somewhere on each of the eight planets in their solar system is a powerful laser. Those lasers work in conjunction with each other in forming a massive wormhole. They call this system the Loop—for the last two hundred years the Loop has enabled the Craing to conquer and subjugate any society they've come into contact with—even those thousands of light-years away."

"Wait a minute," Orion said confused. "So why are we going to the Craing worlds?"

"We need to bring down the Loop. Destroy the Craing's ability to quickly move around the universe. But, primarily, we have less than seven days to stop the Craing from deploying those three warships—warships that may be as advanced, or even more advanced, than *The Lilly*. They call them the Emperor's Guard."

"Why don't we just take a ship into HAB 12?" Orion asked.

"We thought of that. Even our fighters have a larger wingspan than the portal openings. According to Ricket, if you can't enter directly through the portal window, there's no way to enter the habitat. Phase-shifting into a habitat is not an option," Jason said, looking to Ricket for confirmation.

Billy, who'd been quiet up till that point, asked, "So we'll also need to figure out how we'll get from Halimar, where the HAB 12 portal opens, over to the laser fortification. I'm still not clear on that part ..."

Jason nodded. "From what Glenn said, he has people loyal to his cause who will help us with a ship. He's already given me the information, a way to signal them and give them our coordinates on Halimar. After that, they'll rendezvous with us at the portal."

Billy nodded, taking it all in.

Jason continued, "We'll use multiple teams. Here's how they break down: Admiral Reynolds maintains overall Alliance command here at the outpost. We'll leave him the majority of our SEAL forces. If we fail, it will be up to him and what's left of our Craing fleet to hold off this approaching Emperor's Guard ... somehow. Next, I'll be in command of the HAB 12 team. Billy, we'll need the best of the best—an assault team of no more than twenty. Remember what we'll be going up against in there ... we'll need a team that will get us there in less than seven days, then get us back out again. Orion and Ricket, you'll be in charge of equipping our team with the necessary battle suits and any technology that gives us an advantage. Put your heads together; take a look at the terrain and environmental conditions—and don't forget about the Serapin-Terplins. Again, while our team is making its way through HAB12, *The Lilly* will be en route through deep space to the Craing settlement. Admiral, we'll need to transfer Glenn and the two other overloads to *The Lilly*. Apparently they prefer communal living, so XO, set something up in the upper hold. Let them set up their tents there. Just no open fires. The trip shouldn't take us more than a few days. From what I understand, they have no defenses, few weapons. A quick and easy trip! A milk run! We'll keep a few SEALs on board, but a minimal crew.

"Nan, I'm guessing you and Mollie will want to stay onboard *The Lilly*. It's probably still your safest bet. But it's up to you. We'll be leaving orbit first thing tomorrow morning. That's it, people. We have a lot of work to do before then, so let's get cracking."

Chapter 7

The team was nearly assembled when Jason made his way into the Zoo. His meeting with Gunny Orion ran longer than expected—one he'd originally scheduled for the previous afternoon.

The assault team assembled in front of the ten-foot-wide portal to HAB 12. Everyone, including Jason, was outfitted with a new custom-designed camouflaged combat suit. Orion and Ricket had been busy most of the previous evening on sub-Deck 4B at the large, building-sized phase-synthesizer unit. They'd designed the new suits with a combination of solid and flex armor made from composite materials derived from various alternate planes of existence.

"Who are we missing?" Jason asked, as he approached the group. Everyone came to attention, including Billy, a soggy unlit cigar protruding from his lips.

"A few more stragglers," Billy humorously replied.

"As you were," Jason said. Billy went back to inspecting his team of four SEALs. Petty Officer Rizzo nodded towards Jason and smiled.

"Good to see you're on the team, Rizzo. If anyone knows how to fight Serapins, you do."

"Yes, sir—looking forward to it."

Team members were looking out through the portal window. The baren desert landscape looked uninviting, harsh. A small wind cyclone of dust and small rocks twirled across the sand. Seeing Lieutenant Morgan on the team was no surprise. Not one of Jason's favorite people, but a competent SEAL just the same. It was the person standing next to him who was a surprise. Dira was laughing at something Morgan had said and responded by punching his shoulder. But then, it made sense she'd be on the team. They'd need a medic. Ricket, wearing his own small customized combat suit, had his back to everyone and was busy typing something into a keypad at the wall—no doubt in the process of trying to jail-break its security protocols. From what Jason understood, habitats had a range of security levels from one to ten. Some, like HAB 4, where Raja the elephant lived, were security level one. The most dangerous, like HAB 12, were not supposed to be accessible at all—by anyone—and held the highest security level of ten. Ricket continued inputting information at the virtual keypad. He was getting a *beep beep* response from the portal interface. Not a positive sign. Jason had come to realize that if Ricket couldn't bypass the security protocols, no one could. Then the floor began to shake.

Everyone stopped and turned towards the opposite end of the corridor. A procession of ten seven-foot-tall rhino warriors approached. Each was a thousand pounds of muscle beneath thick grey hide, with legs and arms like tree trunks, and bodies strong and ripped without an ounce of fat. Built more hulk-like than human, and with the heads of rhinoceroses—horns and all—the ten beasts moved forward with heavy grace and determination. They carried the rhino warrior weapons of choice: a heavy hammer in one hand and an energy weapon strapped onto the wrist of their other arm.

The beasts halted in unison several paces in front of Jason. His friend, Traveler, battle worn and missing an ear, stood before him. Then, to Jason's surprise, they saluted him. He returned their salute and brought his attention back to Ricket.

Beep beep. Access still denied—but he wasn't giving up.

Orion was positioning a hover cart, stacked high with

equipment, over to the center of the group. Billy rushed to help her and was rewarded with a glare—a glare that spoke volumes: *don't you even come near me.* Obviously, they'd yet to clear up their tiff. Jason only hoped it wouldn't interfere with the mission.

"Listen up, everybody," Gunny Orion announced, while holding up a new kind of rifle. "This is a multi-gun. Do not try to reload it—as long as you are aboard *The Lilly*, or within the confines of HAB 12, it utilizes the JIT munitions. They're automatically phase-shifted to the weapon's micro port." Orion pointed to a round expanded casing at the mid-section of the rifle. "This weapon interfaces with your HUD. Review your menu settings, folks. Three separate plasma bolt configurations, four separate mini-rail gun configurations, two separate micro-missiles with integrated tracking capabilities ... Get to know your weapon. There's also radical changes made to the helmet and HUD systems, as well as to your battle suit configurations. We'll be reviewing these changes once we get going."

"Dad!" Jason turned to see Mollie running down the corridor.

"Hey, kiddo." He gave his daughter a hug. Nan, back to wearing her spacer's jumpsuit, was close behind. Jason noticed Nan and Dira exchanging cordial nods, but something was going on there.

"Mollie wanted to say goodbye before you headed out," she said. Jason saw Nan had applied lipstick and makeup to her bruised face and was smiling. A good sign.

Nan said, "We're staying aboard *The Lilly* this time. I can continue working and communicate via FTL linkups to the outpost. And the safest place for Mollie, if that alien fleet arrives, will be here on board, don't you think?"

"I do, and she feels more at home here than anywhere else right now," Jason said, liking the direction their talk was going. "Do me a favor, though—when you check in with the outpost, see how my father's doing, okay? I'm leaving one of the shuttles behind for him. If things go badly, he'll be able to move underground until we get back. I mentioned this to him, but he may need reminding."

"I'll tell him, I promise. One more thing, and I hope you'll agree to it. While I'm on board, I'd like to go through that procedure, you know—to be nanotized and have that NanoCom thing installed in my head? I never remember what hand signals to use on those damn DeckPorts and it would be nice to be able to keep in contact with Mollie. I'd just feel safer considering what we've been through. Can you authorize that before you go?"

Jason smiled and brought up his virtual tablet. "With both Dira and Ricket being gone, you'll need to work out the schedule with the remaining medical staff. I've gone ahead and authorized the procedure. Also, remember that communications into HAB 12 will be spotty at best." Jason closed down his tablet and looked up to see that Nan was worried looking. "You okay?"

"Watch yourself out there, Jason. If what I've heard is true, you'll be—you'll all be in constant danger."

"We'll be fine. And I'm hoping that things here onboard, while in FTL, will be fairly non-eventful. It'll take a few days for the ship to reach the rendezvous point, so maybe you can use that time to relax a bit, hang out with Mollie, even have some fun."

"I'd like that." She gave Jason a hug and a kiss on the lips, and stood back. Jason got another hug from Mollie; they stood back and watched as Jason and the rest prepared to enter HAB 12.

Impatient, Jason glanced at his HUD's mission countdown timer:

Dys: 06 Hrs: 13 Mins: 22

They'd already burned too much time getting started. There was too much at stake. The last time the Craing had sent warships to Earth, they'd been lucky. Few knew how close the Earth had come to being totally annihilated. With this new threat, these three Caldarium warships—the Emperor's Guard—Earth again might very well be at the precipice of destruction. Truth was, nothing was more important than this mission, not *The Lilly*, not even his own family.

Beep beep beep. Three beeps instead of two. Ricket turned and nodded toward Jason. "We're in; we have sixty seconds before the portal closes, sir," Ricket said.

Jason turned to his team. "Let's move out, everyone."

Chapter 8

The assault team of twenty entered HAB 12. Once inside, three of them, including Jason, fell flat on their faces.

Ricket said, "Gravity here is slightly denser than that of Earth's, Captain."

"Thank you Ricket. That would have been nice to know ahead of time," Jason replied, getting back on his feet. He dusted himself off and looked back through the portal window where he received smiles and waves from inside *The Lilly*. The window itself had a glowing blue frame around it. At the portal's side was a metal sign on a pole that was a combination of strange symbols, something that represented HAB 12—below it was a hinged metal box, which he assumed contained the access keypad.

"Also, as you'll notice, our HUDs indicate the access port we just entered through as a blue rectangle with a corresponding signal level."

"I see it; it's reading level 25. I take it that's what we're looking for with the other one?"

"Yes, sir, but that port will show up purple—we'll see it once we are within thirty miles," Ricket said.

Jason nodded and looked around, ensuring that everyone was present. "Listen up. No one goes anywhere by themselves—find partners and stay with them." At that, everyone broke up into pairs. Jason noticed Dira and Morgan had selected each other to pair off with.

"I thought I'd see more wildlife," Morgan said to no one in particular—looking through his riflescope and panning the horizon. "I'm ready to begin hunting season—right here in HAB 12."

"We've entered the area of the HAB 12 habitat with the least wildlife—basically arid desert," Ricket responded. "Note that the quadrant you are in is indicated on your HUD readout."

Jason looked toward the far horizon and adjusted the optical zoom. First, past this desert, was quadrant 2, with its rocky terrain and dark red cliffs. Next would be quadrant 3, with its open plains and green pastures, and finally quadrant 4, where—at the far end of HAB 12—a forest of tall trees grew. "Okay, we'll work our way through 2 and 3 and finish off in 4 if we haven't found the port sooner," Jason said.

Two blocky-looking large hovercrafts appeared from behind the cliffs in quadrant 2, soundlessly moving across the terrain thirty feet off the ground and headed in their direction.

"How cute, they look like big mail trucks," Dira said, smiling. Jason marveled at her light violet skin and long eyelashes for the umpteenth time. She moved to get a better view. To Jason she seemed to glide with effortless gracefulness. Each battle suit had been custom tailored for each team member based on full-body scan measurements. For that reason, the fit was perfect, comparable to having a second skin. It wasn't that Dira's battle suit fit better than anyone else's, it just seemed to *look* better on her than anyone else. Her long legs, narrow hips, and curvy backside had instigated more than a few leering glances—Jason's included. He wondered if she was aware of the effect she had on men, or perhaps she just didn't care. Then he realized she was staring back at him, eyebrows raised. Caught in the act, he quickly averted his attention to something Ricket was saying.

"Those are the feeding drones," Ricket responded. As if on cue, the two crafts stopped in mid-air. A moment passed before one of them opened a hatch and dropped several large slabs of meat onto the ground, no more than fifty yards ahead of them.

"Something tells me we don't want to be standing this close

to those things at feeding time," Billy said.

"Multiple red icons!" Morgan yelled, spinning on his feet and positioning himself in a protective stance in front of Dira. Jason and Billy exchanged quick glances; both scowled at his overreaction.

Jason inspected his HUD, viewing new life sign icons approaching from three sides.

"They seem to be at a considerable distance. Let's head out, people," Jason said, moving off at a slow jog in the direction of quadrant 2. Orion quickly moved from the back of the pack to the front. Her long, muscular legs gave her nearly twice the stride as anyone else. Once even with Jason, he could see she was smiling. Orion wasn't just competitive, she was a maniac. From arm wrestling Billy's SEALs in the mess, to challenging anyone to beat her run-times in the gym.

"Captain, there are a few things we didn't have time to discuss earlier this morning," Orion said. "I mean about our equipment." Jason picked up his pace a little to stay even with her. In the middle of the pack, Morgan said, "Fuck—what's the rush?" evoking chuckles from just about everyone. Jason let Morgan's comment go.

"What type of *things* are you talking about, Gunny?"

She laughed. Then she was gone.

Jason did a double-take, thinking his eyes had deceived him somehow. He scanned his HUD for her location. Perhaps she'd fallen behind in the pack, although that seemed unlikely. HUD icons included a two-letter name designation. The icon with the *GY* designation was gone. Jason slowed, feeling his heart rate increase. The team slowed down and came to a stop. There was a tap on his shoulder from behind; then a finger pointed toward an outcropping of rocks twenty yards ahead. Sitting lotus-style, like a Buddhist monk, Orion waited for them to catch up.

"Looks like someone's built a phase-shift device into their battle suit?" Jason called up to her.

"Nope," Orion replied, looking smug. "Anyone else have a guess?"

Rizzo spoke up: "It's not the suits, it's our new combat belts."

"And the prize goes to Mr. Rizzo!" Orion said in her best announcer's voice. Everyone looked down at their new combat belts. Several had complained earlier about them being awkward and heavy. Matte black and slightly over six inches wide and an inch thick, the belts seemed overkill for holding their Ka-Bar knives and miscellaneous utility equipment.

"We thought about adding the phase-shift components to the suits themselves, but our rhino-friends don't wear battle suits. But if you'll notice, they are wearing a specialized belt we provided them with." The chattering group turned and looked at the ten rhino warriors. Each wore a new belt—much bigger than their human-sized versions.

Jason *shushed* everyone. "Let's bring it down a notch or two—this isn't play time—we're on a mission here. Go ahead, Gunny."

"Let's start with the rhino-belts." Orion waited for the snickers to subside from the new phrase she'd just coined. "Since our robust warrior friends do not wear helmets and don't have access to our HUD system, that technology has been integrated into their wrist bands." Orion jumped down off the rock and pulled Traveler away from the group. She pointed to the large black band on his wrist. "There's two spring-release buttons on each side. Go ahead, Traveler." With fingers as big as bananas, Traveler compressed the two side buttons on his wristband. The faceplate flipped open and the inside of the plate came alive with a miniature *spatial representation* of the local terrain. "This is similar to what the rest of you are going to see on your

HUDs, and—this is important—once you select your phase-shift location. Go ahead, Traveler—use the touch screen to select the distance and elevation to where you want to phase-shift." Traveler looked at the small display, then looked up and around at his surroundings. Once he'd correlated what he was visually seeing compared to the view on the small screen, he nodded and grunted his approval. He touched the screen. "Okay, folks, he's just activated the unit and set the coordinates. He has twenty seconds to press the *Activate* key. Go ahead and press it, Traveler," Orion said. Traveler disappeared. Everyone spun to see where he'd gone.

"Can I get one of those for my ex-wife?" Billy asked with a wry grin and to more chuckles.

Atop the same rock Orion had shifted to earlier, Traveler stood tall with his hands on his hips. His fellow rhino warriors cheered, then in unison smashed their heavy hammers together over their heads—their own unique version of a high five. The sound thundered and echoed into the distance.

"Several more things you need to know about the belts," Orion said. "First, you need to be extra careful where you're phase-shifting to. Take care not to shift into solid rock or into the side of a mountain. Second, your phase-shift belts are limited to a thirty-yard radius. And third—and probably most important—because of extra-power consumption you're limited to no more than five shifts per hour. Any questions?" Orion asked.

"So, when can we try it out, Gunny?" Rizzo asked, smiling like a kid with a new toy.

Orion looked over to Jason for approval. With his nod, everyone, including Jason himself, began to disappear and reappear within a thirty-yard radius. They were having fun. Even the typically serious rhino warriors were making the equivalent of laughing sounds. Within several minutes, all had used up their five phase-shifts. Unnoticed, twenty-five light blue raptor-like creatures called Serapin-Terplins, more commonly called Serapins, had completely surrounded the assault team.

Chapter 9

"You're going to feel really really sick afterwards, Mom. I mean like you'll want to barf all the time and your head will feel like it's going to explode. But I'll take care of you. Like I did Dad." Mollie watched as the skinny med-tech named Allen helped her mother into the clamshell MediPod chamber. Once situated, her mother reached a hand out for Mollie to take.

"Absolutely no going near the Zoo while I'm in this thing. Do you understand?" Nan commanded, scowling at Mollie, then bringing her attention up to the med-tech. "Allen, you'll keep an eye on her?"

Allen was entering information onto the keypad and had already initiated the clamshell to start closing. "She'll be fine, Nan. I have some work she can help me with around here for the next few hours."

The MediPod closed and Mollie could see her mother's face looking back at her through the little rectangular window. Her mother mouthed the words *you be good!*

Mollie smiled and turned to Allen. "So what do you want me to do? I don't know anything about medical-type stuff." Then she noticed someone else had entered Medical. Both Allen and Mollie looked to see who, but they only caught a glimpse of someone turning the corner to leave the room.

"Alright, off with you Mollie. I have things to do," Allen said, not looking up from what he was working on.

"I thought you said you had stuff for me do around here," Mollie said, looking confused.

Allen finally looked up, annoyed. "I have way too much work to do to be playing babysitter to an eight-year-old.

Your mother will be fine, so check in later. Why don't you go get a bite to eat? Out. Scoot."

Mollie had to take several quick steps back as Allen rushed by, disappearing into the lab section of Medical. She continued to watch her mother sleep for a few more moments. "*Why don't you get a bite to eat?*" she mimicked the med-tech's high-pitched voice instruction. "Dork," she said a little louder. She slowly turned and headed out of Medical. In the corridor, Mollie headed for the DeckPort that would take her down to the second deck of the ship. She knew the layout of this ship as well as anyone. She'd spent hours exploring hidden areas that even her own father didn't know existed. And her parents fussed and worried about her—not having kids her own age to play with. But she did have the best friend anyone could ask for.

"Lilly, want to play a game?" Mollie asked out loud, opting not to use her now-activated NanoCom.

"Good morning, Mollie. Yes, that would be wonderful. What would you like to play?"

"Hot and Cold, of course, silly." Mollie began skipping down Deck 2 corridor. "Give me something harder to find this time, Lilly. Don't go so easy on me."

"Okay, Mollie, I have a real stumper for you. Are you ready?" The Lilly AI asked.

"Give it to me."

* * *

Lieutenant Commander Perkins sat in the command chair and surveyed the bridge. With Jason and the others gone, he'd be pulling double and even triple shifts for a while. Not that there would be much going on. He knew that FTL travel was about as exciting as watching your toenails grow. He leaned back into the seat's wide padded cushion. He could get used to this. He liked the sound of the word *Captain*. Sure, being the XO was nothing to sneeze at, but come on, it wasn't *Captain*, was it?

"Excuse me, XO, we're receiving incoming markers for an FTL transmission," McBride said from the helm. "They're requesting a private channel with the captain."

"Who is it?"

"Um, I'm not sure. It's a deep space communication. It's marked high-priority and confidential."

Perkins thought for a moment, unsure what to do. McBride was still looking back over his shoulder at him and waiting for his answer.

"Send a reply that Captain Reynolds is currently indisposed and is not on the bridge. Let them know that I'm the XO and available."

"Aye, sir."

Perkins knew that McBride's response, depending on the recipient's distance, could take up to several hours. Perhaps he should contact the captain, but then again, Jason had been fairly explicit: *handle the everyday minutia, XO, unless it's an emergency.* No, he'd find out what the FTL communication was all about before contacting Captain Reynolds. Why was he over-thinking this?

"We've got a response, sir," McBride reported.

"That was quick. Have you picked up anything on long-range sensors?"

"No, sir. Not within the last few hours."

"What's the message?"

"They need to speak with Captain Reynolds."

"Aye, sir."

Perkins noticed there was a commotion going on in hushed voices between two seaman first class guys to his right at the tactical station. Both young men were recent recruits from the Earth Alliance outpost. What made the two men unique, and a constant irritation, was they were identical twins. Jeffery and Michael Gordon not only looked the same, stocky and with their heads shaved, they also had identical-looking moles on their right cheek. Inevitably Perkins, and everyone else for that matter, got them mixed up. An order, issued to Seaman Gordon, was given to the wrong twin to fulfill. Under normal conditions the two were never assigned to the same shift.

"What's the problem over there, Seaman Gordon?" Perkins asked.

The two Gordon brothers turned to face the XO. Perkins eyed the name tags on their spacer's jumpsuits. "Seaman Michael, what's the matter?"

"Sir, I picked something up on long-range scans. At least I thought I had. Definitely a vessel's signature. I saw it plain as day, but the AI won't confirm the identification. She would have seen it long before me, too. Jeffery thinks I'm imagining things, but I saw it, sir, plain as can be."

"Alright, just stay on your posts. Lilly, what do you see as showing up on long-range scans?"

"There are no vessels within long-range scans at this time, sir."

Perkins looked at the two identical twins. "Just continue on. Keep an eye out, Jeffery. I mean Michael."

* * *

His mind reeled. Days and weeks had become long drawn-out months. Always told to be patient—that his time would be coming soon. It had been difficult to maintain the charade and hide his hatred, but now, at last, the orders had come through.

The nondescript seaman sat alone in his small dark quarters. A red scar on his arm peeked out below the sleeve of his jumpsuit. He pulled down on his left sleeve, obscuring it from view. The fold-down desktop was strewn with a myriad of intricate tools and small complex-looking devices. He furrowed his brow at the small desk light connected to the bulkhead via an adjustable swing arm. It was obscuring his view, making it difficult to complete his task. He angrily bumped the light aside with the back of his hand and glared at it for being such an irritation. He took a breath, tried to relax, and readjusted the light to where it was *supposed* to be. He added the final high-capacity optical array unit to the substraight and held the six inch square module up, admiring its elegant circuitry. He smiled, something he rarely had an occasion to do, and placed the now-completed module next to the other two off to the side.

Feeling hungry, the seaman pushed his chair away from the desk and stood, his eyes never leaving the three devices. Moving backwards he felt for the doorframe, found it, and stepped out into the corridor. Three minutes later he arrived at the mess. A short line had formed. He glared at the chubby man serving food behind the counter. *What's his name? Oh yeah, Plimpton.* The seaman imagined what one of his little devices would do to the slow-moving server behind the counter—*hell, to everyone in the mess.* He allowed himself another brief smile.

Chapter 10

Even before Jason made the command to take up defensive positions, the ten rhino warriors were already moving to encircle the team. Jason silently cursed himself for dropping his guard in what he knew was a hostile environment. Dira and Ricket moved to the center of the group, staying low and out of the way. Jason, Billy and the rest of the SEALs maintained an inner defensive circle, several steps behind the rhinos, with their multi-guns at the ready. The Serapins approached, moving forward slowly, tentatively.

"Cap, I don't think these are the same guys we ran into on the Dreadnaught," Billy said over their comms.

"Yeah, heads are a bit bigger. And those guys didn't talk," Jason replied. One Serapin was making more noise than the rest. He pointed an almost human-like finger and more Serapins scurried around to the assault team's flanks. Deep growling sounds filled the air. A constant flow of drool, thick and stringy, dripped from bared teeth. At thirty yards out they had completed the circle around the assault team. Jason and the Serapin leader made eye contact. A silent acknowledgment between leaders—both stood immobile for several moments. At over seven feet tall, and easily a thousand pounds of mostly muscle, Jason measured his Serapin opponent. A warrior in his own right, a scar crossed from the left side of his long-flared snout to its other side, continuing up past his right eye. Almost inaudibly, the Serapin leader made one more singular sound. The attack came in a blur.

The Serapin leader came directly for Jason—strategically a good move. Jason was ready for him. He brought his multi-gun up, aimed for his head and squeezed the trigger. Nothing. In fact, nobody was firing their weapons. A rhino warrior had moved in front of the scar-faced leader.

"Ricket, what the hell's going on with our weapons?" Jason yelled into his comms.

"You need to set the firing mode, Captain."

"Shit!" Jason barked. He hastily selected the first firing mode from the menu selection, not knowing nor particularly caring what it was. Unfortunately, firing modes were listed from the least to the most lethal settings—inadvertently, he'd selected a stun-level setting.

He fired directly at the head of a rapidly-charging Serapin leader. At ten feet out, the beast momentarily staggered, then leapt towards Jason. As if in slow motion, Jason saw the approaching jaws gap open before his eyes. He saw bits of chewed meat clinging between jagged rows of pointed teeth as the creatures six-inch long canines thrust forward, like two razor-sharp spears—pointing and angled towards his own jugular—and drool that streamed and whipped back and forth into the air. No doubt, Jason was looking into the jaws of death itself.

Swung two-handed like a baseball bat, Traveler's intervening heavy hammer connected at the side of the Serapin's head, right at the hinge point of its upper and lower jaws. The cumulative force behind Traveler's powerful swing and the weight of the heavy hammer's blow caused the Serapin's jaws to hyper-extend open far wider than nature ever intended. Bone splintered, flesh and muscle ripped, as his now disconnected upper and lower jaws flew off in separate directions. Jason stared, momentarily frozen, at the headless beast before him. Even before the Serapin fell to the ground, Traveler was gone and engaged with another Serapin. When two new Serapins charged him, Jason hoped he'd selected the most powerful level for his multi-gun. Apparently it was the rail-gun setting mode with explosive rounds. Both Serapins charged single file, one in front of the other. Jason squeezed the trigger. Both Serapins lost their heads simultaneously and fell to the ground. For the first time, Jason had a moment to assess the situation. The rhino warriors were still holding their outer circle. Four of them had been killed, with their partial remains scattered about, making it difficult to determine which arm or leg had gone with what torso. Another rhino-beast, also dead, was being dragged off into the desert by two Serapins. Two SEALs were dead and another one down and being attended to by Dira. The remaining SEALs quickly figured out their multi-gun settings, and that changed the tide of the battle. Within seconds, the rest of the Serapins scampered off. Again, Jason turned back and took in the carnage. Where was Ricket? Jason let out a sigh of relief, spying Ricket's active icon on his HUD. But he still couldn't see him anywhere.

"I am here, Captain," Jason heard over his comms, "above you, here in the cliffs." Jason spun around and saw the small robot-cyborg thirty yards away, halfway up the side of a ragged cliff line. "What the hell are you doing up there?" Jason asked, his anger helping to hide his relief at discovering Ricket was still among the living.

"Captain, this man requires time in a MediPod," Dira said. Jason knelt down next to Billy and Dira and the fallen SEAL. She had attended to his left shoulder and upper arm; blood had saturated his field dressing and he'd lost consciousness.

"I'll take them back," Morgan volunteered.

Reluctantly, Jason nodded, not wanting to break up his already fractured team. "You better get going then. Ricket will tell you how to gain access back into *The Lilly*."

"Never mind, Captain," Dira said. "Petty Officer Dolan has expired," she informed as she reassembled her med kit.

"What do you want us to do with the bodies, Captain?"

asked Billy, who stood and surveyed the remains of the fallen SEALs and rhino warriors. "I don't think we can bury them deep enough—the Serapins will get to them."

"I have an idea," Jason said. "Where's that damn Ricket?"

Within ten minutes, eight bodies, both of rhino warriors and SEALs, lay side by side on the ground, body parts reassembled on a best-guess basis and secured together using straps from their own packs. Meaningful words were spoken by Traveler for the fallen rhino warriors, and by Jason for the fallen SEALs. A long silence followed. When the time was right, Jason nodded for Ricket to start. Beginning with the first body, the largest of the deceased rhino warriors, Ricket knelt down, accessed the rhino's wristband, and within several seconds the body disappeared. One by one, Ricket activated each dead body's phase-shift device until all had disappeared. Dira, sharp rock in her hand and standing before a flattened area of the rock cliff, finished inscribing each of their names. She stood back and assessed her work. As if on cue, the remaining twelve assault team members looked up to the rocky cliff where two hundred feet into solid rock, eight bodies would remain undisturbed in their final resting place.

"We need to secure a suitable campsite for tonight. We're losing daylight. Grab your packs and be ready to move out in three minutes," Jason commanded.

In three minutes the team headed off towards quadrant 2. Jason led, with Ricket beside him. "Captain, I believe I have found a suitable camp location for tonight," Ricket said, looking up at Jason. Not getting an answer, Ricket continued: "That rock spire—the tallest one—half a mile ahead."

"When did you have time to investigate potential campsites?" Jason asked, his voice not hiding his irritation.

"I'm uncomfortable around violence. When the Serapins attacked I—"

Jason stopped and looked down with contempt. "You what? Abandoned your fellow crewmembers? You hid while others died fighting?" Jason yelled.

The remaining SEALs and rhino warriors had caught up and formed a semicircle around the two of them. Ricket stared up at Jason, seemingly tongue-tied.

"Let me make something perfectly clear to you, any of you—I don't care who you are—an emperor, or the fucking Queen of Sheba, in battle or otherwise—you don't leave your post—you don't leave your team. I need to know you'd gladly lay down your own life protecting the warrior standing next to you. Next time that happens, any of you, I'll shoot you myself!"

They headed off again in the same direction. No one spoke for a long time. Then Ricket broke the silence.

"I apologize, Captain," Ricket said. "It won't happen again."

"Tell me about your campsite."

"Yes, sir. I hadn't used all five phase-shifts when everyone else had. I looked for locations that would not be easily accessible by the Serapins, or anyone else. I determined that the outcropping or spire on the side of that distant cliff is inaccessible from above or below."

Jason adjusted the optical zoom on his HUD. Midway up a sheer, thousand-foot-high ridge was indeed a protruding ledge jutting out from the cliff face.

"Water is available as well as shelter from the elements. It requires two phase-shifts: one to the base of the spire and one up to the ledge."

"How do you know it's safe?"

"Other than insects and rodent-sized creatures, I detected no other life forms," Ricket replied.

"Alright, let's get up there. Go ahead and give everyone the phase-shift coordinates."

Chapter 11

"You're getting warmer, Mollie. You're definitely going in the right direction."

"When I said I wanted you to be harder on me, I didn't mean this hard," Mollie replied. She hadn't previously ventured above Deck 4. With the other Decks you entered and left the DeckPorts through various corridors. But here, on Deck 5, she entered a large room remote unto itself. The first thing she noticed as she left the DeckPort was the muted lighting and soothing background music. Shaped like an oval, with large-cushioned seating around the perimeter, the room was all about the space above. This was the observatory that she had heard other crewmembers talking about. Mollie stood in the middle of the large room with her head back. Thousands of stars streaked by and disappeared as quickly as they appeared.

"Mollie, are you still playing the game?" the AI's friendly voice asked her.

"Yeah, I guess. This place is so cool." Mollie brought her attention back to matters at hand. She took several steps forward and squinted her eyes against the darkness.

"You're getting colder, Mollie."

Mollie stopped and took a tentative step towards the left bulkhead and then took several steps more.

"You're getting hotter, Mollie. Scalding hot!"

Mollie had gone as far as she could; the wall and the couch were directly in front of her. She made a face. "Hmm, you're being pretty tricky, Lilly. Let's see. There's nothing in front of me on the wall. Nothing on the couch." Mollie smiled. "Maybe I'll look beneath the cushions." She crouched down, put her fingers in between the cushions, and pulled them apart. There, sitting at the back of the couch beneath one cushion, was a little six-inch square device. "What is that thing?" Mollie asked, now unsure if she should be touching something foreign to her. Lilly didn't answer. "Hello, are you there, Lilly?"

"Yes, I'm here, Mollie"

"What is that?" she asked again. The soft music played in the background, but silence from the AI.

"Lilly?"

"Yes, Mollie. For you to win this game, you must complete your task, remember?"

"I'm not so sure I should be doing this. Maybe this thing is something important?

"Would I have you do anything that would get you in trouble, Mollie?"

"I don't think so. No, you wouldn't."

"We can't continue onto the next part of our game until you complete the task—as we outlined when we started."

"Okay, okay, okay ..." Mollie picked up the small device. It was heavier than she thought it would be. *Well, whatever this thing is*, she thought to herself, *it certainly shouldn't have been left lying around, anyway.* She made another face and looked around the room. As part of the rules of the game Lilly AI had come up with, every time she found one of the hidden items, she was to find the nearest incinerator panel and drop the item inside. At the far end of the room was a small bar, and behind that, a kitchenette. She walked around the counter and looked for the characteristic metallic panel. There were hundreds of those things, little trash ports, all over the ship. "There it is," she said in a singsong voice. Without another thought, she pushed open the little metal door and let the device fall inside.

"I win."

* * *

The solemn-looking seaman walked slowly down the corridor. His mind was conflicted. *Why should I be tested? His own brother, and I have to be tested?* He'd accomplished more than anyone. The simple fact that he was here, a trusted crewmember wandering the corridors without suspicion, should not only be enough to prove his loyalty, but his higher intelligence. He was coming up to the wide hatch for the rear hold area. *I can almost smell them*, he thought to himself. He accessed the keypad and entered the code he'd recently hacked, *too easy*. The overheads lighting was off, *they live like vermin*. The hold, basically empty, was as wide as the ship with access from either side. A haze filled the air, smoky, like airborne soot. He squinted his eyes against the darkness. In the distance a small fire burned. Three silhouetted figures spoke in low tones. *There they are, like little piggies*. His instructions had been explicit. No energy weapons that could be detected, no loud noises either.

The seaman pulled a long slender knife from his sleeve. He was brought up to have one or more hidden weapons upon his person at all times. He'd seen others in his clan pay the ultimate price for not being prepared. Hell, his own uncle had been gutted while taking a crap—lesson learned the hard way.

He stepped out of the darkness. Flames of the small fire illuminated half of his face.

"Fires are not allowed onboard this ship," he said

Glenn looked up and saw the knife. "They sent you."

"I'm afraid so," he replied. As awkward and unskilled in the art of killing as the young seaman was, the three elderly Craing overlords were no match. Their throats cut, each died watching their lifeblood spread across the deck plating.

Chapter 12

Jason was the first to arrive at the rock outcropping. Easily three hundred feet in diameter, he'd shifted to an open clearing close to the middle of the site. He was unprepared for the untouched natural beauty of the place. Behind him the sheer rock face continued up another five hundred feet to the top of the cliff. A waterfall fell into an azure pool, causing a mist to rise and eventually dissipate in the warm air above. Looking straight out, away from the cliff face, Jason saw a small forest of trees—several precariously angled out over the far edge of the rocky ledge. Rizzo was the next to appear; then, one by one, everyone else arrived.

The rhino warriors spent little time goggling over their new surroundings, preferring to get right to work preparing the campsite. Multiple tent-like enclosures, called Retractable Camp Modules, or RCMs, unfolded from small, paperback book-sized contraptions in mere seconds. A fire was built and soon shish-kabob skewers were sizzling over the open fire. Traveler had informed Jason that rhino warriors required much nourishment, primarily meat—and they needed to eat often. They'd brought along provisions but had made it clear they would hunt and eat from the land itself in HAB 12. Subsequently, four of the rhino warriors had arrived from below carrying expertly butchered Serapin carcasses. The meat was carved and prepared with spices and rubs that they'd brought with them.

Jason could not imagine a more secure site. Just the same, he would not be taken off-guard again. With the exception of Dira and Ricket, a revolving sentry duty of two rhino-beasts and two SEALs was instigated. As darkness fell over the camp, the team took up seats, mostly tree stumps and rocks, around the fire. The rhino-beasts shared their Serapin kabobs and, to Jason's surprise, the meat was succulent and full of flavor. Sitting next to Billy, who tore chunks of meat off with his teeth, a phrase came to mind—*to be consumed by his conquerors.*

Rizzo broke the silence. "Hey, Cap, any chance we can hit that pool before we head out tomorrow?" he asked, looking over to Billy to see if he too was open to the prospect.

Jason looked over at Billy; the smoke from his cigar hung in the still night air.

"Only if we make it quick. We'll take a few minutes in the morning, but then we have to double-time it to make up for time lost. Truth is, we could probably all use a bath."

On the other side of the fire, Dira and Morgan sat shoulder-to-shoulder deep in conversation. Jason had purposely avoided any eye contact with her, still embarrassed from his early morning scrutiny. What was he thinking, anyway? If Alliance regulations were anything like those of the Navy, there were strict rules about fraternization between officers and NCOs. His schoolboy crush would need to stay just that: a crush—and a secret one at that. Looking away from Dira, Jason saw Billy staring at him. He smiled and shook his head. *Shit.*

"What are you working on over there, Gunny?" Jason asked, seeing Orion entering something on her virtual tablet.

"I'm reconfiguring our HUD weapon interfaces," she said, looking up. "What happened today, the multi-guns not being properly set. I thought we'd have time. I wanted to show everyone how to configure the menus." Orion abruptly stopped talking. Her eyes welled-up with tears and she started to shake. Billy got up and sat down beside her. He reached an arm around her shoulder, but she pushed it away. He tried again, and this time she didn't fight it. She turned and cried into his shoulder for what seemed a long time.

Jason was quiet, and then said, "You know, this is new for all of us. We're all winging it as best we can. No one's blaming you, Gunny. Without those amazing guns, we would not have survived today."

She nodded, her face still buried into Billy's shoulder. Jason looked away to the star-filled horizon. As the last vestiges of light slipped away, his eyes focused on a red planet, a planet with Saturn-like rings. It looked close enough to touch.

"I believe that planet is called *Evam*," a voice nearby said.

Jason turned, seeing Ricket had taken the rock where Billy previously sat.

"The name fits, " Jason replied, keeping his eyes on the magnificent view.

Jason looked over to the mechanized alien, wondering just how much Ricket was analytical and machinelike, and how much an actual sentient, feeling being. Still irritated at Ricket's previous actions, Jason stood. All eyes followed him. "It's my turn to take watch."

* * *

Jason overslept. He'd stayed awake, covering two sentry duty shifts overnight, and only crawled into his sleeping bag at 0600 as the sun started to rise. He'd heard yelling and laughing for the past hour and realized it was his team having a little R&R in the pool. By the time he'd gotten up and made his way over to the pool, things had settled down. Traveler was the last one still in the water.

"Good morning, Traveler. How's the water?" Jason asked.

"The water is a gift from *Baruke*. Like fire and air, one of the elemental forces."

Jason realized that the phrase 'how's the water' was an English-language colloquialism and he'd taken the question literally. Over the past few weeks, Traveler had picked up English fairly quickly. Jason saw no need, nor did he have the energy right then, to correct him.

"I will leave you to some private time of tranquility, Captain."

Traveler pulled himself out from the rock pool. Seeing him now, naked, and without his heavy outer leather coverings, the years of battle were clearly evident. Scars—some were long and traveled the full length of his upper torso, and others were jagged, round-like clusters where his hide had been punctured. Seeing he was now alone, Jason activated his battle suit to disengage from his body. The torso and leg panels, as well as his boots, silently hinged open and allowed him to step out from it. The suit's materials were extremely lightweight, yet sturdy enough for the battle suit to remain standing on its own. Wearing only his underwear, he jumped into the water. He'd expected it to be cold and invigorating, but it was more warm and relaxing—which was just as well.

"Mind if I join you, Captain?" came a voice from behind him. Jason pushed away from the side of the pool and turned as he treaded water. "Please, come on in," Jason said, trying to sound nonchalant. Dira stood at the edge of the pool, looking down at him. Smiling, she turned away and activated her own battle suit to disengage from her body, as Jason had, and now wore only bra and panties. Jason, averting his eyes from her, dove under the water and came up on the opposite side of the pool. Dira sat on the opposite edge, her legs in the water.

"The water's surprisingly warm," she said, then slowly slid the rest of the way in. "Captain, I've been meaning to ask you something, if that's okay?"

"Sure, shoot."

"What are the rules about—" she hesitated, as if unsure how to ask. "What are the rules about ... um ... dating on board *The Lilly*? You know, for officers and the like?"

Jason's heart skipped a beat before realizing the reality of the situation. Lieutenant Morgan was the officer she was asking about. She treaded water several feet in front of Jason and was slightly out of breath. Waiting for his reply, she tilted her head all the way back and immersed her hair for a quick moment, exposing her wet, now see-through, bra.

"To be perfectly honest, I haven't checked the Alliance regulations. But if they're anything like the Navy, and I'm fairly sure they would be, relationships between Alliance officers and an Alliance NCO crew member would be considered fraternization."

"Suppose it was an officer and someone who was not an Alliance crew member, but someone who was simply on loan from a civilian hospital?" Her Jhardian accent sounded almost Australian, but then again, different too.

Dira had moved a little closer, their faces no more than a foot apart.

"Like I said, I'm not up on Alliance rules and regs, but if you are a civilian, then dating Lieutenant Morgan may be—"

Dira burst out laughing, which soon turned to coughing and choking as she inhaled a mouthful of water. Jason took her arm and helped her over to the side of the pool. Once her coughing subsided, her smile returned.

"You OK?" he asked.

"Yeah, I'm just showing you how sophisticated I can be."

Jason laughed. "Well, at least you didn't throw up; sophistication goes right out the window at that point." He was aware she had put her arm around his neck when he'd helped her over to the edge. She'd left it there and turned her face towards him—now only inches away.

"Morgan is certainly a good friend," Dira said, starting to laugh again, but she then turned serious. "I wasn't referring to myself and Lieutenant Morgan, Captain." She didn't elaborate. She didn't need to. She let go the edge of the pool and brought her hands forward to encircle Jason's waist. She brought her lips close to the side of his face and he felt her lips lightly brush against his ear as she whispered, "Can I say something without the risk of being insubordinate?" Jason looked into her Jhardian eyes, with their flecks of violet and amber, her long lashes tickling his cheek with every blink.

"You might as well. No one else seems to worry about it," Jason said, in an equally soft whisper.

"I think you are doing everything you can to hide something."

"What would I have to hide? I think I'm pretty much an open book."

"I said *trying* to hide, not successfully hiding, something. There isn't a soul on board *The Lilly* who hasn't noticed there's something going on between us. People notice things—they see how you look at me." Jason felt his cheeks flush. Had he been so obvious? Was he that transparent? She became serious and said, "Why don't you stop thinking so much?" Dira was pulling him backward, first beneath the cascading waterfall and then to the dark recessed space behind it. She brought her lips up to his and kissed him long and hard. Her arms and legs came up and encircled him. All too quickly, she pushed him away. "Okay, that's enough of that."

Speechless, Jason simply looked into those incredible eyes.

"You can't tell me that you weren't wondering what that would be like—now we know," she said.

"And now we know," Jason replied, finding it hard to keep the smile off his face.

"But ... Well, maybe you need to figure out what you want. I mean, are you back playing house with your ex-wife or are you really interested in me? You need to understand, I'm not human, Jason. I'm Jhardian. There are things about me, things that..." She stopped talking, embarrassed.

"Go on, Dira, please," Jason coaxed. He saw how important it was to her, and he wanted her to know he didn't take her concerns lightly.

"Courting a Jhardian girl. God, that sounds so old-fashioned."

"Go on."

"Courting a Jhardian girl is different—unlike how it's done on Earth. Not that I'm an expert on the goings-on with Earth relationships. And, unfortunately, I won't be able to tell you how it's different."

Jason could see there was more she wanted to say. She was flustered. His hands rested gently on her hips. Immersed, they nestled closer together behind the waterfall—their faces inches apart.

"There's more... "

"Tell me, I want to know," Jason said.

"Oh, God. We're ... I'm ... physically not the same as a human," she said, barely loud enough to hear over the cascading water.

"Oh." He let that sink in for a moment. "So things don't work ..?"

Dira smiled, "No, they actually work just fine. Things definitely work. You'd be surprised how well things work. But, I'm not human." She smiled, more flustered. "How about we just leave it at that for now, OK?" She gave Jason a friendly shove, making him disappear back under the waterfall. "Cool off, sailor, I'm getting out."

Chapter 13

The mess hall was packed. Mollie sat with four of the fighter pilots—two men and two women. Lieutenant Wilson was telling a joke, but was switching out certain words—words she knew replaced bad words she wasn't supposed to hear. Everyone laughed when he finished. Mollie looked up at their faces and wondered why they thought that was funny.

One of the women pilots, whom everyone just called Grimes, put an arm around Mollie's shoulder and gave her a quick hug. "That's a stupid joke; we only laugh so Wilson doesn't get his feelings hurt," she said, which evoked a few more giggles.

The XO entered the mess and approached their table. He smiled at Mollie, then looked over to Wilson. "I need you to start rotating your officers into bridge duty shifts."

"Yes, sir. From what I've heard there wasn't going to be a need—not much to do during FTL travel, is there?"

"Long-range scans are acting flakey. So we're periodically dropping out of FTL, doing some short-range scans and making any minor course changes as necessary. With Gunny gone, I need someone familiar with *The Lilly*'s weapon's system. Shift rotation's coming up ... I want three people," Perkins replied.

"I'll take this shift," Grimes chimed in.

Wilson nodded, "I'll be there, sir, and add Dak to the roster as well."

Wilson, Grimes and Dak all stood in unison, picked up their lunch trays, and left the table.

Perkins brought his attention back to Mollie. "How's your mom doing?"

"Not so great. I don't think she realized how bad she was going to feel."

"Well, let her know if there's anything she needs or I can do for her—I'm just a NanoCom hail away." Perkins smiled and strode out of the mess. Others were returning to their shifts as well. Mollie turned around in her seat and eyed the activity of crewmembers coming and going. She'd had the strange feeling she was being watched, and this was the third time she'd spun around to find no one looking at her.

"It's ready, Mollie," came Plimpton's friendly voice from behind the counter. He held a tray filled with covered food items up in the air and then set it down. "Let her know this is my own special recipe—designed to alleviate MediPod hangovers."

"Thanks, Plimp."

"Oh, so now I'm Plimp? You know, now everyone's going to start calling me that," he said, not too thrilled.

Mollie smiled and shrugged. She got up from the table, bussed her tray to a large bin, and walked over to the food tray Plimp had left for her. Again, she felt like she was being watched. In the minute she had turned away, something had changed—someone had moved. After picking up the tray, she headed toward the exit. She scanned the lunch tables; only a few stragglers were still in the mess finishing their meals.

* * *

The Seaman First Class watched the little girl in his peripheral vision walk toward the mess hall exit. He was fairly certain it had been her who had found and then destroyed one of his devices. He felt his anger rise up seeing Mollie Reynolds' smiling face. Soon enough that smile would be gone. Soon enough, she, and everyone else on board, would be dealt with. The seaman let his mind wander. What would Admiral Reynolds' reaction be when he heard that both his granddaughter and son were dead? *If only I could see the expression on his face ... Payback's a bitch.* But right now he needed to keep his head in the game. Having only two phase-disruption modules left would not be optimal, but there was nothing he could do about that now. His primary concern was the AI. What a magnificent piece of technology. *These morons have no idea what her true capabilities were. Perhaps that's best.* For a brief moment, the seaman let a small smile invade his typically-solemn face—then it was gone. *That fucking Craing cyborg monstrosity wasn't the only one who could hack the AI.* It had taken time. He'd had to mirror Ricket's workstation—without either the AI or the cyborg being any the wiser. Now, with his every new hack into her core system level rules engine, the AI was losing her capability to manage key ship systems. And, with his most recent set of parameters, she was incapable of divulging the truth of what was happening. *If that's not ingenious, I don't know what is ...* The seaman got up from the table, leaving the tray and remaining scraps of food behind. He had a lot to do and little time to do it.

* * *

Mollie put the food tray on the side of her mother's bed. "The cook said this will make you feel better, Mom." Mollie watched as her mother looked down at the tray of food, removed one of the plate covers, and quickly replaced it.

"Thank you, sweetie, that was kind of you to do that. But I'm not quite up to solid food yet."

Mollie picked up the tray and took it into the kitchenette down the hall. When she returned, her mother had sat up and actually looked somewhat better than she had the previous day.

"You look a little better, Mom."

"I think I'm getting there. What have you been up to? You're staying away from the Zoo, right?" Nan asked, watching Mollie's face for any sign of deception.

"Nope. No Zoo." Mollie said, then looked into her mother's eyes.

Nan frowned, then she relaxed her face and smiled. "So that's what that's like."

Mollie nodded and relayed another NanoCom text message to her mother: "If you have any questions on how to use your comms, I can help you." Mollie then texted her mother another message: "It takes a while to get the hang of, but it's kinda fun."

"Okay, I'll practice," Nan said out loud. "I'm going to lie back for a little while, get some rest. You be good—stay out of trouble."

* * *

Lieutenant Commander Perkins tensed. With the captain off ship, he was expected to make good decisions and, like the captain, be able to think fast on his feet. They'd received a distress call. Strange, though, that long-distance scans weren't showing any vessels.

The three fighter pilots had taken their posts with Grimes at comms. Wilson, who'd relieved McBride, at the helm, and Dak on tactical, as well as roving and helping out on multiple other stations as needed.

"Helm, let's ease out of FTL and take a look around," the XO commanded.

"Aye, sir."

The only indication that anything had changed was what appeared on the overhead wrap-around display. Distant stars were now stationary. But what really caught their attention was sitting off their forward bow. A ship.

"She's twenty-five miles off our port, sir," Wilson, said.

Perkins looked over to Dak, "And that wasn't showing up on long-range sensors?"

"No, sir. Long-range sensors are clear."

"Lilly, why didn't you report the location of that vessel?"

"Short-range sensors indicate that this is a Bromine freighter out of the Lom-Cornice system. She's been damaged and her propulsion systems are offline. There are currently three life forms on board," the AI replied.

"That's not what I asked you. I specifically inquired about your long-range sensors," the XO responded, irritation building in his voice. There was no response from the AI.

The XO exhaled and looked closer at the ship. "Zoom and fill screen."

The Bromine freighter had obviously been damaged. Blackened scorch marks dotted her hull. Her stern, two drives, had been targeted and much of that area looked to be open to space.

"We're being hailed, sir," Grimes reported. "They're requesting assistance, they've got injured aboard. Numerous casualties."

Perkins said to no one in particular, "Perfect, half our security personnel are away as well as our primary medical doctor. Who's covering Medical?"

"Allen Moppet. Like Dira, he's not military—He's one of her medical technicians."

"He'll have to do. Dak, get a team together with necessary supplies and shuttle over. Until we know who they are and what's happened, I don't want them anywhere near *The Lilly*."

"Aye, sir."

"Sir, more ships are showing up on short-range scans. I'm at twenty-three and counting." Dak reported.

"Belay that order, Lieutenant. That freighter will have to wait until we see what's going on."

"Pirates," Perkins said. "I recognize that fleet of junkers. The Alliance had more than a few altercations with them. Thought they'd learned their lesson, but then again, they don't really know who we are."

"We're being hailed, sir. A Captain Stalls from the ship directly off our stern," Grimes said.

"There are now several hundred ships within a hundred mile radius. Most are old and of no real threat, but a few would pack a punch—like those three destroyer-class vessels off our stern," Dak said, referring to the overhead display where three larger vessels were located.

"Put Captain Stalls on screen."

"Captain Stalls, I'm Lieutenant Commander Perkins, XO of this vessel. How may I be of assistance to you?" Captain Stalls fit the look of a stereotypical pirate captain: long hair, beard, broad smile and something unexpected—likable.

"Lieutenant Commander Perkins, thank you for taking a moment to speak with me. I wish this could be a meeting under more agreeable circumstances. Unfortunately, by coming out of FTL at this particular time and place, you have inadvertently trespassed into a restricted space."

"We would be happy to be on our way. We would like to offer our assistance to the surviving crew of the damaged freighter, then we'll be out of your way," Perkins replied cordially.

"I'm sorry, Lieutenant Commander Perkins. The damage is done. Please prepare to be boarded. There is absolutely no need for anyone on board your vessel to be injured or, God forbid, killed," Captain Stalls said, and then offered up that friendly smile again.

"Captain, we're actually in a bit of a hurry. I'm hoping our AI is translating things correctly for you, so there are no misunderstandings. Now I'm going to expedite things. According to our short-range scans, you are currently, and I mean your ship personally, sitting directly off our stern. In fact, your ship is positioned between two similar destroyer-class warships, correct?"

"That is correct. And there are several hundred other warships targeting your vessel as we speak." The captain's smile remained, but he had lost some of his confidence.

"We have something on board this ship we've just recently started to refer to as Orion's Revenge. To be perfectly honest, I wouldn't wish this on my worst enemy. But Captain Stalls, you're forcing my hand."

"Dak, deploy rail guns and take out both vessels to the port and starboard of Captain Stalls' ship."

"Aye, sir"

"Helm, prepare to phase-shift to open space."

The Lilly's forward and aft rail guns emerged from her underside, snapping into place. Both guns commenced firing their munitions with antimatter characteristics. The two destroyer-class vessel's shields did little in warding off *The Lilly's* rail munitions onslaught. Both ships were destroyed, nearly vaporized, in less than five seconds. *The Lilly's* rail guns retracted into the hull and *The Lilly* vanished, only to reappear again several miles away. Perkins continued to watch the display. Captain Stalls' smile was gone. He'd also turned several shades of grey.

"Captain, the next vessel to be targeted will be yours. It's up to you, but I'm betting you'd like to reconsider things. No?"

Captain Stalls didn't reply right away. When he did, the smile was back. "Lieutenant Commander Perkins, please forgive my rudeness. You are always welcome here. Please help those on the distressed freighter; take your time. Until we meet again ..." The display went black. One by one, the fleet of pirate ships headed away.

Chapter 14

Jason took one more circuit around the campsite, not only to ensure they hadn't left anything behind, but to avoid all the sly glances, uncomfortable silences, or out-and-out smirks from both Billy and Orion. Dira's words still rang in his ear: *There isn't a soul on board* The Lilly *who hasn't noticed how you look at me.* Had he been that obvious? The last thing he'd wanted to do was hurt Nan, or push her away—and he'd undoubtedly done both. On the flip side, he'd had just about the most spectacular morning he could remember. He needed to get his head back into the game and, if at all possible, complete the mission. In a few days, the Craing Emperor's Guard would be entering the Sol solar system.

At the far edge of the rock ledge where several trees were growing at what seemed to be unnatural angles—as if being pulled over the ledge itself—Jason looked to the far horizon from five hundred feet above ground. From this perspective he could clearly see all the other quadrants. He wondered what perils lay ahead for his team. If they were anything like quadrant 1, they had a ton of work cut out for them and very little time to do it.

Dys: 05 Hrs: 13 Mins: 12

The next obstacle was a rocky gorge over a mile wide. Jason studied the terrain ahead and searched for an easier way to cross it, but it zigzagged from one horizon to the other—casting a brutal scar across the landscape. What made this gorge more of a concern, above and beyond its sharp rocks and deep canyons, was the constant expulsion of steam from below that was rising up in the air. Whatever lay at the bottom of the gorge was more than a little hot. But staring at it all day wasn't going to get anything accomplished. The actions he and his team took over the next 48 hours could very well determine the fate of mankind.

Jason joined the assault team where they had converged in the clearing. Everyone was back in battle gear with helmets on. Orion was giving an impromptu demonstration of the multi-gun weapons system. Jason listened and followed along with her instructions on how to access menu selections quickly, as well as how to set default favorites ahead of time.

When Orion completed her overview and answered everyone's questions, she looked over to Jason.

"It's time we head out," Jason said. "Pair off and stay alert." Dira and Morgan were paired off again. Morgan had removed his helmet and Dira and Billy were looking at something on his neck.

"What's the problem over there, Lieutenant?" Jason inquired, moving closer and taking in Morgan's exposed shoulder and lower neck area.

Dira said, "Morgan has some kind of parasite growth." Now seeing his bared skin up close, what surprised Jason—beyond the fact that the growth seemed large, easily an inch thick and irregular in shape—was that it showed signs of movement under Morgan's skin. "Can't really remove it at this time—dangerously close to his carotid artery. I've taken a sample and it's being analyzed."

Billy asked, "Does it hurt? I mean can you feel it wiggling around like that?"

"Yes, I can feel it wiggling around—it's doing fucking cartwheels on my neck!" Morgan spat back, frowning at Billy.

"Where could he have picked up something like that?" Jason asked Dira.

She shrugged and then opened her eyes wider. "I imagine the pool."

"Okay, everyone, take a few minutes and check yourselves," Jason said, wasting no time in activating the release mechanism to his own battle suit. The others did the same. As it turned out, no one else seemed to have picked up a parasite. Morgan was uncomfortable, but it hadn't adversely affected him otherwise, at least not yet. Once all were suited up again, Jason ordered the team to phase-shift back down to ground level, and they quickly complied.

They marched in pairs in the direction of the gorge expanse ahead. Jason's HUD showed the outside temperature was rising steadily. Each battle suit was equipped with an internal climate control, but Jason wasn't sure what extremes it was capable of handling. He opened a direct NanoCom channel to Ricket, who walked by his side.

"Ricket, what can you tell me about our suits ability to withstand heat?"

"The materials themselves are nearly impervious to extreme heat. How the suit will compensate and maintain survivable levels, I'm not sure. I'm reading extremely high temperatures below ground."

They'd reached the gorge. The terrain was even more perilous than Jason had thought. Thousands of jagged spires pointed toward the sky. In between were crevasses and deep canyons. In some spots, he couldn't even see bottom.

"Looks like some of this terrain will be impossible to traverse on foot. For those areas, we'll phase-shift to suitable flat areas. Like stepping stones. Who wants to go first, show us how it's done?"

Jason was not surprised when Orion moved to the edge with her hand raised. "Let me give it a try, Cap," she said. She took a step back and assessed the gorge, eyeing places where she'd phase-shift to and the areas where she would climb or walk. Then she was gone. Twenty yards into the gorge, Orion was already walking across a rocky plateau before disappearing from sight.

"Who's next?" Jason asked. "Follow where Orion is going. Watch where she's phase-shifting to and where she's walking and climbing."

"I'll take Morgan across," Dira said. They both walked to the edge and disappeared. One by one, everyone did the same. Jason and Ricket brought up the rear.

Jason hailed Orion.

"Go for Gunny, Cap."

"Where are you, Orion?" Jason asked.

"Three quarters the way across. Moving a little slower now—terrain is worse here. I've used all but one of my five phase-shifts. I was going to hold here for a while and recharge."

"Good idea. The rest of us will get close and hold for a recharge as well—good work Gunny," Jason said. Now, looking across the gorge, he saw his assault team—some in pairs and some a distance apart from each other—but all were slowly making their way to the other side. The six remaining rhino warriors seemed to be having a difficult time finding adequate locations to shift to, capable of holding their substantial girth.

Four hails came in at once. "Go ahead, Rizzo," the first one to make contact.

"Captain, something's happening below. It's heating up and there's lots more steam. My HUD readout says it's close to three hundred degrees." Jason received virtually the same information from the other three hails. Jason and Ricket were now halfway across the gorge. Most of the others were almost even with Orion, three quarters the way across.

"Captain," Ricket said, "It's now clearer to see that we are traversing a volcanic river of lava, and apparently it has tides. The lava is steadily rising and at its current rate we will be vaporized within seventeen minutes."

Jason did the calculations in his head. No one had more than one phase-shift left and none was close to either side of the gorge.

"Get moving everyone; do whatever you can to get to the far side. Move it!"

One sure thing about a life and death situation was getting that boost of adrenalin coursing through your veins. The capacity for almost superhuman feats kicked in. Everyone was moving quickly now. One glance downward and it became apparent the lava was rising—fast. Beneath billowing clouds of white steam, glowing red lava flowed mere yards below their feet. Heat rose in waves, distorting visibility. Jason hopped from the ledge of one rocky spire to the next and helped Ricket along the way.

Fifty feet ahead, but at an elevation lower than Jason and Ricket's, a rhino warrior was frantically looking around. He was trying to find a way to move higher. Without full battle suit gear, his leather-thong sandals had begun to melt. Then one caught fire. Jason opened his visor and yelled directly across the divide: "Phase-shift back to us—you can make it!" He pointed to an open area close by. The rhino-beast turned in their direction and immediately started to input coordinates onto his wristband. *Come on, come on, hurry up!* He was taking too long, looking up and then back at his wrist several times. Just as it seemed he might have figured it out, the red glow of lava appeared all around him. He screamed in agony as molten rock flowed over the tops of his large feet. As if melting, the rhino-beast's legs merged with the fiery molten river. He toppled over, hands outstretched to break his fall, only for them to disappear into the lava as well. The echoes of the rhino warrior's screams lingered as his entire body caught fire, disappearing into the molten lava.

In seconds, the rest of the assault team would face the same fate. There simply was nowhere to run, no place to hide. Jason picked Ricket up and placed him on his shoulders. In the distance, he looked for Dira. Had she already succumbed to what their fate might inevitably be?

A cloud passed overhead. Both Jason and Ricket looked up. Not a cloud. Two boxy mail truck-looking crafts were lumbering along in the direction of quadrant 2, a mere thirty feet overhead. Calculating the flat space on top of each vehicle to be about fifteen feet by twenty, Jason was encouraged. He opened a channel to the group.

"Look up! We're going to phase-shift to the roof of those feeding drones. One at a time. Jump to the middle—once you're up there, get over to the sides. We don't want to phase-shift right on top of each other. Let's start with you first, Orion," Jason commanded.

One by one, starting with Orion, they phase-shifted onto the top of the drones. With the weight of each additional person, the drones lost a little altitude. Jason noticed that the rhino warriors were not phase-shifting as their turns came around. Jason and Ricket were the last to make their phase-shifts. Weighted down, both feeding drones barely skimmed above the tops of the rocky spires. Once above solid ground, everyone jumped from the drone rooftops. Within seconds, the drones rose back up and slowly continued on with their deliveries. At the edge of the gorge, Jason and the others looked back to the remaining rhino warriors. Two separate screams of agony were immediately followed by two more bright bursts of fire. Only three rhino- beasts, those fortunate to be on higher spires or plateaus, remained.

Chapter 15

The Lilly was back at the freighter's starboard side. Lieutenant Dak had assembled the few remaining SEALs still onboard, as well as the med tech, Allen. Perkins watched the display with the various segmented helmet cam POVs. The team had used the shuttle to ferry over to the freighter and was currently in the process of clearing their airlock. Something about this situation made Perkins uncomfortable. Why only three survivors? Sure, there was damage, but nothing so catastrophic to the point that so many hands would have been lost. And why hadn't the pirates taken the ship, or destroyed her? By the time Perkins had connected the dots—dots that led to one singular conclusion, it was too late. It was a trap.

"Signal general quarters," the XO yelled.

* * *

At the sound of the klaxon, the solemn seaman was ready. His instructions had been clear. Trigger the three devices simultaneously. Only two remained, but that would be more than enough for their purposes. The only deviation he would make was to ensure that he would be there to greet them. With *The Lilly* AI now completely at his control, and with the impending breech, he was aware of something unfamiliar: *A feeling of confidence.* He walked with his head up, taller. A feeling of importance engulfed him. He reached into a small pouch at his side, found the square object, and let his thumb roll over the smooth protruding button. *Not yet.*

He picked up his pace, entered the DeckPort, and emerged

on Level One. His two devices were well hidden and he was sure hadn't been discovered. How that annoying little girl had found the one on Deck 5 was still a mystery. The AI had been reprogrammed—there was no way she could have told that little brat the location. *I'll figure it out.* He brought his hand up and let it gently slide across the bulkhead as he walked. His bulkhead. His ship. The arrangement would have to be changed. There was no way they were going to hand this ship over to the Craing. *Who was doing all the heavy lifting here?* Their new high priests were nothing but conniving little shits. No, his brother had promised he wouldn't let that happen. He'd already killed the three Craing dissenters for them. Whatever the Craing were paying for this ship, it wasn't enough. Maybe he'd rename her. *What kind of name is* The Lilly, *anyway? Too girly.* No, he'd change it to something appropriate. *Like* The Guardian. *Yeah, I like the sound of that.*

Two crewmembers were running down the corridor toward him; they both looked at him. "What are you doing? Where you going, Bristol? Get back to Engineering—don't you hear that fucking alarm?"

Bristol continued down the corridor. The first of his devices was secured to the bulkhead behind a protruding ventilation duct. Bristol stopped in front of the duct and reached a hand above his head to the narrow open space behind it. *There you are.* He brought his hand down and looked thirty yards further down the corridor. There, up above, behind a similar duct, was the other device. *They have no idea of its complexity. Simply elegant.* Sure, Ricket did the lion's share, building those crazy phase-shift belts. *But who came up with this implementation?* And the best part was that the ship, his ship, would not be damaged. Bristol continued on down the corridor until he was midway between both devices. He brought out the small transmitter and fingered the smooth button again. If everything went as planned, both devices would activate at the same moment. Two ten-yard radius sections of the ship would disappear for one hundred and twenty seconds—briefly phase-shifting to a parallel layer in the multiverse somewhere. *The Lilly* would never be completely exposed to open space. They'd thought of that. The pirates would have more than enough time to bring their vessel alongside and then access the ship. Then those same sections would return. No harm done. Bristol was ready. It was time. He pressed the button.

Chapter 16

It took another two hours for the remaining rhino warriors to rejoin the group. Jason was happy to see Traveler was among the living. Tired as they all were, Jason wanted to continue on—at least until they made their way out of quadrant 2 and into quadrant 3. Dira was finishing up tending to the scalded feet of one of the rhino-beasts.

Morgan sat off by himself on a rock. He was having trouble securing the top of his battle suit over the now substantially larger growth on his neck.

"Come to gawk at the freak?" Morgan asked him without looking up.

"What did the test results say?" Jason responded.

"They came back inconclusive. Dira said something about her portable diagnostic device having limited capabilities."

"Let me see it," Jason said, gesturing towards Morgan's neck. Reluctantly, Morgan pulled the field dressing away enough so Jason could peer beneath it. "Has anyone looked at this in the last hour or so?" Jason asked, trying to keep his face as expressionless as possible.

"No. I think Dira is heading over here next. Why? What's wrong? What's it doing now?" he asked, craning his head to do the impossible: see the back of his own neck.

"Stay calm. I was just wondering if—maybe it had grown—you know, a tad more."

"Grown a tad? Holy mother of God, what the hell does that mean?"

Dira arrived and wedged herself in between Morgan and Jason. Seeing Morgan's state of anxiety, she furrowed her brow at

Jason as if to say *What did you say to him?*

She untaped the dressing and exposed the parasitic growth. Both Dira and Jason had to fight the urge to jump back. It was moving beneath the skin. Something dark—a complex shape. "*I don't get it*" Dira said to herself. "*His nanites should have extracted this abnormality from his body. That's one of the things they do, remove foreign matter from the body.*"

"Well? What is it? What are you looking at?" Morgan asked, closely watching Dira's expression. "Did it grow a little?"

"You could say that," Billy said, leaning in from above.

"Just back away, Billy," Dira said, holding her hands out and gesturing for him to give more space. Ricket was now inspecting Morgan's neck as well and started to poke at it with his finger. It moved.

"I can feel it moving. I can feel it moving all around there," Morgan said nervously.

"And you say it's grown over the last few hours?" Ricket asked, looking up at Dira.

"As much as two hundred percent. That's in the last hour alone," she replied. "Truth is, I think his nanites are leaving it alone because they don't consider it a foreign body. From the few tests I've taken, the only DNA I'm seeing is Morgan's. Not really sure how that's possible."

"It needs to come out," Ricket said.

"I don't have the proper instruments here to conduct that sort of surgery," Dira replied with incredulity.

"I will do this myself. Please sterilize and provide an anesthetic to the localized area. I'll prepare myself." Ricket turned and hurried off toward his backpack.

Morgan looked up at Jason. "Shouldn't the doc ... Dira, be doing this, Captain? I mean, is that robot equipped to be digging around in my neck?" Morgan asked, watching Ricket in the distance.

Jason was no fan of Morgan, but he certainly wouldn't wish this parasitic growth on him or anyone. "Don't underestimate Ricket. He brought my daughter back to life, didn't he?"

"Yeah, only after shooting her in the first place," Morgan replied shrugging his shoulders, which only seemed to agitate the parasite. The dark mass beneath his skin scurried from his lower neck to the middle of his shoulder and then back up again.

Dira had her medical pack open and had retrieved a small device. Being careful not to inject into the mass itself with the anesthetic, she began numbing the area around his neck and shoulder.

"Okay, let that take effect for a while. Just sit tight, Lieutenant, while Ricket gets prepared."

Morgan nodded, but said nothing. Dira stood and gestured for Jason to follow her a few steps away. "I didn't want to alarm Morgan, but his condition is worrisome."

"Seems so," Jason said. "But we're going to cut that thing out of him and he'll be done with it, right?"

"It's not that simple, Captain. According to the scans, that organism not only shares his blood stream, but his nervous system as well. What's interesting is I didn't pick up any foreign DNA indicators."

"What does that mean?"

"It means that *thing* is more of a growth than an actual parasite. Still—something, perhaps an organism back in that pool, infected him. I don't know. As of right now, with the amount of nerve clusters tied directly to Morgan's brain stem, I don't see how Ricket will be able to do anything without killing both him and that *thing*. I just wanted to mention that—if it were up to me—I'd let it stay along for the ride, so to speak. At least till we get back to Medical on *The Lilly.*"

"Noted," Jason said. "Let's just see what Ricket comes up with. Here he comes now."

Ricket was back at Morgan's side and poking at his neck again. "Umm, this is better. The effects of the narcotic has also effected the organism. It seems to be sleeping," Ricket said.

"I thought you'd have a set of medical devices. Scalpels—that sort of thing," Jason said with a furrowed brow. "What were you doing over there?"

"I was accessing The Lilly AI's medical database. I now have the necessary programming to continue with the procedure. I can get started now, with your permission." Ricket's face was expressionless. Jason glanced over to Dira, who shrugged and shook her head.

"Do it," Jason said, staring down at Ricket. "Just don't kill him."

Most of the team had huddled in close and were also watching Ricket. "Let's give them some privacy; we'll be moving out as soon as possible."

Billy took the cue and marched twenty yards out into the open desert. "Let's go everyone, over here. Give them some space to work."

A folded-up tarp was placed on the ground. Ricket told Morgan to lie down on his side and to try not to move. Jason wasn't exactly sure what he'd expected from Ricket. He didn't have any medical devices, scalpels, or anything useful other than his partially mechanical hands. Once Morgan was situated and had become still, Ricket placed his right hand over the protruding mound on his neck. Ricket's hand moved very slightly and then was still. Sitting, with his legs crossed Indian yoga-style, Ricket closed his eyes. Quietly, Jason and Dira also sat and continued to watch. An hour later Ricket's eyes opened. Keeping his right hand on Morgan's neck, Ricket gently slid his other hand beneath it. With his two hands cupped together, Ricket stood.

"The procedure is complete—neither organism has suffered any adverse effects," Ricket said.

Jason looked over at Morgan's prone body. The skin on his neck and shoulder was exposed and the mound was gone. Whatever Ricket was holding in his hands was awake and moving—to the extent that Ricket's arms were being jostled about.

"Can we see it?" Jason asked, gesturing toward his cupped hands.

"Yes." Ricket brought his hands down to the ground and slowly separated them, releasing what he held. The organism was black. Short fur covered its entire body, including its six stubby legs. Slightly larger than a hamster, the organism was fully conscious and didn't seem to be nervous or afraid. Its small head was wide, with a protruding muzzle and ears that flopped down—dog-like. As much as they were looking at it, it was staring right back at them.

"What the fuck is that?" Morgan asked, now up on his elbows.

"The short answer is this organism is ninety-eight point nine percent—you," Ricket replied.

"Is it dangerous?" Jason asked, moving a little closer to inspect the creature.

"Does it bite? Or worse, will it infect or get inside someone else?" Dira asked, also coming closer.

"I believe it would have extruded itself fairly soon from Lieutenant Morgan's body. It's self-sustaining and not parasitic in nature. At least now that its incubation period is over." Ricket looked at the creature with indifference.

"So it's not dangerous?" Jason asked again.

"I do not believe so. It does not produce toxic poisons or infectious enzymes. And again, since it's basically Lieutenant Morgan's DNA, it should be safe."

"It doesn't look like me," Morgan said, seeming somewhat confused.

Ricket shrugged.

"So what do we do with it?" Jason asked nobody in particular.

"I can terminate the creature if you wish," Ricket replied.

Although the creature did not seem to understand the conversation, it was paying attention to who was talking and watching as each person spoke.

"Kill it? Why would you kill it?" Morgan protested. "Look at it. It's not hurting anyone."

"Should we feed it? Maybe—give it some water?" Jason asked, reaching a hand out to the tiny dog-like creature with six legs. The creature backed away from Jason's hand, and then tentatively moved forward, as if to sniff his fingers. Dira retrieved a water bottle from her pack and poured some into the palm of her hand, holding it out in front of the creature's face. Again, it stepped back and then came closer. A blue tongue lapped at the water. Jason broke off a small bite-sized piece from an energy bar and held it out for the creature. It sniffed it and then licked it several times before taking a bite. Seeming to like the taste, it finished chewing and looked up.

"I think it wants more," Morgan said smiling. "Here, give it to me, let me feed the thing." Jason handed Morgan the rest of the energy bar and they continued to watch him feed the creature.

"We need to get moving," Jason said, getting back on his feet. "Morgan, if you're going to keep that thing, make sure it doesn't get in the way of your duties. Understood?"

Morgan watched it for several more seconds before

answering, "Yes, sir. I guess it can stay in my pack," but Jason was already heading off in the direction of the team.

* * *

The transition from quadrant 2 to quadrant 3 was dramatic. The jagged rocky landscape first changed to deep red soil, then to lush green grasslands atop gently rolling hills. Separated by the volcanic gorge, it was as if they'd entered a different world. Jason wondered if Serapins were among the wildlife. Perhaps this was a gentler, kinder type of environment. One could only hope. Jason heard the familiar melodic tone in his ear; he was being hailed via his NanoCom.

"Go for Captain," Jason said. "XO, I wasn't entirely sure we'd still have comms this far in."

"Captain, we have a situation—"

That was all that Jason heard before the transmission dropped. He tried several times to reestablish contact, but had no success. *Something's not right*, Jason thought to himself. Hopefully, Perkins would be able to handle the situation on his own. Jason had been testing the comms link every few miles up to this point. But now, not having communications with *The Lilly* had other implications. Undoubtedly he'd need to talk to Glenn—*who exactly were they meeting at the portal? Had he arranged for a ship?* This was far more serious than simply a lack of communications; this put the whole mission at stake.

Jason looked for Ricket. "I've lost comms with *The Lilly*. Any way you can boost the signal, or something that will open a channel again?"

Ricket listened, then appeared to be testing the comms himself. "Communications with *The Lilly* will be impossible this far into the habitat."

"This is important, you can't do anything?"

"Sorry, Captain, no."

Irritated, Jason was about to push Ricket to try harder.

"Cap," Billy said, diverting his attention. At that moment, all hopes of quadrant 3 being a kinder, more peaceful environment were squashed. The ground began to rumble and each member of the assault team turned this way and that to see what was happening. Traveler, easily the tallest in the group, pointed a meaty finger toward the distant horizon. Jason adjusted his HUD's zoom optics. What he and the others were looking at defied comprehension.

There were two chariots, each drawn by a bright blue Serapin. Side by side, the chariots were racing across the plains and headed in their direction. As they drew closer, it soon became apparent who held the reins of each chariot: small Craing warriors clad in leather battle garments. Secured at the rear of each chariot, a long a spear reached into the air. Billy and Jason ordered the group into defensive positions simultaneously. The remaining three rhino warriors moved to the front of the group. Jason and the SEALs took up positions in a semi-circle behind them. Both Ricket and Dira kept back and stayed low to the ground.

"They've changed directions, Cap," Billy yelled. It soon became apparent the charging Craing chariots were heading away from three other chariots in fast pursuit. Those other chariots, each drawn by two Serapins, were configured differently. Wider in size and carrying two Craing warriors instead of one, the figures wore black capes which fluttered in the wind behind them.

"What the hell!" Billy said. "Since when did the Craing grow a spine? And what are they doing here?"

"Something tells me they aren't the same Craing we're used to," Jason replied.

"HAB 12, in all probability, is not experiencing the same time frame as the one we currently exist in. We could be viewing a period of time in their ancient past—even thousands of years ago," Ricket interjected from the back of the group.

"I didn't think this habitat was large enough to support that kind of civilization," Dira said.

"When the Caldurians created these habitats, whatever or whoever was present within the confines of this specific area would have been duplicated—or, better put, their alternate dimensional counterparts would be represented here also," Ricket replied.

"They appear to be all male warriors. Certainly they would have died off fairly quickly," Jason interjected.

"Yes, an interesting observation. Obviously, we aren't seeing the entirety of the habitat's inhabitants." Ricket was quiet a moment while he looked off toward the chariots speeding across the plains. "My sensors indicate that somewhere out there beyond the plains there are close to one thousand Craing life forms—males, females and young offspring."

Excited yells and cheers rolled across the open planes as the black-caped Craing closed in on their slower counterparts. Jason shook his head, amazed. The speeds of the Serapin-drawn chariots were easily double, perhaps even triple the speeds of what Earth's Egyptian horse-drawn chariots would have been capable of many centuries earlier. The pursuing warriors had the obvious advantage—not only having multiple fighters, but also a second Craing in their chariots who was able to throw spears—which evidently was now their intent. With arms pulled back, poised to throw, they moved in closer. Looking behind now almost as much as looking forward, the fleeing Craing warriors began to weave their single-driven chariots back and forth. But when each of the three black-caped Craing let their spears fly, their aim was true. Two spears entered the back of one, and a single spear pierced the back of the other. Both fell dead to the ground. Their chariots continued on for a while, then slowed, then came to a stop. The three pursuing chariots pulled alongside the two dead Craing. Two Craing stepped off their chariots. They were speaking to each other. They both unsheathed what looked to be a small sword.

"Are they going to do what I think they're going to do?" Billy asked.

No one answered. There was no need to. In the distance, the two black-caped Craing warriors raised their swords over their heads and swung their weapons down in an arc across the exposed necks of the two dead Craing. Heads rolled free and were quickly fetched up and thrown into their empty chariots. The warriors walked over to the fidgety, unmanned teams of Serapins and brought them around and in close to the others. All the Serapins seemed to be getting agitated. One stood up and nearly upended the chariot behind it. The headless Craing bodies were deposited at the Serapin's feet. In a flurry, jaws ripped and tore at the bodies, devouring everything in a matter of seconds.

"I could have gone all day without seeing that," Billy said to no one in particular.

"Captain, the portal indicator just became active," Rizzo said.

"I see it. Thirty miles away—straight ahead into quadrant 4," Jason replied.

Ricket took several steps forward, watching as the black-caped victors in their chariots disappeared over the horizon. "Accessing that portal may be more difficult than we had anticipated."

Chapter 17

By the time Perkins had warned Dak of the trap and to get off the freighter, it was already too late. Craing security hover drones, hundreds of them, seemed to appear out of nowhere. Helmet cams showed what came next. An ambush. Bright plasma bolts targeted the team members quickly and efficiently. In less than five seconds, Dak, along with five SEALs, was dead. Perkins sat mesmerized.

"XO, our hull's been breeched; we've been boarded, sir!" Grimes shouted, now working both tactical and comms.

"Damage?" Perkins asked.

"Um ... Actually, none, sir," Grimes said, confused. "And the AI continues to be unresponsive."

"Get a security team—"

"Sir, those SEALs—they were our security team."

* * *

Mollie recognized the sound of the general quarters' klaxon. She also knew exactly what she was supposed to do. Before that, she needed to get to her mother.

"Lilly, what's going on?" Mollie asked aloud as she headed down Deck 4's corridor toward their cabin. "Hello? Lilly? Are you there?" Mollie yelled above the sound of the alarm.

Nan rushed from their cabin, still zipping up her jumpsuit. "Mollie, what's going on?"

"I don't know. But Dad told me what to do if ever I heard that sound."

"What?"

"Hide."

Nan grabbed Mollie's hand and together they headed for the DeckPort.

* * *

They wore old and battered combat suits, which only covered their torsos and upper thighs. Tattoos covered thick, muscular arms. They moved with purpose. Their energy weapons held at the ready. Bristol raised his hand in a gesture to let them know he was one of *them*. He counted forty raiders in all as they continued forward, away from the two breeched areas. Moments later, the missing sections returned. One of the raiders, the largest, stood before Bristol.

"Good work, little brother. I knew you could pull this off. Now take me to the bridge."

Bristol was unprepared for his brother's abruptness. Where was the gratitude? If anything, he should be asking for permission to come aboard *his* ship.

"I don't have all day. Lead on, Seaman Bristol," his brother said smirking.

Bristol moved to the front of the group and led them to the closest DeckPort. Bristol entered first. The pirate captain hesitated and then followed. One by one, they reemerged on Deck 4. Captain Stalls stopped in his tracks. Nan and Mollie stood before him. Stalls made a gesture and twenty of his men continued on toward the bridge. He ran his fingers through his long, black, somewhat messy hair.

"Please excuse the commotion," he said in an accented voice. He was smiling and obviously taken with Nan. "I am Captain Stalls."

"You're a pirate?"

"That I am."

"What are you going to do with us?"

"We have no interest in hurting you. It's the ship we want."

Realization was dawning on Bristol. Obviously he'd been misled. His brother never had intended to hand over the ship to him. He'd been naïve. *How could I have been so stupid?* Bristol continued watching the enamored pirate captain speak to the woman. All of the men seemed to be transfixed by her. *Seriously?* He'd seen this before. More than a few of the men onboard *The Lilly* had a major hard-on for that one. Bristol's own sexual orientation was no secret—simply put, he played for the other team. But he wasn't blind; she was striking. He just didn't care.

Nan was smiling, engaging Stalls as well as some of the others. *They're not buying this, are they?* That's when Bristol noticed Mollie was no longer standing at her mother's side. She had slowly slid her way back down the bulkhead. Before anyone noticed, she was sprinting toward the DeckPort.

"Run, Mollie!" Nan screamed in the distance.

"I'll get her," Bristol said, rushing after her. He had no idea what deck she was headed for, so he took a guess and used his nano-configured devices to take him to Deck 2.

* * *

Halfway down the corridor, Mollie heard him yell after her.

"Wait. Please. I'm not going to hurt you." She ran fast, but every time she looked back, the tall, solemn-looking man in a battle suit had further closed in on her. Halfway down Deck 2's corridor, she knew she wasn't going to make it all the way to the Zoo. He was too fast. She wished Lilly could help her—*why won't you help me, Lilly?*

"Hey, I'm not going to hurt you, kid. Just stop running. Truth is, they're after me too."

Mollie yelled back, "You're trying to trick me. I'm not dumb enough to fall for that. Go away!" She had a stitch in her side and she was spent. Half walking and half running, she turned to face the man behind her. "My daddy will hurt you if you come near me. You know who he is, don't you?"

"Of course I do, and I'm not going to hurt you. I want to help you. But I need to hide too. I've, um, made a big mistake."

Mollie had given up running and was stopped several paces in front of her pursuer. "You were going to steal my dad's ship and give it to that bunch of pirates."

As Bristol moved closer, Mollie stepped back, keeping her distance. He smiled down at her. "I need your help. It's Mollie, isn't it?"

They circled around, now both facing in the opposite direction they had been in. Jack, broom in hand, emerged from the Zoo. Once behind Bristol he swung, Mickey Mantle style, striking the back of Bristol's head. The broom handle snapped in half and Bristol fell unconscious to the deck.

"This way, hurry," Jack said, grabbing Mollie's hand and heading back toward the Zoo.

"Did you kill him?" Mollie asked.

"I don't think we were that lucky. He'll definitely have a bad headache, though."

Mollie looked back over her shoulder. Bristol was defiantly still alive. "Jack, he's moving. He's getting up."

Jack went directly to the access panel for HAB 4. Several keystrokes, and the portal window opened. Jack took Mollie's hand again and they stepped into the habitat.

"He's coming, Jack. Close it!" Jack hesitated, then scurried over to the inside panel and started to enter the code again.

Beep beep. "Damn!" Jack said under his breath.

The sound of Bristol's running footfalls was getting closer. Mollie looked over at Jack. "What are you doing, Jack, he's coming!"

"Well, I usually just let the thing time out. It's a different code to close the thing."

Mollie saw Bristol running toward them. He was looking from one side of the corridor to the other, seeing which habitat they had gone into. Then he was directly in front of her, but facing the wrong way. He turned and saw her. He dove.

Beep beep beep.

Bristol's forehead impacted the portal window even before his hands did. Again, the seaman was sent to the deck in a heap. Still conscious, he turned and looked directly up at Mollie. She couldn't hear his worlds but she definitely could read his lips.

You're dead, little girl.

* * *

Captain Stalls entered *The Lilly*'s bridge. His men were already positioned and pointing their weapons. The bridge crew stood together with their arms raised.

"First things first. Who, may I ask, is Lieutenant Commander Perkins?"

"I'm Perkins," the XO said, taking a step forward and looking as defiant as possible under the circumstances.

Captain Stalls tilted his head and smiled. "Mr. Perkins. I have been looking forward to meeting you. It's not every day one meets someone with such strong convictions." Stalls continued to walk around the perimeter of the bridge while he spoke in a soft, unthreatening voice. "To have the stones to fire on—not one, but two vessels, destroying them and taking the lives of hundreds of men and women so easily ... Well, that really does take a certain kind of man, doesn't it?

Until that particular moment, Perkins hadn't really considered the lives of the pirate crews—or thought about the implications. He suddenly felt sick. Sick and ashamed.

Red-faced and out of breath, Chief Horris rushed onto the bridge. Startled, pirate weapons pointed in his direction.

"What the hell's going on here?" Horris barked, his eyes now leveled on Captain Stalls.

"Isn't it obvious? Your ship has been boarded and I am now in command. Who are you? What is your position on this vessel?"

"I'm Chief Horris. I'm chief of engineering. You won't get away with this."

"Seems I already have, Mr. Horris," Stalls said, and gestured to one of his men to move the chief over to where the rest of the bridge crew stood.

Stalls brought his attention back to Perkins. "You see, Mr. Perkins, even for a pirate, there is a code of conduct. Now don't get me wrong, I've done some very disagreeable things in my life. Things I'm not proud of. But killing hundreds of men and women before a single shot has been fired ..." Captain Stalls stopped walking and now stood directly in front of Perkins. The pirate was easily one of the largest men he had ever seen, and Perkins could not hold his stare. He looked away. Stalls grabbed him by the chin, forcing him to look up into his eyes.

"And that is why I am forced to do something particularly unpleasant. Better I do it than make someone else do it, don't you think?"

Captain Stalls pulled a dagger from his inside sleeve, so quickly, it was as if the knife had always been there in his hand. Coming closer now, face to face in an almost intimate gesture,

Stalls thrust his knife upward, piercing the skin directly below the sternum, driving the blade into Perkins' heart—rupturing his right ventricle. He was dead on his feet. He toppled to the floor. Captain Stalls continued to look at Perkins' lifeless body. The screams from the bridge crew pulled his attention back to the here and now.

"Throw him out an airlock," Stalls said to his men.

"No, wait!" Chief Horris said, taking a step forward, hands up in submission. "Please. At the very least, let us conduct a brief memorial service for him. He was a highly religious man. We have a morgue on board."

Stalls looked at the portly chief, his red face looking ready to explode. "Very well, never let it be said I don't have compassion. Take his body, but return back here directly." Stalls turned to one of his men, "Watch him, stay with him," He then turned to the remaining crew members.

"I truly apologize. Understand, the crews of those vessels were my family. So careless an act could not go unpunished." With that, Captain Stalls headed off the bridge, then stopped momentarily and addressed a fellow pirate. "Find my brother. We need to have access to the ship's AI."

"Aye, Captain."

Chapter 18

Two hours later, Jason and the assault team had made good progress crossing quadrant 3. Periodically phase-shifting forward across the plains, they followed the chariot tracks. They aligned nearly perfectly with the direction their HUD's indicated they needed to go. Jason fell back and watched the team move ahead of him. He'd noticed Morgan had been slowing down, and Jason wondered if he was having ill effects from his surgery. Watching him now, the problem became apparent. The weight of his backpack was stretched to capacity, billowing out nearly twice the size of anyone else's.

"Hold up there, Morgan," Jason commanded.

"I'm all right, Cap, it's all good." Morgan picked up his pace and continued on, even catching up to the others.

"Hold up," Jason said again.

Reluctantly, Morgan came to a stop, but was obviously irritated. The others in the group held up as well, turning to see what the hold-up was.

"Take off your pack, Lieutenant."

"Sir, there's nothing to be concerned with—"

"Come on. Off with it."

Morgan released the waist strap, slipped his arms out from the shoulder straps, and let the pack gently fall to the ground.

"Open it," Jason said, eyeing the now-moving pack on the ground.

Morgan hesitated, then started to unzip the back portion of the pack. Halfway through the unzipping, the creature sprang out, ripping the pack wide open in the process. Now the size of a medium-sized dog, the creature took off.

"That thing is huge!" Billy said from the front of the group. "Morgan, what the hell have you been feeding it?"

"Just water and nutrition bars, same thing we're all eating."

Jason noticed the creature was headed back and running at full speed. All six legs moved at different intervals, but that seemed to work for it okay. When it reached the group, it veered off and continued to run tight circles around everyone. At times it seemed to forget to pull in its big blue tongue.

Dira started laughing. Characteristically, her hand covered her mouth though her helmet was still on. She laughed until everyone else caught the laughing bug. "She's playing!"

Sure enough, the thing was enjoying itself. It charged each of the individual team members, then quickly skirted off—daring anyone to chase it. Dira took the bait and chased after it as best she could, but she wasn't nearly fast enough. When she gave up and turned away, the creature darted back and, dog-like, laid at her feet on its back. Dira reached down and tickled the creature's belly, which caused its six legs to gyrate in the air, obviously in some kind of happy ecstasy. Dira looked over to Morgan and said, "It's a female. So what's her name?"

"Hadn't thought of naming it," Morgan said. "Call her Alice. Had a dog as a kid called Alice."

"Alice it is," Dira said, giving the creature one more round of tickles. She caught Jason's eye, and gave him a quick wink.

"You're not going to be able to carry that creature ... Alice ... in your pack, you know," Jason said to Morgan.

"Yes, sir. I was really struggling towards the end there," Morgan replied.

"This is as good as any place to set up camp," Jason said, looking around their surroundings and removing his own pack. "Billy, set up a sentry rotation—don't include me this time."

Billy nodded, "You got it, Cap."

The group spread out into a circular configuration similar to the previous night. Jason brought out his own small RCM device, set it on the ground, and pressed the release button. Within seconds, it unfolded to its standard size, nearly seven feet high at its center point and ten feet wide, large enough to fit four adults comfortably. With all the amazing technology Jason had been introduced to over the last month, for some reason this contraption fascinated him more than most. As Jason unzipped the front flap, he noticed there was one difference in how the other team members had configured their modules— Dira had moved closer and was now his next door neighbor. A soft, overhead lamp illuminated as Jason entered his RCM. A virtual display came awake and hovered high up at the back of the module. He let his mind reflect back to the previous day with Dira at the rock pool. As he stepped out of his battle suit, he wondered how far he wanted things to progress. That was a lie; he knew perfectly well Dira was already a part of his life, like it or not. But, then again, so was Nan. Maybe he *was* playing house with Nan.

A request icon flashed onto the virtual display and Jason snapped back to the present. There was a high-priority communications file from *The Lilly* waiting. Jason touched the icon.

Hello, Captain Reynolds. I am Captain Stalls. I was disappointed you were out when I dropped by today. Apparently, wherever you are, communications are tenuous at best. Which is strange unto itself, since even FTL transmissions are commonplace. Where could you be? Unfortunately, you will not have heard your ship has been boarded and, as you can see from where I am seated, I have taken command and ownership. I realize this is a lot to take in, and I sincerely apologize—but there really isn't a nice way to communicate this sort of thing.

Now, there are a few things I'm sure you will want to know straight away. First of all, your wife, who by the way is simply magnificent, and your daughter have not been harmed in the slightest. But to be perfectly honest, Mollie has run off and hidden herself, quite effectively by the way, but we will find her, of course— there are only so many places for a little girl to hide on a ship, yes?

As Jason listened, he felt his blood pulsing through his ears; it took every measure of self-control to keep from firing a plasma blast into the display.

Now for the less pleasant news. There have been casualties. But that should be expected from a forced takeover. You realize that, of course. Piracy is a messy business.

I am a reasonable man, Captain. From what I understand, you were asked to deliver two things: your ship and the emperor— Emperor Reechet. Now I already possess your ship—no worries there. That makes things easier—all that's left is for you to deliver the emperor. I would hate for anything unfortunate to happen to your wife, excuse me, ex-wife, and your daughter. But Space is a dangerous place, my friend—very dangerous.

Well, I must attend to things. I so wanted to make your acquaintance; you've built quite the reputation in such a short time. It is quickly approaching the dinner hour, and tonight I will be dining with your lovely ex-wife—captivating is an understatement.

The file closed. Jason's mind immediately flashed to Mollie and Nan—at present they seemed to be safe, and Nan hadn't been thrown into another Craing cage.

Jason hailed the team. "I'm forwarding a file to each of you. Please watch it. Obviously things have changed. We're breaking camp—be ready to head out in ten minutes."

Jason emerged from his RCM fastening up his battle suit. The team had already assembled and was ready to move out. After retracting his own RCM, he moved forward to the point position and headed off towards the blinking purple rectangle on his HUD. They needed to cross twenty-three miles, avoid confronting Craing locals, and figure out how to find and retake *The Lilly* and rescue the crew, including his daughter and ex-wife. And he had to figure out how to divert those three advanced alien warships, the Emperor's Guard, from annihilating Earth. Truth was, he wanted to abandon the mission here and now, head back across HAB 12 and reenter *The Lilly*. *But what about the Emperor's Guard? How do you weigh the needs of one family against the possible destruction of an entire planet?*

They were maintaining a fast jog. Billy, Orion and Ricket—and even Alice—hurried to catch up with Jason. Within minutes, they were brought up to speed on *The Lilly's* situation.

"Ricket, what can you do to get us more distance with these phase-shift belts?"

"They can be reconfigured beyond safe parameters."

"What does that mean?"

"A ten mile phase-shift radius, with thirty minutes re-gen time."

"That would put us at the portal in an hour!" Jason said, encouraged by the news.

"Be aware that overheating is a distinct possibility; this is a dangerous configuration," Ricket added.

"Overheating? You mean the belt gets overly hot?"

"No! Approximately ten percent of the time, the belt will explode."

Jason looked back at his team: Counting himself, they were still ten strong. If he moved forward with the reconfiguration of the belts, one or more of them would most likely be killed. His eyes lingered on Dira, now jogging at Morgan's side. He wasn't willing to risk anything happening to her.

Jason slowed and brought everyone to a stop. He opened

a comms-channel to the team. "Okay, we're splitting into two teams. Traveler, Billy, Rizzo, Ricket, and myself—we're team Lion. Morgan, you'll head team Zebra with everyone else. Team Lion will be moving ahead to the portal with reconfigured phase-shift belts. Team Zebra, you'll make all haste to catch up when you can. Morgan and Orion, keep your team safe." Immediately a private hail came in from Dira.

"Go for Captain."

"What are you doing, Jason?"

When had he become *Jason* to her and not captain, he wondered to himself? "We're reconfiguring our belts. Truth is, there's a good chance they'll explode. I like you better in one piece."

"Yeah? Then I'm fine being in Team Zebra. Just make sure you don't leave us in this place. You and I still have a bit of unfinished business, you know."

"I know." Jason smiled and cut the connection.

Chapter 19

It took Ricket less than five minutes to recode the belts. Instructions were minimal—pretty much point and click. But at ten miles, HUD zoom and night optics would be stretched to their absolute limits. Risks of shifting into a rock or tree or anything else was significantly higher. For that reason, Ricket instructed them to calculate phase-shift locations to several feet off the ground. No guarantee, but one small safeguard. Ricket was huddled up with Dira and Morgan. The codes required to open the second portal were fairly complex and needed to be followed in a precise order. Jason saw Dira nodding and making notes into her virtual tablet. Team Lion assembled in a straight line, side-by-side—everyone looking toward a tree-lined horizon off in the distance.

"Team Lion, are your coordinates set?" Jason asked over their comms. "Ricket, double-check each of their coordinates." Ricket stood still for a moment, obviously reviewing information on his internal HUD display.

"Drop location coordinates are all acceptable, Captain," Ricket said, looking up at him.

"Let's go ahead and phase-shift," Jason said, and immediately disappeared.

Simultaneously, Jason and his team reappeared two feet above the ground ten miles away. When Traveler's thousand-pound bulk landed, the ground shook. Now, ten miles closer to the tree line, the team settled in for a thirty-minute wait time while their belts recharged. Jason took a deep breath, relieved none had gone up in a ball of fire.

"Any ideas on what we're going to do once we clear the

portal, Captain?" Billy asked, now standing at Jason's side.

"Not really. Problem is, we have no idea what we'll be walking into. We'll be emerging into the Craing world of Halimar. The limited meta-data provided gives us nothing to go on regarding their current population, or even the technological levels of their populace. All we know is the air is breathable, and the planet is roughly the size of Mars. My main concern is getting back to *The Lilly*.

At the thirty-minute mark, the team lined up again, reset their coordinates, and phase-shifted at the same time.

* * *

"They must be a thousand feet tall," Billy said, as they eyed the massive redwood-like tree trunks that reached into the nighttime sky. Above the treetops, looking close enough to touch, a nearby red planet with Saturn-like rings hovered in the heavens. Three other neighboring planets, smaller and fading into the distance, were also observable in their shared concentric orbit. Jason assessed his HUD display and the now-blinking purple rectangle.

"Two point five miles, Captain, through that break in the trees," Ricket said, pointing off toward the right where amber lights flickered in the distance.

"Campfires," Billy said, "and quite a few of them."

Traveler, towering over the others, took a step forward. Standing tall with his hands on his hips, he said, "The portal is there within their encampment. It is there amongst the indigenous people."

Jason subconsciously nodded his head. "Of course it is. Why should we expect things to become any easier now than the way the mission has gone so far? Let's move out; stay together."

The five team members headed off toward the distant campfires, skirting twenty- and thirty-foot diameter tree trunks. Several inches of long pine needles covered the ground, quieting their progress.

"I suggest we go dark, Cap," Billy said.

Jason turned around and saw four backlit faces staring back at him through their helmets. He, and then the others, laughed out loud. They'd taken such care to sneak up on the Craing encampment, but had ignored the fact they were lit-up like Christmas trees. One by one, their helmets went dark.

They reached the outskirts of the encampment. There was a large clearing in the forest with what appeared to be some sort of stable—no less than twenty thatch-roofed structures— each illuminated by a small, slow-burning torch. Jason opened his helmet visor. Typical stable-like smells permeated the air: leather, manure, and saddle oil. Team Lion crouched down low when movement ahead was detected. To Jason's surprise, it wasn't a Craing warrior on sentry duty but a seven-foot-tall Serapin. The beast walked leisurely by, then stopping to check various locations before he continued on out of sight.

Jason signaled for the team to move forward. Passing in front of a structure's open doorway, they could see inside. Curled up into circular balls, with their tails wrapped snuggly around their bodies, ten Serapins slept together on a hay-covered floor. Jason had assumed these beasts were held captive, used like horses back on Earth. But it was evident their relationship with the Craing was an entirely different one. After passing a large corral, and what looked like an arena with numerous chariots parked and aligned in parallel rows, they headed towards a wide path that led deeper into the forest.

From behind the trunk of a massive tree, a Serapin sentry guard emerged. Startled, the Serapin froze in his tracks. Without hesitation, Traveler moved forward, pushing Billy and Jason aside. His thick, muscled arms came up—his fingers extended wide, encircling the Serapins neck—all in one fluid motion. The Serapin's feet left the ground as Traveler slowly lifted the beast's thousand-pound body into the air. As his grip continued to constrict, the Serapin's tongue frantically flicked forward, his eyes widened. Without access to his airway, no sound escaped. The eyes lost focus and the tongue fell limp. Traveler continued to hold the beast in his grip for several more moments. He stared into now lifeless eyes, then casually let the Serapin fall to the ground in a heap. The team moved forward without exchanging a word.

They arrived at another large clearing, the size of several large football fields. Numerous small campfires encircled the area, with a larger campfire in the center. Several hundred Craing warriors knelt on the ground. Jason had seen this before. A repeating mantra had begun and droned in the background. Each Craing kept his head lowered, as if in reverence or submission. Just like weeks earlier onboard the Craing battle cruiser, there was a loud cracking noise—one that sounded like snapping twigs or small bones being broken. The sounds echoed into the night.

The Craing suddenly turned in unison and faced in another direction, bowing several times in rapid succession. When the sound came again, in unison they turned forty-five degrees and bowed again. They did this ritual four times—bowing north, south, east, and west. When the strange sounds stopped, the Craing sat up and faced a solitary figure standing on a raised platform several yards ahead in front of the fire.

With a stubby sword at his side and dressed in elaborate leather garments with reflective metal fittings, the figure addressed the crowd. Jason had no idea what he was saying; he hadn't realized that when he retracted his helmet's visor, the rest of his team members had followed suit. Not a problem, unless you needed to access any of the HUD readouts. Readouts that would have signaled the approach from behind of thirteen Serapins and the oversized net they carried between them.

When the net was cast high into the air and caught by another team of Serapins, there was no time to phase-shift away or to use their weapons. In mere seconds, Jason and his team were forced to the ground, immobilized.

Jason lay with his face on the ground. Billy, inches away, was still struggling against the netting and then stopped.

"Didn't see that coming," Billy said, smiling.

"Can you move? Anything?" Jason asked him, trying to see more of the approaching crowd around them.

"Maybe. My right arm seems to have some movement."

Jason could see why. Traveler was on that side of Billy's arm. His bulk raised the netting just enough for Billy's arm to have some freedom of movement.

"If I could just reach my Ka-Bar," Billy said as he moved his arm closer to his belt. "Another few inches …"

Struck in the head from behind, Jason never saw if Billy managed to get hold of his knife.

Chapter 20

When he awoke, he was naked. Naked and tied to a pole several feet off the ground. His head throbbed and something was wrong with his side. Looking down, Jason saw the flesh on his right hip had been ripped open. *Is that my hip bone?* The pain caught up with what he was seeing, and he moaned.

"That looks like it hurts," came a voice close by. Jason turned his face as far as the leather straps holding his head back against the pole would allow. Billy, too, was strapped naked to a pole. Then, as his vision cleared, Jason noticed two more bodies propped up on poles: first Rizzo, and then Traveler, at the far end, who was secured to three poles. Arms and legs spread wide to smaller cross beams. Jason saw that each could move somewhat.

"Everyone all right?" he asked.

Billy answered first: "Couldn't be better, Cap." Then Rizzo, "I'm good, Cap." Then Traveler, "This is not an honorable way to die."

"Well, you're not dead yet," Jason said, turning his head in the opposite direction but not seeing another pole there. "Any idea where Ricket is?"

"I'm here, Captain."

Jason heard the mechanical voice coming from below. Ricket, helmetless, seemingly unhurt and still in his battle suit, stood below him looking up. Behind Ricket, in a semi-circle, were at least one hundred Craing warriors, and behind them, just as many Serapins. A murmur of quiet talking filled the air.

"I could use an update about now, Ricket. What the hell's going on?"

"They are deciding your fate as we speak," he replied.

"Is there a reason I'm pinned up here on a pole with blood streaming down my leg, while you're standing down there, perfectly fine?"

"First, they believe I am no threat. Second, they are intrigued by my ... mechanical qualities. They're quite intelligent, Captain."

"Fine. What are they going to do with us? I don't suppose you could reason with them?"

"Yes, sir, I've been actively doing that. Seems the killing of their sentry guard has complicated matters. Theirs is a clan steeped thousands of years in tradition. We have dishonored them. They fully believe in an *eye-for-an-eye* form of justice."

"Perhaps we can give them something they want or need," Jason said, seeing the same Craing who had spoken earlier making his way through the crowd. Jason then noticed in the distance other Craing beings—a handful of females with their small breasts exposed and small Craing children holding their hands.

"In speaking with their leaders, I found they need for little," Ricket said. "I had noticed very few females lived among the tribe. When I mentioned this and that we had the medical capability to assist them with that imbalance, I detected elevated heart rates, although they showed no outward signs of interest. That same condition is borne by both Craing and Serapin."

The Craing leader had joined Ricket at his side and was looking up at Jason.

"Can you translate for us, Ricket?" Jason asked.

"I will do my best. I'm learning this dialect as I go, sir." Ricket turned to the Craing and spoke in a strange, highly-guttural language. The Craing listened and then slowly nodded his consent. They both looked up at Jason.

"I'm sorry for the death of your ..." Jason paused: *What the hell should I call him?* "The death of your fellow ..."

"No offense, but you're kinda fucking this up, Cap," Billy intoned with a wry smile.

Jason ignored him. "I'm sorry we killed your sentry. There is no excuse. We acted impulsively when he discovered our whereabouts. We are simple travelers and only wish to move on," Jason explained.

The Craing spoke for an extended period of time, first looking at Ricket, and then up at Jason. Similarly to how humans speak, he used his hands in gestures and to emphasize his points. Jason and the Craing looked to Ricket for the translation.

"His name is Wik-ma—at least, that's the English phonetic equivalent. He says he is inclined to just kill the lot of us, me included. They are especially excited about the amount of meat that would be available from Traveler. He mentioned another tribe, the ones we saw on chariots earlier. They are currently not completely at war. He phrased it as a brief lull. That tribe has far more Serapins. From what I understand, Serapin are the lifeblood of a tribe. For many years now, the other tribe has possessed the singular female Serapin, the queen. Many times this tribe has attempted to abscond with her. All attempts have failed. The other tribe is too strong. He said if we could bring the queen here to his tribe, that it would go a long way towards getting us our freedom."

"Like kidnap her? That's ridiculous. He'll just have to do that himself," Jason said, while maintaining as much of an impassive expression as possible.

"I advise you to reconsider, Captain. He is quite serious about killing us. He fears the other tribe. Overtly breaking the peace treaty would be catastrophic."

Jason's mind went to Mollie and Nan and the pirates. Time was running out. "Well, how does he see this working? We certainly can't do anything tied to these poles," Jason said, looking at the Craing leader.

"They'll release three of you. But Traveler stays."

Jason noticed the Craing leader and Ricket were looking at his private parts. *What the hell are they looking at? No ... not at his private parts ... his injured hip.* Over the last few minutes, the nanites had worked overtime; the wound had completely healed. Wik-ma turned and walked into the crowd, which parted, leaving a wide opening. At fifty yards out, the Craing leader turned back around and faced them.

Jason looked over at Traveler. "You going to be okay up there a while longer, Traveler?"

"Yes, I am fine," he replied stoically.

"Listen, we'll be rescued. Zebra team is no more than a half-day out, can you hang in there that long?"

"That will not be a problem, Captain,"

Thump thump. Two arrows, one in each upper thigh, pierced Traveler's thick grey hide. Blood spurted and flowed freely down his legs. He made no sound. He continued to look straight ahead, no indication of what must be excruciating pain. Jason turned to see that Wik-ma was now holding a long wooden bow and had knocked another arrow at the ready.

"Ricket, tell that son a bitch that if Traveler dies, or is further mistreated, all bets are off. He can just kill us all right now."

Ricket conveyed Jason's words to the approaching Craing leader. "Wik-ma says that no additional harm will come to the prisoner, but we need to make extra haste, for without attention he'll surly bleed to death within several hours." Jason realized that waiting for a Zebra team rescue was no longer an option.

* * *

Rizzo, Billy and Jason had their eyes on the proud rhino

warrior secured to the three poles. "Ricket, keep an eye on him. The way they're licking their chops around here, I'm not so sure he'll be alive until our return. Try to get him released from that pole, if you can. And one more thing: Look around for the portal. It has to be close by."

"I'll do my best, sir," Ricket replied.

Jason's team was not allowed to go anywhere near their battle suits or weapons. Using an assortment of leather-like garments, similar to short skirts and strapped sandals, the three SEALs quickly made preparations to head out.

"We look ridiculous like this," Billy said. "Rizzo, so help me God, you mention this to anyone—"

"Why would I want anyone knowing we're wearing dresses?" Rizzo countered, looking equally humiliated.

"Knock it off, you two, we have bigger issues at hand," Jason said.

Earlier, Wik-ma, who seemed to be tribe leader for both Craing and Serapins, had made a crude map in the dirt with the tip of an arrow. He provided the location of the black-caped tribe in respect to their current location. After an extended debate between Ricket and the tribe leader, Jason's team had been allowed to carry three of the tribe's stubby swords. As Jason studied the lines in the dirt, he estimated the distance to be no more than eight miles, but he was only guessing.

Jason brought his attention back to Rizzo and Billy. "I don't like this—it's wrong at so many levels. But our priorities have to be saving Traveler, getting back to *The Lilly*, and ultimately defending Earth. So we'll grab their Serapin queen and get right back here, understood?" Billy and Rizzo nodded. "I've been in contact with Morgan via NanoCom. Seems they're making good progress crossing the plains. I've instructed them to avoid being captured—watch their backs as they approach the encampment."

* * *

The three-man team moved quickly through the forest, following the same path out through the trees as they had taken in earlier. Once out on the open plains, they headed in the opposite direction they had come. The terrain was fairly flat and visibility wasn't a problem due to the multiple nearby planets high in the night sky. There were several landmarks they needed to watch for along the way—a large rock shaped like the letter "T", a snake-like river or brook, and an area where nothing grew. What Wik-ma described as *scorched earth*—whatever that meant. Supposedly, the enemy tribe would be close, within a few hundred yards back into the tree line.

Billy had taken point, Rizzo followed, and Jason brought up the rear. They were running fast, their pace consistent. Each one had been through the same SEAL training. They were in the 'zone.' They'd learned to move past exhaustion, past the pain.

Chapter 21

In the distance, the top of a large rock formation came into view. Only when they were even with it, at the crest of a small hill, did they recognize that the rocks were situated in a large "T" formation. Jason, relieved they were still headed in the right direction, focused on his teammates. Streams of sweat poured down the backs of both Rizzo and Billy. Without hydration, sooner rather than later, they would be hitting a wall. Something big moved. What had appeared to be large rocks or clusters of rocks, Jason realized, were actually massive animals. Heads down and grazing, they looked similar to bison, but larger. These animals had thick, fluffy, white sheep fur. Clearing the next hilltop, they discovered hundreds more of them—a massive herd grazing as far as the eye could see.

"What the hell," Billy said, dodging one of the animals. "Won't be able keep this pace up now, Cap."

Jason pointed. "Over there, to the right. Looks like a small river."

They altered direction, dodging several more of the large animals and bringing their run down to a slow jog. They walked the last few yards. Jason lowered to his knees and inspected the water. The last thing they needed was to get the trots from drinking contaminated water. It was more of a brook than a river. No more than six feet wide, but fairly deep. Lots of rocks and pebbles, and up the hillside there looked to be several small waterfalls.

"You going to stare at it all night, Cap, or you going to take a drink?" Billy asked Jason. He hadn't hesitated before bringing his own cupped-hands up to his mouth to drink the water. Rizzo did the same ... then smiled with relief.

"Nothing has ever tasted so fine, Cap," Rizzo said smiling. "You forgot about your nanites, Captain?" Rizzo asked. "I think you're safe."

"Hadn't thought of that—thanks." Jason, too, began to drink.

Two minutes later they were jogging, then running again.

"So what are we looking for now?" Billy asked.

"Scorched earth, or a place where things won't grow," Rizzo answered.

They found it fifteen minutes later. The plains had flattened out and the grazing animals were nowhere to be seen. The grass-covered plains were gone, replaced by a near-perfect circle the size of a city block. The earth here was blackened and charred. They stopped running. Bent over, with hands on their knees, the three gasped to catch their breath. Jason knelt down and felt the charred soil with his fingertips.

"There's nothing natural about this. Looks to me like something from a ship's thrusters," Jason said. He stood up and turned toward the tree line. "There's a wide break in the trees. I think that's where we're supposed to go."

Jason ran off in that direction. A moment later, Billy and Rizzo followed close on his heels. Several hundred yards into the forest, just as the Serapin leader had described, they found the other encampment. It had nearly the identical layout. A large stadium made from hewn and stacked logs stood to the right of the path. Several hundred of the two-man chariots were parked along the side of the structure. They reached the Serapin stables. Silently, they moved to the side of the first thatch-roofed structure.

"So, how do you tell a female Serapin from a male, anyway?" Billy asked in a whisper.

"Ricket told me the females have utters or teats down here, low on their bellies," Rizzo whispered back, pointing to his own belly.

"So, how do we know where to find them?" Billy asked.

"The Serapin Queen will be kept isolated, in separate quarters, somewhere around here," Jason replied.

Moving as quietly as possible and keeping low, the three SEALs scurried from one structure to the next. Similar to the stable area of the other encampment, these structures were also open at the front; multiple Serapin, curled up into tight balls upon hay-strewn floors, were seen sleeping.

After the twelfth structure, Billy whispered into Jason ear, "Cap, I don't see anything that looks like the Queen. These are all males."

"Let's skip over to the other side of that path." Jason gestured to another grouping of thatched structures in the distance. Jason led the way. *Snap!* Rizzo had stepped on a tree branch. Still out in the open with no place to hide, the three stopped in their tracks, motionless. Once they felt it was safe, they headed toward two small, and one slightly larger, structures. They split up, with Jason heading for the bigger structure. It was quickly apparent that Jason had hit pay dirt. He signaled for Billy and Rizzo to join him. Once at his side, Billy and Rizzo took turns peering around the corner into the corral's interior.

Rizzo made a face and mouthed the words, "Look at the size of that thing!"

Jason removed one of two things they had been allowed to bring along. At over six feet long, the belt had needed to be wrapped twice around Jason's waist. Ricket had convinced the Craing leader that without Traveler's belt and associated wristband, there was no chance of success. Jason flipped open the display he had secured to his own wrist. The return phase-shift coordinates had been entered at the other Craing encampment. Theoretically, all he had to do was position the belt around the Serapin Queen, confirm the coordinates, and, within twenty seconds, press the activate button. But several factors had complicated things. First was the sheer size of the animal. Easily two thousand pounds, she was a mass of flab and flopping teats. There was simply no way Traveler's belt would fit around that Serapin. Second, and of equal concern, the Queen had four baby Serapins suckling at her four teats. They took several steps backwards, away from the corral's opening.

"What do we do now, Cap?" Billy asked in a whisper.

"Nothing changes. At least she's sitting up. Here, hold this." Jason, handing the big belt to Billy, took both of its ends and secured them together by locking the clasp. "Think about it. All we have to do is get this belt around her head. Anything making physical contact with her will be phase-shifted over to the other camp."

"You're going to phase-shift the babies too?" Billy asked with a furrowed brow.

"Would you have me leave them here? They'd probably die," Jason replied.

Billy and Rizzo nodded, seeing the logic.

"I need one of you to sneak in there, drop this belt over her head, and quickly get the hell out of the way," Jason said, looking from one to the other. "I need a volunteer."

"I'll do it," Rizzo replied, but not happy about it.

"Excellent, Rizzo. Don't worry—that thing will be miles away before it wakes up," Jason said, giving Rizzo a reassuring look. Jason needed to get things moving along. Every extra second they took, Traveler's life became more in jeopardy.

Rizzo took the belt in both hands and held it out in front of himself. He made several practice throwing movements. Both

Jason and Billy gave appreciative nods. A noise came from up the pathway. Two Craing sentries were making their way down the hill in their direction. Both had swords hung from scabbards at their hips and partially-shaved heads. Long braids fell below their shoulders.

"Hide," Jason needlessly whispered, and the three ducked behind the rear of the corral structure. The small warriors walked directly to the Queen's structure and looked in on her. Once satisfied all was fine, they moved on down the path and out of sight.

Jason hailed Ricket via his NanoCom.

"Go for Ricket," came the mechanical voice.

"We're just about ready here. Be prepared, she's a lot bigger than other Serapins."

"Understood," Ricket replied. Jason cut the connection.

"You ready?" Jason whispered to Rizzo, double-checking the wristband coordinates one more time.

"I guess—sure. Ready as I'll ever be."

"Good. Let's do this," Jason said. He gestured for him to get going. Jason scurried over to the other side of the opening and peered into the corral. Billy took Jason's place, and with his nod, Rizzo stepped into the Queen corral. Although the mother, the Queen, seemed to be asleep, the baby Serapins were not. Jason watched from behind, and off to the side, as Rizzo approached the Serapins. Rizzo forced himself to smile as four sets of eyes locked on him. With one exception, the young continued to nurse. Five feet away, a second young Serapin stopped nursing. Rizzo looked back over his shoulder; Jason waved him on to continue. At three feet from the Queen, all the young Serapins had stopped nursing and had brought their full attention up to Rizzo. A new sound, similar to purring but far louder, emanated from each of the young.

The Queen stirred. Not fully awake yet, but not asleep either. Rizzo brought the belt forward with his hands far apart in order to make its opening as wide as possible. Jason bit his lip. *Why doesn't he just throw the damn thing?* The Queen opened her eyes. In the split second that it took for full consciousness to return and objects to come into focus, Rizzo threw the belt. But she was already on the move and trying to stand. The belt struck the Queen several inches beneath her lower jaw. With surprising speed and agility, she sprang up and forward, jaws opened wide—far wider than it would be necessary to engulf not only Rizzo's head but his entire upper torso, as well. But Rizzo, feeling excruciating pain in his left calf, had bent over and reached for his leg. The Queen's massive jaws and teeth snapped into empty air an inch above Rizzo's head. As if everything was happening in slow motion, Jason watched as it transpired in a blur. Although it was apparent the belt never made it around the Queen's neck, it had, somehow, gotten itself wrapped around one of her stubby arms. Jason pressed the button. Nothing. Jason cursed himself for forgetting that phase-shifting was a two-part sequence. He now had twenty seconds to *activate* the phase-shift. He pressed the button again. The Queen Serapin and three of her young disappeared. The fourth young Serapin was still present, its jaws firmly secured around Rizzo's left calf. Both Billy and Jason reached Rizzo at the same time. Jason covered Rizzo's mouth with a hand to stifle a scream he knew was coming. Billy, doing his best to pry the baby Serapin's jaws apart, was not having any luck. Billy brought his hands down around the creature's neck and squeezed. *Crack.*

"I guess that did it," Billy said.

Upon closer inspection, Jason saw the bite on Rizzo's calf wasn't terrible. He'd need a few stitches, but he'd live. And most importantly, he'd be able to run.

"Good job, Rizzo," Jason said, getting back to his feet. "You'll be okay."

Billy peeked out the corral structure, first looking left, then right. "I think it's clear."

Once they had cleared the tree line, Jason let himself somewhat relax. Then he heard new sounds from behind them. All three had heard these same sounds before—the sounds of Serapin- drawn chariots.

"So much for a clean getaway," Jason said, looking over his shoulder toward the tree line. "We've got two chariots, four Craing warriors, quarter of a mile back."

"Any ideas?" Billy asked.

"Yeah, make it to the rocks up ahead." The three picked up their pace. The sounds of the approaching chariots and yells from the approaching Craing warriors increased. It was clear they weren't going to make it to the rocks, not even close. The three SEALs slowed and separated. Turning to face their pursuers, they pulled their short swords. The approaching chariots were coming fast, close together, side-by-side. Each was pulled by a single Serapin—with one Craing at the reins and another poised to throw a spear. Jason had witnessed just how effective these Craing warriors were at bringing down their quarry. At thirty yards out, the first spear was thrown. Billy ducked to his left. The spear pierced the ground several inches from his feet. The chariots sped past and separated. Jason didn't wait for the second spear to be thrown. Earlier he'd noticed these stubby swords were fairly well-balanced between hilt and blade—workable. He flipped the weapon end over end and held it by its broad blade. With the closest chariot no more than ten yards out, Jason threw his sword. The Craing warrior's spear was already in the air, headed for Jason. Caught spinning sideways, it glanced off his upper left arm, splitting the skin. Blood flowed. But Jason's sword had found its intended mark. The dead Craing warrior lay on the ground, sword buried to its hilt in the middle of his chest.

The chariots were circling again, one of which now had a single driver. Both chariots separated and then came back together and charged directly at Rizzo. He waited, and at the last moment jumped to his left. He'd waited too long. Although he'd gotten out of the way of the Serapin, the chariot hit Rizzo with a glancing blow to the head. Rizzo hit the ground and didn't get up. Jason and Billy retrieved two of the Craings' thrown spears. Both made the split second decision to go for the Craing warrior at the reins, and with luck, the thousand-pound Serapins would veer away. Jason threw his spear and caught the closest, the single Craing driver, in his lower torso. The Craing fell to the ground and the unmanned chariot eventually rolled to a stop. The Serapin snorted and huffed, but seemed to have lost his willingness to run. The second chariot circled, then quickly closed in on Billy. He followed its movement, turning as it drew near. Billy threw his spear. It hit the Craing driver in the forehead, catapulting him end over end off the chariot and landing ten feet back. The remaining Craing warrior grabbed up the reins and circled the chariot in a tight circle, and charged again. But without gaining sufficient speed, Billy was able to not only dodge the chariot, but also grab on and pull himself aboard. In a blur, the Craing's neck was snapped and his body tossed to the ground. Billy slowed the chariot and stepped off. The Serapin glanced back once, ran on for several more seconds, and finally came to a stop alongside the other Serapin.

Jason raced toward Rizzo, but slowed when he saw that he was alert and up on his elbows looking around.

"Have a nice nap?" Jason asked, but was relieved the young SEAL hadn't been killed.

The Serapins were getting agitated. Drool streamed from

their mouths, and their heads turned in the direction of their fallen drivers' bodies.

"When in Rome," Billy said, shrugging his shoulders.

"I guess," Jason replied.

They fetched up and unceremoniously deposited the dead Craing at the feet of the two Serapins. The bodies were ripped and torn in a blur. Sounds of snapping bones and frenzied biting and chewing continued as if the two Serapins were competing with each other for every scrap of meat. Finished, they continued to snap angrily at each other.

Jason turned away and looked toward the tree line. Six more chariots and twelve Craing warriors were headed in their direction.

"Rizzo, you're with me, hop in," Jason said. "We need to go. Right now!"

Jason took up the reins of his Serapin, stole one more glance over his shoulder, and snapped the straps against the Serapin's hindquarters. The beast leapt forward, quickly running at a full gallop. Billy, close behind, pulled even with Jason and Rizzo. If they hadn't been fleeing for their lives, Jason would have enjoyed this. Looking to his left, he noticed Billy, at the reins of his own chariot, was smiling.

"They're gaining on us, Cap," Rizzo yelled into his ear. Billy had pulled farther ahead, but neither was going fast enough to outrun them. They'd passed the big "T" shaped rock, as well as the winding river. Another look over his shoulder and Jason knew they wouldn't make it to the entrance to the other Craing encampment in time. Both of their chariots had slowed under their weight. Only halfway up the hill, the Serapins were struggling. Jason's mind flashed with images of his own body being thrown at the feet of a group of hungry Serapins. He snapped the reins again, then again, harder. He could hear the sounds of the six approaching Serapins and their chariots. A spear streaked by, inches from his head. "Shit!" Jason veered his chariot to the right. More spears streaked by. Jason's Serapin was huffing and puffing, its pace slowing even more. He peered over his shoulder again—he counted twelve warriors, or was it ten? Up ahead Jason saw that the crest of the hill was finally in sight. Billy's Serapin had begun to slow as well and was unresponsive to Billy's continuous snapping of the reins. Two arrows pierced the inside of Jason's chariot, missing his legs by inches. Three more arrows flew by, imbedding themselves in the hindquarters of his Serapin. The beast reared up and spun its head, frantically biting at the protruding arrows caught in its flank. The Serapin stumbled, then fell to the ground, dead. Chariots closed in around Jason, Craing warrior screams of triumph filled the air. Billy was out of his chariot, rushing to join Jason and Rizzo. Together, they'd make their last stand.

But it wasn't Billy's approach that had caught Jason's attention. Confused, what he saw didn't register at first. Then it did. Orion. Magnificent Orion standing tall at the crest of the hill—the muzzle of her multi-gun pointing back in their direction. She ran forward. Now, close enough to see the expression on her face, she was clearly angry. Her weapon flashed, and the ground erupted all around them. One by one, the Craing warriors took the brunt of her continuous fire. The few Craing that had survived her initial barrage had circled back and quickly fled the way they had come. A handful of abandoned chariots lingered nearby. Billy, Jason and Rizzo took the reins of their own chariots. As Billy approached the crest of the hill, he slowed, and without missing a beat, Orion jumped on next to him. All three chariots picked up speed on the far side of the hill—halfway down, they changed direction toward the small break in the trees.

Chapter 22

Jason, Billy and Rizzo pulled their chariots up to where they had left Traveler. The poles he had been secured to were empty—dark rust-colored stains remained.

"Billy, check on the Queen. I need to find Traveler."

"Over here!"

Jason turned to see Dira waving at him from a thatch-roofed structure at the edge of the encampment. She had removed her helmet and her hair was wet with perspiration. The top of her battle suit hung open, revealing enough cleavage to catch Jason's eye. She ushered him inside, where Traveler lay prostrate on a large table. Both legs had been bandaged. He lifted his head up and acknowledged Jason with what looked to be a smile.

"Thank you, Captain," Traveler said, his voice weak.

"I'm glad you hung in there, my friend," Jason replied. He turned to Dira, "How is he doing?"

"Needless to say, he's lost a lot of blood. Fortunately, that's something I can manufacture in the field, so he'll be fine—just needs a few hours of rest."

"When did you arrive here?"

"About two hours ago. They tried to sneak up on us with that net thing, but we were ready for them. Two of their little warriors were killed. Orion headed out right away to find you."

"She found us. Just in time. I take it our delivery arrived here earlier?" Jason asked.

Dira started to laugh and shook her head. "Oh yeah, Queen Serapin appeared out of thin air, along with her screeching babies. I have a feeling, as far as the locals are concerned, you are nothing short of a miracle worker. To say there was a commotion

154

would be a serious understatement."

"OK, that's my next stop." Turning to leave, Jason looked back. "I'm glad you made it here in time, you know, to help Traveler."

"Me too," she replied. They both held each other's gaze for a moment before Jason left, heading off toward the large crowd of Craing gathered on the other side of the encampment.

Jason hailed Billy.

"Go for Billy"

"Status?"

"Apparently Team Zebra was ready for the guys sneaking around with the net. Several Craing were killed in the process. Morgan and Orion located their leader, Wik-ma, secured the camp, and set up a roving perimeter. We have a total of seven men, three rhino warriors, plus Dira and Ricket." Jason nodded to Billy and cut their comms connection as he approached. Jason was unprepared for the reception. The entire camp population turned and greeted Jason with smiles, several reaching out to touch him. The Craing moved aside, making an opening to where Wik-ma stood waiting. Several yards beyond him, on a mound of hay, sat the Queen and her three suckling offspring—apparently no worse for wear. An excited, equally large group of Serapins had formed in a semicircle behind their queen. When Jason turned his attention back to Wik-ma, he saw that Ricket was there, listening to something the Craing leader was saying. Both turned to Jason; Wik-ma bowed his head, then looked up and spoke. Ricket translated: "I am in your debt; we are in your debt. We didn't believe you would have the slightest chance of success. Now, with the return of Queen Serapin, our citizens rejoice. But the true miracle is her three offspring. One is female—a future queen. This is a great day, an historic, momentous day." The crowd of Craing cheered and little hands reached out to touch Jason again.

Ricket continued to speak. "Wik-ma wishes to offer you a gift. Your choice from among their maidens." Wik-ma gestured toward a group of five smaller looking Craing, who peered out from the opening of a nearby hut. Jason nodded and smiled appreciatively. The memory of the Craing leader shooting two arrows into Traveler made it difficult for him to not kill the little shit where he stood.

"Thank you, and I am honored by your kind gesture. We look forward to a long friendship between our people, but now we must move on." Jason looked over to Ricket. "Have you asked about the portal? Do they know where it is?"

"Yes, sir. The portal, apparently similar to the other one, is nearby, and a sacred place among these people. They believe it to be a window to God. He was quite adamant that no outsiders are allowed there," Ricket explained.

"Is that right? We don't have time for this. Please translate what I have to say about that:

We do not wish to offend their customs or beliefs, but accessing that window is crucial."

Ricket translated as Jason spoke, but the way the Craing leader was frowning and shaking his head, his answer was obvious. Jason caught Orion's eye and spoke to her over NanoCom.

"Orion, I take it by now the leader is aware of the damage your weapon is capable of, right?"

"Yes, sir, they are all more than aware."

"Good. Put two plasma burst into the ground—make it as close to their Queen's fat ass as possible."

Orion stepped to the side of the group, pointed her rifle, and fired off two bright-blue plasma bursts. Several inches from the Queen, the ground erupted—sending dirt several feet in the air. Orion stepped in closer, the muzzle of her rifle pointed at the Queen's head. The Craing leader dropped his non-negotiable stance. He spoke, and Ricket continued to translate.

"When you are ready, I will take you myself. It is not far."

* * *

When outfitted again in their battle suits, along with weapons and equipment packs, Wik-ma and four Craing warriors guided Jason's team of nine and three rhinos to a rocky area less than a quarter mile from the camp. Here they found the entrance to a large cave. The Craing leader offered Jason and Billy two lit torches. They declined, illuminating their own battle suit head lamps instead. Wik-ma bowed again, but gestured for them to proceed on alone—the portal would be found at the far end of the cave. The five Craings found this humorous for some reason, their faces all smiles.

Alice, seldom far from Morgan's side, was the first to approach the entrance. Crouching low, she sniffed the air, took several tentative steps forward, then jumped backwards and made a series of sounds not so different from barking.

"Cap, I'm betting there's more to this cave than the location of the portal," Morgan said, nodding toward Alice.

"Yeah, I don't like this. Why don't you hang back here, cover our backs, while we check things out."

The other eleven team members headed deeper into the cave.

Traveler limped along slowly. The two surviving rhino warriors stayed close by his side, there if he needed assistance, although he'd never ask for it.

Thirty feet in, the cave narrowed from twenty feet across and that high, to half that. Something crunched beneath their feet, like gravel or twigs. Jason pointed his helmet lamp down and realized it was actually small bones.

"Creepy," Dira said. She slowed her pace and held to the back of the group, where she found Alice cowering and looking over her shoulder. Alice looked up at her, then quickly turned and ran back in the direction they'd come. "Figured she'd want to stay with Morgan," she said disappointedly.

"I think I see something," Rizzo said over his comms. As they continued forward, the cave veered slightly to the right. There was definitely movement ahead. Something was reflecting the light back from their lamps. Jason, Billy and Orion, at the front of the group, saw the creatures first. Large enough they needed to walk single-file, the big cockroach-like creatures were heading in their same direction. So far, they'd shown no signs of noticing anyone behind them. Then the last creature slowed, stopped, and then turned. It reared up on its back two legs as if attempting to crawl up the cave wall and flipped back to face the assault team. Seemingly wanting to hold its ground, the insect activated its two protruding pinchers.

"They're disgusting!" Dira yelled. "I hate roaches, and those fucking things are much bigger than any of us. Can't we just go another way?"

Like two curved swords, or scissors, the pinchers continued to rapidly open and close.

"Cap, is it just me or do those things look familiar?" Billy asked.

"Yeah ... was thinking the same thing. Kinda look like miniature Craing battle cruisers. Hold up, everyone—doesn't look like we're going any further until this one is dealt with," Jason commanded.

One of the two remaining rhino warriors, whose name translated to Stands in Storm, was already on the move. Jason watched and was somewhat surprised by his fearlessness. As the rhino drew closer, the bug's pinchers increased their activity. Without turning his back on the insect, the rhino held out his left hand toward Traveler. Traveler made a grunt, but relinquished his own hammer. Now, holding two heavy hammers, Stands in Storm moved forward.

The enormous bug was back on its feet, exposing a series of thick mucous-coated plates along its underside. With no neck to speak of, the bug's segmented head angled down further into its own body. This allowed it to see the rhino standing before it. It continued to move its pinchers. The rhino probed forward with his left-hand hammer—making a stabbing motion. The bug's attention was completely focused on the outstretched hammer. The rhino pulled back too slowly and the extended hammer was firmly caught in the pinchers. Stands in Storm didn't hesitate; obviously, that was his plan, as the other hammer was already moving. With his arm straight out, he spun the hammer around in a circular, counter-clockwise arc. As the weapon's centrifugal force increased to the point the hammer was nothing more than a blur, it struck the bug's head from beneath, and continued on, taking with it the bug's head. The bug stayed vertical for several moments, then tipped over onto its back.

Stands in Storm returned Traveler his hammer, turned back to the dead insect, grabbed up the bug's two skinny, stick-like back legs in one fistful, and dragged the dead bug behind himself. After maneuvering around the team and depositing it away down the cave, he returned to Traveler's side. They all moved forward again. Dira had moved from the back of the pack to Jason's side. He had noticed it earlier, but now it was louder, much louder. A squealing sound. One look at the walls up ahead, and he knew what it was. More of them. Much smaller—perhaps their offspring. Hundreds of the six-inch-long cockroaches rushed forward. On the walls. Up above their heads. Soon they were several inches deep at their feet. With every step, Jason felt their bodies crunch below his feet. Above the constant screeching sound were Dira's screams. He turned to face her, to console her. The bugs covered nearly every inch of her body. Trails of sticky wet mucus glistened in the dim light. He brushed several bugs from her visor and looked into her eyes. "They can't hurt you, Dira. They can't penetrate your battle suite. Take deep, slow breaths. You're going to be fine." She nodded but didn't look happy.

As they continued on, fewer and fewer cockroaches remained. The cave widened around the next bend and angled down. The way was steep to the point they needed to slow their pace and watch their step. Jason also noticed the temperature readout on his HUD had been fluctuating— forty-five degrees down to thirty-five. He glanced behind and noticed the rhinos were now walking single file, each had an arm outstretched to the shoulder of the rhino before him. With a nod to Traveler, Jason felt a heavy hand on his shoulder. He knew first hand that rhino warriors were virtually blind in low-light situations.

At a half-mile in, the ground leveled off and the cave widened into a large circular cavern, fifty paces wide and just as lofty. Multiple other tunnel openings encircled the room. Even in the near total darkness, subtle movement could be seen at each of the openings. Jason was leery of the insects, or anything else that may be lurking close-by. The portal, similar to the first one in blue, had a purple border and hovered just up ahead. Where the first portal was a window into the *The Lilly's* domain, this portal looked out onto, Jason assumed, a metropolis somewhere on the planet of Halimar. Jason took in the view—not dissimilar to looking at Manhattan's skyline at night— bright lights emanating from high-rise buildings, and the frenzied activity of a large populace. Here, the sky was lit with countless airborne crafts of varying sizes and shapes. And similar to the other portal, there was a metal sign affixed to a pole with the HAB 12 alien character designations. Below it was a small metal box. Ricket moved to the box, flipped open its hinged lid, and began entering the access code.

"Hold on a minute, Ricket," Jason said, then hailed Morgan. No response. He tried again as he began jogging back, thinking the half mile of solid rock must have interfered with their comms. He made it to the cave's opening, where he found Morgan. His headless body was covered in blood and sprawled across the cave entrance. His battle suit showed signs of damage, with numerous scrapes and gouges. It didn't seem to have been penetrated. Apparently, the suit's primary weakness was the neck cowling. Looking around, Jason found no sign of Morgan's head. He didn't get it. Morgan had been heavily armed with a multi-gun. He also had his HUD, which would have warned him of anything approaching. Crouching down closer to the body, Jason noticed something peeking out on Morgan's exposed upper neck. There appeared to be another black growth. Jason released the upper portion of Morgan's battle suit and let it fall open. Hundreds of growths covered his upper body. Jason stood up and backed away, noticing that more than a few had burst. "Damn, Morgan. Why didn't you say something to us?" He spoke the words aloud, angrily. Morgan hadn't fought back against the insects because the growth had already killed him.

As if on cue, Ricket was at Jason's side. "I can remotely program his belt."

Jason retrieved Morgan's unused rifle, sidearm and pack from the body. Ricket went to work, and within two minutes Morgan was phase-shifted somewhere deep into the rocky hillside. On the way back outside the tunnel entrance, Jason let the team know via their comms. No other words were spoken between Jason and Ricket as they neared the portal.

Dira had several questions about the condition of the body, but eventually sagged under the weight of her emotions. Jason pulled her close, where she sobbed into his shoulder. The three rhinos watched in silence. Traveler wiped at a single tear from his own cheek.

Ricket was back at the portal's keypad. Twenty seconds later, the telltale *beeb beeb beeb* indicated Ricket had been successful.

"What about Alice?" Dira asked, looking back toward the tunnel they'd come from.

"She'll be fine. Maybe we'll see her on our way back. Right now, we need to go."

One by one, the remaining eleven team members stepped up and into the portal window.

Chapter 23

They emerged on the planet of Halimar, high up on the side of a hill. Here amongst trees and tall grass was another metal sign. Jason assumed alien characters represented the same HAB 12 designation. Another access box was secured below the sign. The portal window itself was gone.

Ricket said, "To keep their locations secret, portals can be configured to be hidden, Captain."

One thing was immediately apparent: they were anything but inconspicuous. The five fairly tall Alliance crewmembers, striking in their battle suits, were uncommon enough, but the three seven-foot-tall rhino warriors would, beyond any doubt, draw attention. Although Ricket was indeed Craing, he was unmistakably their long lost emperor. Jason had little doubt he'd be recognizable even behind his battle suit's visor.

Jason looked out at the bustling city in the distance. A thick layer of smog, more like soot, filled the air. He had been unsure if the laser they were looking for would actually be visible. Ricket approached and stood at Jason's side, and both gazed out at the distant horizon.

Ricket said, "Assuming the laser is powerful enough, the heating of atmospheric gasses changes its index of refraction. The difference in the index of refraction of the ionized air and that of the surrounding air could cause the light to scatter enough to be visible." Jason looked down at Ricket and shook his head, somewhat irritated. He'd done it again. He knew what Jason was pondering.

"There," Ricket said, pointing his mechanical-looking finger at the left horizon. A blue line stretched from ground level up to the heavens. The rest of the team converged together; all gazed up at the laser beam's skyward trajectory.

"What's the approximate distance?"

"Close to two hundred and fifty miles, maybe more," Ricket replied.

"Let's get out of sight. We need to signal Glenn's contacts here on planet for a rendezvous. Hopefully he was able to work that out on his end," Jason said, not sounding confident.

Ricket was quiet while looking out at the landscape below. "I've generated the signal, and provided our coordinates as Glenn instructed, Captain," Ricket said.

"Now we wait and decide our next move," Jason said, already heading off to the cover of a nearby cluster of trees.

* * *

Huddled together and out of sight, the group sat on the ground; several were leaning against trees. Impatient, Jason glanced at his HUD's mission countdown timer again:

Dys: 00 Hrs: 5 Mins: 33

Discouraged, he stood and paced, then decided to take a walk. Startled, he nearly walked into three Craing males standing mere feet in front of him. All three held small energy rifles, which were pointed in Jason's general direction. One spoke rapidly. He looked and sounded angry. Ricket moved in between them, his hands held up conciliatorily. Ricket spoke, but they seemed too astonished to listen. All three fell on their knees, heads bowed low. Ricket stopped talking and glanced back up toward Jason, exhibiting a rare expression of irritation.

"Are they the ones sent to meet us?" Jason asked.

"Yes, apparently they expected us yesterday; they've been waiting here," Ricket replied.

"Tell them to get up ... we don't have time for any of this."

The three Craing rose up on their own, still staring at Ricket in reverence. Ricket continued to speak to them as they intermittently gestured toward the horizon and the blue laser in the distance.

Jason, growing impatient, interrupted their chattering. "Are they going to take us?"

"Yes, but they are nervous. Their ship is small and old. They are concerned about the rhinos and their substantial weight. Also, Halimar is heavily policed. They, and others too, are politically aligned with the one you know as Glenn and his cause. But they are few in number and would face certain death if discovered. Just being here with us could be a death sentence."

"Ask them to lead us to their ship, so we can see what they're talking about. It can't be that bad."

Ricket relayed what Jason said, and they seemed agreeable to that. They took another tentative glance at the rhinos and headed off deeper into the trees. It was a quick walk before they reached a clearing to where a small craft waited.

There were several groans, and Billy was the first to speak up. "Come on, Cap. You can't tell me this death trap is our only option." Somewhat bug-like, the craft was obviously old. An assortment of varying-color rusted panels, perhaps from other ships, comprised its outer hull. One of its landing struts hadn't completely deployed, which caused the ship to tilt awkwardly to one side.

As they approached, a hatch slid open mid-ship. The three Craings scurried in first. Jason waved the others to get in. "We won't know if it'll fly unless we try. Come on, nothing ventured

..." Jason was making light of the situation, but he was more than a little leery.

The rhino warriors were the last to climb aboard. They had to stoop down on their hands and knees and crawl to the back of the already-cramped main compartment. Traveler was moving slow and his bandage oozed, his wounds infected.

Since there were no seats, Jason figured it was some sort of small delivery craft. Like Halimar's version of a cargo van. A fourth Craing appeared from the cockpit area. Naked like the others, she must have stayed behind on the ship. Jason realized she was one of the few female Craing he had seen. Unlike the males, she had a full head of hair. She began barking orders at the other three Craings, obviously in command. Jason had been watching Dira. Since Morgan's death, she had kept herself busy attending to Traveler, but she was uncharacteristically quiet, even withdrawn. He wanted to reach out to her, console her somehow.

"Captain, this is the ship's commander, Gaddy—she is a relative of Glenn's. Actually, she is his niece," Ricket said, pulling Jason back to matters at hand. "Attempts to sabotage the Loop are not all that uncommon. There is much civil unrest amongst the people of Halimar. But no one, to date, has ever been successful destroying a sub-station. If we are to have their help, they wish to discuss several things first. Primarily, they'll want safe passage to the Craing settlement where her uncle will be. Gaddy would also like to know our plan."

"Perhaps it would be best if she'd loan us her vessel— "

The Craing commander shook her head, apparently understanding enough of what was said without Ricket's translation. She spoke in heavily-accented broken English, "We came too far. We all go or no one goes. Give us passage, and we trust you know what you're doing."

"Fine. You'll have your passage to the settlement," Jason answered. "As for our qualifications, know that this is what we do and what we have been trained for." Jason waited for Ricket to translate.

With that understanding, the young Craing commander withdrew into the cockpit and sat at the controls. She had pulled her long black hair into a ponytail and it swung back and forth as she moved. After several false starts, the main drive caught and noisily droned in the background. The vessel shook and the drives kicked into a high-pitched whirling sound. Through a small window on the hatch, Jason could see the ship had left the ground, but it seemed to momentarily stall. Then, with a jolt, the craft lifted higher and was headed in the direction of the laser.

Having to yell over the noise and looking at the three male Craings, Jason asked Ricket, "What can they tell us about the location? What's security like?" The three Craings talked amongst themselves and Ricket for a brief spell. While they conversed, Jason huddled close with Billy and Orion. "What are our weapons, our multi-guns, capable of now that we're on Halimar?" Jason asked.

"Captain, our weapons have a full load of rail and missile projectile munitions," Orion replied, "but they are finite. Once you're out, you're out. Energy weapon settings will operate same as before."

Turning his attention back to Ricket and the three Craings, Jason enquired again about the layout. Ricket explained, "It's commonly referred to as the Loop sub-station. Although the numbers can vary, there are never less than seventy-five armed guards or sentries within and around the outer perimeter. The compound itself is fortified behind sixty-foot-high concrete walls and multiple turret-mounted plasma cannons."

"Any weaknesses?" Jason asked.

"None that they are aware of," Ricket said. "They again asked if we are confident we will have success?"

Billy spoke up, "Just tell them not to worry. We have been trained for this type of thing," Jason looked at the young Craing dissidents and tried to look as confident as possible. He glanced at his HUD's mission countdown readout. Time was quickly running out. They now had less than three hours. Jason suspected the Emperor's Guard would be making preparations or already underway to enter the worm hole. "How close are we?" he asked.

The cabin noise changed pitch. They were descending. Looking out the hatch window, the Loop sub-station was clearly in view. The laser was massive. A consistent hum and vibration filled the air. Then it stopped.

He looked again through the window. The bright blue beam of the laser was gone. "What the hell happened? Why's it off?" Jason asked, alarm in his voice.

The three Craing males looked to one another, confused, then spoke rapidly to Ricket.

"They said this is common and not to worry. The laser is turned off for maintenance at least once a day," Ricket replied.

"Then how will destroying it make any damn difference?"

Ricket listened to them, spoke back a few short sentences, and turned to Jason. "They are unsure what the problem is, but Glenn was well aware of it. They're not sure why we are just learning of this shutdown now—they want to know how it will impact our mission," Ricket said, translating their comments to Jason.

"What mission? Obviously, not all the lasers need to be operational simultaneously. And the truth is, that actually makes sense. Of course they would need to have the ability to make repairs, do maintenance work, or have a back-up at the ready in case someone does something like we're planning to do," Jason said.

The hatch slid open and everyone scrambled out of the tight compartment. They had set down in a rural farm area—what looked to be some kind of vegetable field. At no more than five miles away, the grey Loop sub-station compound loomed nearby. The sky was bright with three neighboring planets suspended overhead.

Jason walked several paces into the field, still looking up, "Those lasers, they're not stationary?"

"No. Even though we are at the planet's southern-most pole, the laser, all their lasers, are always tracking the convergence point in space. They constantly move, rotating and pivoting."

Jason said, "What if we don't destroy this facility?"

Ricket was now looking up as well.

"What if we use this laser to destroy the others? Use it as a weapon. Would that be possible?" Jason asked.

"No. Couldn't destroy them all, but perhaps several," Ricket replied. "I would need the specific coordinates of each of the seven planet sub-stations. I would also need access to their overall system control AI," Ricket said, looking back up at Jason. Behind his helmet's visor, his illuminated-face again revealed more expression than Jason was used to.

"You'd need to hack their network."

"Yes, and most assuredly they will have numerous safeguards in place."

"Can you do it?"

"I designed it."

"What do you mean you designed it?" Jason asked. The rest of the group had migrated over to where they were standing.

"Captain, I believe I was the scientist, the one who designed this system in the first place."

"That must have been hundreds of years ago, Ricket. How—"

"Two hundred and thirty, to be exact. My memories, for the most part, have been wiped. With that said, it was necessary to leave core-level sub-routines—required for me to maintain a minimal sense of continuity and time. Although specific events, memories, are gone, I have been able to build new logic paths and make qualified assumptions about my past. In all likelihood, it was my work as a scientist, and the eventual construction of the Loop, that subsequently lead to me becoming emperor."

"Everyone knows this. Emperor Reechet, of course, was the Loop scientist," Gatty interjected. "Your story is taught to our young in school at early age."

Jason, at this point, was not surprised by news of another incredible Ricket accomplishment. He found it interesting how quickly Gatty picked up their language, and again, how Ricket's expression was becoming more animated. "The Craing have a unique aptitude for languages, Captain ... they are highly-intelligent people. Back on board Craing warships, I learned they typically speak hundreds of languages—it comes easily for them." Ricket turned his attention back to the sub-station.

"Gatty, what do you know about the inside layout of the sub-station?" Jason asked. "I questioned Glenn if facility schematics could be provided."

Gatty looked perplexed and crossed her arms under her breast. "No, we have nothing like that. How could we? A stupid question."

Rizzo, off to the side of the group, chuckled—quieting when Jason glanced his way.

Speaking to the group, Jason said, "We need to get in closer before we phase-shift. We'll go in with a small team, do some reconnaissance. Ricket, my HUD's picking up several large crafts in the area, perhaps Craing battle cruisers?"

"Correct, Captain. My long-range sensors, which I might add operate quite effectively here, tell me there is a military base less than twenty miles from our current position. Stationed there are eight light-destroyers and three heavy battle cruisers—not to mention an array of many smaller vessels. There are fifteen thousand, two hundred three combat-capable vessels in Craing space, including three warships, and although smaller, they have similar signatures to *The Lilly*. They comprise, undoubtedly, the Emperor's Guard."

"Cap, we have little more than minutes before all hell drops down on us," Billy said. "And it sounds like you, Ricket, will need time to interface with their network. How's this going to work?"

Jason looked in the direction of the sub-station. Using his HUD's zoom optics, he could make out more detail. Overall it appeared to be about the size of the U.S. Pentagon building—an immense structure. Octagonal in shape, there were four outside wall watch-tower turrets; each was covered and had some sort of pivoting energy weapon. A fifth watch tower rose from the back of the compound, nearly twice as high as all the others. It also had its own compliment of independent energy weapons. "Billy, Orion, Ricket, you're with me. Traveler, sorry, you're in no shape for this."

"My legs are fine, Captain," he replied.

Jason looked to Dira.

She shrugged. "No way, he's got some kind of infection. He can barely walk." Dira looked apologetically over to Traveler.

"Okay, Stands in Storm, you're with us. Traveler—hang back with the team here. Rizzo, you're team leader—stay on comms and let me know what's happening if the shit hits the fan."

"Aye, Cap."

"I go with you," Gatty said with her hands on her hips.

"No, too dangerous. We have battle suits and are trained for this stuff. Stay with your ship, be prepared to get out of here at a moment's notice," Jason said, but liking the little Craing woman's moxie. With that said, he and his small team headed off across the open field in the direction of the sub-station. Jason received a hail.

"Go for Captain."

"How come you never say goodbye, Jason?"

Jason was caught off-guard by how much he enjoyed the sound of her voice. "I'll see you soon, Dira."

The ground started to vibrate again. Ozone filled the air. In a burst, the laser shot up towards the heavens.

Jason opened a channel to his group. "Ricket, can your sensors provide some kind of facility layout?"

"Somewhat, Captain ... nowhere near what *The Lilly* would be capable of, but I can detect walls and open areas."

"We'll need a drop location. Somewhere that's not showing a lot of traffic," Jason said. At three miles out, Jason signaled for them to hold up.

"I've forwarded a virtual layout," Ricket said. "It's an approximation of the facility. I've gone ahead and marked the probable location where the facility's network communications hub most likely is. Massive amounts of data are being funneled through there."

"I see it. I also see a hell of a lot of Craing. What's this area you've outlined in blue—looks to be subterranean?" Jason asked.

"I don't know for sure, but it gets virtually no traffic and it's fairly close to the network hub," Ricket replied.

"Guess there's only one way to find out. Can you provide me coordinates specific enough that I don't phase-shift into a wall or something else?"

"I believe so, Captain; I've already configured your HUD settings."

"Got it. You hang tight here until you hear from me. If everything's clear, the rest of you can follow." Jason phase-shifted away.

Chapter 24

It was pitch black. Jason's HUD strobed a warning, along with an accompanying audio alarm. Radiation levels were high. Jason hailed Ricket.

"Go for Ricket."

"There's radiation here."

"Your battle suit will shield most of it—you should be fine."

"That doesn't give me a warm and fuzzy feeling, Ricket. Do I need to get out of here?"

"Unless your suit is damaged, you are protected," Ricket replied.

"I'll do some exploring. Continue to hold there." Jason increased the amount of light emitting from his head lamp. Walking slowly, he found that the room was large and the vibration was stronger. He guessed it was some kind of pump room. He was reminded of the Craing Battle Cruisers, with their strange mix of older outdated machinery on one hand and highly-advanced technology on the other. At the far end of the football field-sized room, eight gargantuan dark-green containers that looked to be big boilers or holding tanks stood against the back wall. Upon further inspection, they towered at least fifty feet high. Jason walked to a side wall and hailed Billy. "Come on over."

The first to arrive was Billy, then Orion, Stands in Storm, and Ricket. As if on cue, the pumps in the room activated and the noise increased, even through their helmets' insulation, to a near-deafening level.

Billy yelled into his comms, "I guess we know why nobody hangs around in this area."

Jason was on the move. "There's a doorway over here. Stay together." He'd seen this type before. The Craing had a unique latching system for doorways. Nothing like what you'd find on Earth. Theirs had an indentation at the middle of the door, lower down to accommodate their height, and a lever mechanism that swiveled left or right. Definitely not an improvement; if anything, more cumbersome. He swiveled the lever to the left and leaned his weight into the door. Heavy, as expected, it moved slowly on well-lubricated hinges. Bright light streamed in from a corridor. The door, as well as the surrounding walls, was easily three feet thick. The last one out, Stands in Storm, had difficulty maneuvering through the door's narrow opening. Fortunately, the ceilings were close to ten feet high. They came to a juncture where three corridors converged. Ricket took point and headed off down the middle hall. Jason glanced at his mission countdown readout on his HUD; the Emperor's Guard would be leaving the star system at any time. He let his thoughts wonder to the plight of Mollie and Nan and the rest of the crew aboard his pirated ship. *Damn, we really need to hurry things up here.*

"They will have safeguards," Ricket said, "most likely imbedded in their code, as well as real physical barriers to keep us from repositioning their lasers. That's the way I'd do it."

Billy responded, "Well, it's probably the way you *did* do it. You just don't remember."

At the next junction, three Craing males turned the corner and walked into Ricket. Irritated at first, they froze, paralyzed in shock seeing their emperor standing before them. But it was seeing Stands in Storm that triggered a fear response. Billy was ready. Three quick pulses from his multi-gun sent the three Craings to the floor. Each was wearing a white uniform, and a clip-on type metallic tag.

"They'll wake up with a bad headache in about four hours," Billy said.

"Good—grab those tags," Jason said, "We may need them."

Ricket moved down the corridor again, with Jason and the team following.

"Captain," Ricket said, "I believe the network control hub is at the end of this corridor." He stopped and turned towards Jason. "Unfortunately, I'm detecting other readings as well. Security hover drones. Thirty of them and they are moving."

"Can't we simply phase-shift into the control hub from here?"

"Yes, but we may phase-shift into equipment we need to use ... damage things to the point it effects our mission," Ricket replied.

"How much time will you need, once we breech the control hub?" Jason asked.

"I believe I can accomplish what needs to be done in less than four minutes."

Orion stepped closer to Jason, pushing Billy out of the way. "As you know, Captain, our energy weapons are less than effective against drones. Suggest we set our multi-guns for rail munitions—at least until we run out."

"Got that, everyone?" Jason asked, accessing and adjusting settings on his own HUD multi-gun menu.

"Also, Cap," Billy said, pushing Orion back out of the way and exchanging friendly smiles, "Did you notice there's another life form here? I mean other than Craing, rhino or human?"

"What are they, Ricket?" Jason asked. He looked at the multiple icons showing up on his HUD display. "Whatever they are, there's quite a few of them."

Ricket stood quietly for a moment, contemplating his own HUD readings. "I have no idea."

"Fine. Billy and I will take point; Orion, Ricket and Stands in Storm, you bring up the rear." Jason signaled to Billy and they headed off down the corridor. Almost immediately they started to slip and lose their footing. Stands in Storm fell on his backside—everything shook. A white powdery substance, like flour, billowed into the air. They stopped. Jason looked at the bottoms of his boots. They were caked with the stuff.

"What is this?" Billy asked no one in particular.

"Silicon waste," Ricket said, bent over and examining what lay on the floor.

"Waste?"

No one had time to comment, as multiple six-foot-tall, ball-like creatures rolled directly toward them from opposite directions.

"Pill bugs! Big f-ing pill bugs!" Billy said aloud. As if on cue, the first of the white crustaceans unfurled and stood on two legs, almost humanlike in its stance. Hundreds of expanding and contracting curved segments twitched along the back of its torso and legs. Its head was also humanlike. More of that same white powdery substance seeped from in-between its constantly twitching segments.

Other pill-bug creatures, three in front and three behind, rolled to a stop and unfurled to a stance as the first one had. The closest one spoke. It sounded like gibberish to Jason. This was typical of the Craing, who'd used rhino warriors and Serapins to do their fighting and now, apparently, were using these bug things. It didn't seem particularly dangerous until a wet substance squirted from a gland at its abdomen area. The liquid streamed forward and hit Jason directly in the chest. The outer layer of his battle suit hissed and spattered. Black smoke rose up in small spirals. Looking down, Jason saw a smoldering, six-inch crater had been etched several inches below his chin. He dove to his left, seeing another stream arching through the air. That one, angled a bit higher, caught Stands in Storm in his right shoulder. A pink misty cloud blossomed and hung in the air. Flesh, muscle, and tendons started to disintegrate—leaving only exposed bones where his shoulder and upper arm had been connected. Now, with nothing to hold it in place, Stands in Storm's left arm fell to the floor.

Chapter 25

Billy was the first to return fire. His multi-gun burst took the creature's head clean off at its segmented shoulder area. As the creature died, it slowly contracted back into a ball.

The other pill bugs attacked in force—streams of liquid flew through the air from multiple directions. Within seconds, the acid-like liquid was taking its toll on their battle suits. Jason felt a white hot flash of pain below his left knee. Looking down, he saw that his suit had been completely worn away. Returning fire, Jason and his team advanced. The creatures began to wrap their segments tightly around themselves—creating their own version of an exoskeleton battle suit. Using short bursts to conserve ammunition, both Jason and Billy fired forward while Orion concentrated her fire on the creatures moving up behind. With each burst of rail-gun munitions, large sections of the bugs' exoskeleton segments exploded into dust—revealing their inner soft body-tissue beneath.

Jason fired double bursts, the second shot mortally wounding them. He noticed Ricket was in the fight as well, shooting forward several bursts, then turning to help Orion destroy the bugs at their rear. Jason stumbled over Stands in Storm's legs. He was dead. His body was almost completely liquefied; even his bones looked small and insignificant. As the last of the pill bugs died and reflexively contracted back into balls, the team continued forward.

An alarm klaxon had started at some point, but Jason couldn't remember when. They reached another expansive compartment holding ten security hover drones. The room was square; one wall had floor to ceiling windows. The drones held their position in a straight line several feet in front of the windows. This time prepared, with time to react, both Jason and Billy phase-shifted right behind them. At point blank range, their multi-guns made quick work of four drones. Their shielding and metal housings quickly failed under the barrage of close-range fire. Like a tag team, once Billy and Jason phase-shifted away, Orion phase-shifted in from the other side, keeping up the attack. In minutes, all ten drones were destroyed and lay smoldering on the floor.

"This way," Ricket said, jumping over one of the drones and entering a door along the glass wall. They followed him and were surprised to see the room busy with many Craing workers. Jason and his team pointed their weapons and ushered them to stay back. Ricket hurried through the middle of the group. Wide-eyed and open mouthed, they moved aside. He rushed to one particular terminal and gestured for the worker to get out of his seat.

"We're at the sub-station's hub, I take it?" Jason asked.

"Yes." Ricket's fingers flew over an odd-shaped data entry device.

Jason took in the room. Completely circular, with floor to ceiling windows all around, it looked surprisingly modern compared to what he'd seen of the rest of the facility. Large displays encircled the room; each showed one of the eight planets in the solar system. The largest display hung directly above Ricket. There, on what looked to be a video image, showed all eight planets orbiting their red giant sun, each slowly rotating in a counterclockwise spin. An icon hovered a distance away from each of the planets, directly below what would be their southernmost poles.

Ricket must have done something: a blue vector line stemming from the southern pole of each of the planets was now connected to the eight outlying icons below the other planets.

From those, more vector lines converged together to a distant point further out in space.

Ricket continued to speak while he worked. "What you are looking at are the eight planets of the Craing worlds. Those eight icons hovering below each planet make up the array subsystem. They are basically large mirrors. The array subsystem tracks the location of not only its own lasers, but those on the other planets as well. They work as a unit, and together they concentrate the beams of all these lasers to a singular point in space— subsequently creating their unified wormhole. There are seven lasers active at any one time. The eighth one shuts down in a set rotation for purposes of maintenance, cooling, repairs and that sort of thing. What makes any kind of sabotage difficult is the redundancy aspect. Every laser sub-station has a room identical to this one. Anything I do here, that deviates from the norm, will trigger this station to be excluded from the Loop."

Billy and Orion had taken up positions in front of the windows, while Jason leaned in close to Ricket's shoulder.

"How do we get around that?" Jason asked. "That seems like it would be an insurmountable problem."

"It is, actually. There is no way to alter their code or to jail-break it, as you would say."

"So what are you doing then? That obviously hasn't stopped you."

"I'm starting over. I noticed their core software allows for periodic soft-updates. In effect, I'll be replacing one version with a whole new one. I'm writing just enough new code to keep the sub-stations and array operational, but that's about it. It only needs to operate for several minutes. Enough time to cycle on and off each of the lasers, upload the latest version, and power back on."

"So how does that help us?" Jason asked, looking back at the window where more security hover drones were lining up.

"When they cycle back on, four of them will no longer be positioning their individual mirrors in the direction of that central point in space. They have been assigned a new set of coordinates. These mirror arrays will now target a sub-station on one of the neighbor planets."

"Not just one, but four sub-stations will be destroyed?"

"That is correct."

"Where is Halimar in this scenario?" Jason asked.

"Last, of course, although we will need to make haste to evacuate this facility." Ricket turned to face Jason, no longer keying in information.

"We've got a lot of company out there," Orion said. "In addition to security hover drones, there's more pill-bug guys, as well as armed Craing soldiers."

Jason was hailed.

"Go for Captain."

"Captain, I guess you could say the shit's hit the fan," Rizzo said, sounding out of breath. "We've had to pull back; there's two battle cruisers hovering above the sub-station and one is on the ground. Armed combatants are filing into the facility from multiple sides."

"Where exactly are you now, Rizzo?"

"We've found cover in a barn-like structure—about ten miles away, Cap."

"Hang tight there—looks like we're almost finished here."

"Cap," Billy said, pointing to another monitor. They were looking at video footage of the outside of the facility. A red banner with bold symbols scrolled across the bottom of the screen.

Ricket said, "That's local news footage, the equivalent of your CNN."

The feed changed to what looked like overhead security

footage of the inside of a facility.

"That's us!" Orion exclaimed. The announcer was talking excitedly and the video had zoomed in on Ricket sitting at the workstation.

"What is he saying?" Jason asked.

"They're reporting that after analysis of the security footage, they've definitively concluded it's Emperor Reechet—that their emperor has returned. Apparently, this is causing quite a stir..."

Jason continued to watch Ricket, his head turned upward toward the display. Time and time again his loyalty had been put to the test. At some level, wouldn't he have mixed feelings? This is—*was*—his home wasn't it? Will there come a time when he chooses Craing over human? There was still so much Jason didn't know about his father's relationship with this part alien, part mechanical being. What had inspired Ricket's seemingly unfaltering allegiance to him fifteen years ago?

The news feed had changed again, this time showing open space and a group of small vessels.

"What's the announcer saying?" Jason asked excitedly.

Ricket said, "The Emperor's Guard are minutes from leaving Craing space. They've held up temporarily."

"Because you're here?" Jason asked.

"That's a possibility. Me being here has complicated things. Under normal circumstances, their directive is to stay with their charge, the emperor. Leaving the star system would violate that. High Priest Lom's successor and his brethren without doubt would want the fleet to continue on to Earth. Now that my presence here among the Craing worlds is public knowledge, they have a dilemma," Ricket said.

"It seems to me we have an opportunity here. If you're up for it. I mean, as far as the populace is concerned, you are their emperor, yes?"

"Yes. Their perception is that I am Emperor Reechet."

"Why not give them their marching orders? You ... we ... may not have an opportunity like this again," Jason said, wondering if he was crossing the line into an area with which Ricket would be uncomfortable.

The room had gone quiet. Billy and Orion, as well as the Craig lab workers, had their full attention on Ricket. He looked directly at one of the workers and spoke in their native language. Flustered at first, the worker stuttered, hemmed and hawed, then nodded agreeably.

"What did you ask him?" Jason asked.

"If their security system records audio as well as video."

"... And?"

"Yes, it does," Ricket replied.

"You don't have to do this. It's not for me to tell you to do this," Jason said.

Ricket got up from his chair and stood beneath the security camera. He began speaking in his native tongue. In unison, the workers in the room fell to their knees with their heads bowed. On the other side of the glass wall, the Craing there did the same. Ricket continued to speak softly but with determination. Jason had no idea what he was saying. The news feed was now live and showing Ricket addressing the Craing populace. It was uncanny how similar this was to a typical Earth news report, even down to multiple video-feed windows being displayed. They showed what appeared to be the reactions from other locations, other Craing worlds. Jason imagined thousands, millions of Craings had stopped in their tracks. The feeds kept changing. Crowd after crowd, all on their knees, heads bowed. Mesmerized, they saw that their emperor had returned and was addressing them. With his palms up, Ricket gestured to the camera for everyone to rise up. Jason watched the Craing workers in the room, their faces expressing a mixture of fear and astonishment. Whatever Ricket was saying blew their minds—and one by one they stood. They looked to Ricket and then to one another. Astonishment had turned to something else. An expression on the Craings' faces Jason had come to recognize: They were smiling—some were laughing. The feeds from around the star system reflected the same response. The populace was now on their feet. Cheers and clenched fists were raised in triumph. Then the feeds all went black. The news bulletins went quiet.

"What the hell did you say?" Jason asked, bewildered.

There was that same expression. Jason wondered if he'd ever seen Ricket smile before.

"I've started something."

"What?"

"A revolution." With that, Ricket turned back to the console and entered one more set of commands.

The display above him changed—specifically, something on Halimar's neighboring planet. The blue vector line from its south pole sub-station out to the mirror array, and then out to deep space, disappeared. Then the icon representing both the sub-station itself as well as its corresponding mirror array out in space disappeared. Several moments passed before the icons returned. The blue vector line reappeared from the sub-station to the mirror array, but it no longer extended out to space. A new vector line connected the mirror array to another planet on the far side of the solar system—to that planet's south pole sub-station. Moments later, that sub-station icon went dark.

"The process has begun. The wormhole has collapsed. The Craing can no longer travel to the far reaches of the universe."

Jason stared at Ricket in disbelief. What he'd just accomplished would change the lives of millions, perhaps billions across the universe. For those on Earth it meant no less than their survival.

"Captain, within five minutes, this facility will be destroyed," Ricket said.

"Let these people know they need to evacuate—get far away from the sub-station."

Ricket spoke to one of the lab workers. In a frenzy, he turned to his other coworkers. Someone activated another alarm. Mayhem broke out on the other side of the glass wall. Only the security hover drones remained at their posts. Jason checked the display again. Three sub-stations had been destroyed.

"We need to get out of here, fast." Jason noticed new phase-shift coordinates had been entered into his HUD.

"We are all set, Captain," Ricket said.

"One question. What's happening with the Emperor's Guard? Jason asked.

"I no longer detect them within this star system, sir."

"Damn! So they made it out before the wormhole closed down?"

Ricket didn't answer right away. "Yes, I believe so, Captain. In all probability, they will reach Earth within the next day or two."

Chapter 26

They'd phase-shifted five hundred feet from the side of an old barn. Five Craing battle cruisers now hovered in the air. Four were on the ground. The sub-station's alarm klaxon howled in the distance as Jason answered an incoming hail.

"Go for Captain."

He saw a large wooden door slide open. Rizzo peeked out and waved, "We're inside here, Cap."

Jason, Orion, Billy and Ricket ran. Halfway to the barn, ten miles across the open field, an intense white light engulfed the sub-station. Their helmet visor-shields compensated for the intensity of the flash. The ground beneath their feet shook violently. They watched spellbound; within several moments nothing remained of the distant facility. Like a blast furnace, the heat wave that followed seeped through Jason's less-than-perfect condition battle suit. HUD readings spiked, then returned to normal.

The small Craing cargo ship took up most of the open space of the barn. Jason found Dira attending to Traveler. Rustling Leaves, the other and last of the surviving rhino warriors on the team, sat upon something similar to a bale of hay. Dira had removed her battle helmet, and her hair was moist with perspiration. Both of Traveler's legs had been elevated, and she was in the process of cleaning the wounds. They both looked up at Jason's approach. He knelt down next to them.

"How's your patient?" Jason asked, giving Dira a quick smile and gesturing to Traveler.

"He's hanging in there. Without nanites, I'm forced to use old-fashioned medicine to fight off some pretty aggressive infections. My guess, those arrows were tipped with poison."

Irritated, Jason said, "We'll have an opportunity to speak with Wik-ma again. I'm betting he has an antidote for that poison."

"I'm sorry, Traveler, Stands in Storm did not make it. He died in battle. A brave warrior to the end."

"That is good, Captain. Stands in Storm was a friend, but he lacked real skill with the heavy hammer. I'm surprised he survived this long. I will miss him, but now things will change."

"How so?"

"He was my brother. I am obliged to take his wife and child on as my own."

"Well, I'm sorry for your loss—but happy for your gain as well," Jason said, not real sure he was offering the right sentiment.

Traveler propped himself up on his elbows, a curious expression blossomed on his deeply creased face. "I look forward to breeding with her. Yes, thank you, Captain Reynolds—this is a good day."

Dira and Jason exchanged glances. She bit her lip to keep from smiling.

"You'll need to prepare him to move. This place is on the verge of anarchy—best if we're not around," Jason said, noticing that Gaddy was standing close by.

"What you do? We hear reports, but cannot believe it true. Tell me now what you do."

"We did what we came here to do."

"No trick talk. Is it true?"

"Is what true?" Jason asked, getting back to his feet.

"Emperor Reechet has evoked, is that the word? Evoked? He has evoked Ramp-Lim."

"If that means he's freed the people of the Craing worlds, yeah, he probably did."

"You do not say this so casually. There has never been a Ramp-Lim. Thousands of years, never a Ramp-Lim!" Gaddy seemed on the verge of an all-out rampage.

"I thought this would be a good thing, no? Isn't this what you wanted?" Jason asked.

"A good thing? A good thing? You ask such a stupid question as this?" Gaddy replied, looking around to the others as if Jason was a total idiot.

"This is best thing to ever happen to Craing people!" Gaddy was smiling now. "Our ancient teachings, written thousands of years ago, spoke of this day. Ramp-Lim means *beginning of the end*. Nothing will ever be the same here among the Craing."

Moving fast, she took two quick steps and leapt into Jason's arms. She kissed him square on the lips, brought her face away and looked into his eyes. "I thank Emperor Reechet, and I thank you, Captain Reynolds." She jumped down and scurried off into her ship without looking back. Jason saw Dira in his peripheral vision, her hand back up to her mouth. "Don't even say anything." he said, and headed off to look for Ricket.

Jason was having a difficult time keeping his mind off of his family and the plight of *The Lilly*. In all probability, Mollie and Nan were fine. Pirates were a nasty bunch no matter how you looked at it, but in most cases they could be reasoned with. Or paid off. He needed to get back there, as soon as humanly possible.

Ricket was talking to the three Craing dissidents. Seated before him like grade school students, each had questions. Ricket spoke softly and gave them his full attention. Again, Jason wondered if Ricket was making a choice. He was Craing. They needed a leader—was he blind to that?

"Cap, there's no way we can make a move with those battle cruisers hovering overhead," Billy said, standing next to Orion and peeking out the barn door.

Jason joined them, took a look up at the sky and nodded. "Guess we've kicked the hornet's nest, huh?"

Jason noticed Orion had Stand in Storm's wider belt slung over her shoulder.

"I grabbed it after he fell. It's a little beat up, but I thought it might come in handy." Orion handed Stands in Storm's phase-shift belt, along with his wristband control unit, over to Jason.

"Good thinking, Gunny." Jason looked for Ricket and found him at his side. *How does he do that?* "Any way we can make use of this? Perhaps jury rig the ship?" Jason asked, holding up the belt.

Ricket took the belt and the control unit. "Depends on whether I can interface to the ship's power control unit." He looked at it for a moment, shrugged, then scurried off in the direction of the ship.

"Guess I'll see if I can give him a hand," Jason said. "Let me know if anything changes out there. I have a feeling we'll need to move out of here soon."

Jason found Ricket talking to Gaddy. She had come up with some tools, and they were accessing the main drive beneath a floor panel at the rear section of the ship. When she got up to leave, Jason sat down in her place.

"This might work," Ricket said, angling his head deeper into the compartment. Jason found what looked to be a flashlight in the box of tools and handed it over to him. Ricket pulled his head back out and concentrated on the belt, stripping the backing off the clasp casing.

"Don't you need wires or cables?"

"No, it won't be necessary to hardwire anything. Even this old ship uses wireless interface modules. It's more a matter of interfacing frequencies and data rates. And as long as the belt's circuitry is making contact with the ship's power storage unit, similar to a battery, the proximity alone will drive the belt's phase-shift capabilities. This should work surprisingly well," Ricket said.

Jason wanted to take advantage of this alone-time to speak with Ricket. In light of what had happened—and what was going to happen on his home worlds here—he wanted to clear the air.

"You mean a lot to these people. What you started ... They'll need help," Jason said.

Ricket brought his attention away from the belt and looked at Jason. "Are you asking me if I'm staying?" he asked, somewhat perplexed.

"Well, yeah ... These are your people. This was your home. I just assumed— "

"Captain, this body—this quasi-mechanical organic construct—is not the Emperor Reechet or even the Scientist Reechet they believe me to be. That being died well before your grandfather discovered me beneath the scrapyard. But even if I were still that being, the last thing the people of the Craing worlds need is another emperor. With your society's faults, and there are many, your democratic process achieves things that this society has just now begun to hope for. The Craing people are aware of Earth. They have been for a long time. Now, the seeds of freedom are taking root here as well. Glenn and the other overlords ... Gaddy and the other dissidents—they will be the future of Craing. As for me ...?"

Jason continued to watch the mechanical-alien cyborg talk. Small, intricate, mechanical devices beneath his near-transparent skin were constantly moving, always at work doing a thousand different things all at once. But Ricket was far more than the accumulation of sophisticated parts. Ricket, seeming to contemplate his next words, began to speak again.

"I was destined to spend an eternity beneath rock and soil. Aware just enough of my surroundings to be miserable, but incapacitated enough not to be able to move. I've yet to discover the events that led to me being here, but it was the worst hell one could possibly imagine, Captain. When your father unearthed *The Lilly* and reactivated me, I was reborn. Right then and there I dedicated my life, my new life, to your father, and now you, my brother. Wherever that takes us."

Jason didn't respond. He didn't know how to respond. Both Gaddy and Dira were standing at the ship's open hatch, emotion evident in both their faces.

The barn began to rumble; several planks fell from above.

"We've got a battle cruiser landing right outside!" Billy yelled out. "They know we're in here."

"How long do you need to finish up, Ricket?" Jason asked, running over to the door and peering out.

"I am done here. I just need to interface to the controls up front. We'll have the capability for three mile phase-shifts with ten minute recharge times," Ricket said, scurrying to the front of the ship.

"We're leaving, everyone. NOW! Dira, get Rustling Leaves to help move Traveler onto the ship."

Jason heard more sounds from outside. Too many Craing soldiers to count were rushing down the warship's gangway.

Chapter 27

Everyone was on board, with the exception of Jason and Billy, who had been exchanging fire with the Craing. Temporarily held back, the Craing foot soldiers had taken cover wherever possible.

"They're on the move, Cap," Billy yelled, his voice getting lost in the loud whirl of both the Craing Cruiser outside, as well as their own small ship. In the distance, multiple ships were landing, while others lifted off into the air. With the destruction of the Loop, Jason surmised chaos had replaced order.

"Two more ships inbound, coming fast," Billy said. Jason put on his helmet and watched as his HUD came alive with activity.

"Looks like another Craing warship and something else," Billy said.

Jason saw it coming in low from the horizon. It was a smaller light cruiser, about half the size of *The Gordita*, he estimated. What he hadn't figured on was that it would be firing its weapons. The distant *thud thud thud* vibrated up through the soles of his boots.

"What the hell are they shooting at? They're not shooting at us." Billy asked.

"No, they're not—"

The light cruiser and a smaller vessel running alongside it were both firing their weapons—not in their direction, but at the Craing battle cruiser on the ground. Taken by surprise, the large cruiser's shields had not been raised and the subsequent explosions were catastrophic. The barn swayed, and one of the rafters above fell, just missing their ship. The attacking cruiser circled twice, then sped off. The smaller accompanying ship headed directly for the barn.

"Now I remember where I saw that little ship," Jason said, as if he'd just tasted something unpleasant. The sleek little vessel continued to fire on the Craing foot soldiers. Within moments they were all dead. The ship landed close to the barn. Jason and Billy watched as the ship powered down and a small gangway extended. A moment later, Brian Reynolds emerged, waved, and ran across the field to the barn doors.

"Didn't expect to run into you here. That's quite an entrance," Jason said.

"How'd you get here? Wouldn't have believed it possible you're being here on Halimar," Brian said, ducking inside.

"We can talk about that later. What's going on, Craing fighting Craing? What's that about?"

Brian acknowledged Billy with a nod. "Yeah, well, seems things have changed around here. Thanks to you. Emperor Reechet—Ricket—proclaiming Ramp-Lim, that's what. Thirteen billion Craing have been given their freedom, their independence. The military is fractured. Half have aligned themselves with the populace and the other half don't acknowledge Ramp-Lim. High Priest Lom, you remember him, he's proclaimed himself interim emperor. You're witnessing a revolution."

"Good. And with the Loop gone, they'll all have to stay here and fight it out amongst themselves," Jason said.

"You're lucky you're still alive. What are you doing? What are you waiting for here? You don't honestly think you haven't shown up on multiple scans, do you?"

"We were trying to keep a low profile, make some modifications to our ship."

Brian looked over at the ancient cargo vessel and snickered.

Billy said, "So what side of things do you fall on, Brian?"

"It doesn't matter. Part of my assignment was to bring back

Emperor Reechet—In light of what's happened, I don't know if that holds true anymore."

"Who, specifically, made that assignment?" Jason asked.

Brian didn't answer, shrugged off the question.

"Whatever, Brian. We have to go. Have a good life." Jason turned to leave, but Brian took hold of his arm.

"In light of you turning down my earlier offer, the second part of my assignment was to capture that ship of yours, by any means possible."

"What are you telling me? You're responsible for sending those pirates? Even you wouldn't agree to that."

"It's just a ship, Jason. I didn't know your ex-wife and Mollie would be onboard. All you had to do is take the deal I proposed. Hand over Ricket and that damn ship and the Craing leaves Earth alone. All this could have been avoided."

Jason was finding it harder and harder to contain himself. "Just shut up. You'll contact whoever has taken the ship, and my family, and have them released. Do it now."

"Perhaps that could have been possible, if you hadn't dismantled the Loop. Any FTL messages sent will arrive at their intended destination in about three to four hundred years. Don't you get it? We're all stranded here. I'm sorry. But whatever happens with your ship or your family is completely out of my hands."

"I should kill you. Brother or not, I'd be doing the universe a favor," Jason said.

"I'll do it for you, Cap," Billy said, taking a step closer.

Jason put his hand up to hold off Billy. "He's not worth the energy. Tell me, what is it you promised those pirates, anyway?"

"We were going to give them access to the Loop—the wormhole and all the access points. Give them the ability to move about the universe in seconds versus weeks or months or even years."

"I could see that would be quite useful for pirates. What are they going to do when they discover the Loop is history?" Jason asked, already knowing the answer.

Brian shrugged, "The ship is collateral, Jason."

"Nan and Mollie are on that ship; how could you do such a thing?"

"First of all, I didn't know they would be aboard. But even if I had, it's the bigger picture. I was keeping the Craing at bay, away from Earth."

"None of that matters now. If I can't rescue them, you're going to have to think of something else you can give them."

Brian laughed out loud. "What, are you in a dream world here? The Loop is gone. I mean, I'm really sorry, brother, but none of us—not you, me, or anyone else—will ever see that ship, or Earth, again."

"No. The only ship never to be seen again will be that one out there in the field. Grab him, Billy. We need to get out of here."

The already tight compartment got substantially tighter with Billy, Jason, and now Brian added to the mix. Jason didn't bother making introductions.

"We've plotted three consecutive phase-shift points, plus actual flight coordinates," Ricket said, seated in the cockpit with Gaddy. Using the small interface control, Ricket phase-shifted out of the barn.

* * *

Back on the hillside overlooking the city, the small ship landed behind a cluster of trees. Everyone was filing out. Jason waited for Rustling Leaves to maneuver Traveler outside. The more Jason thought about it, the more frustrated he became.

Re-crossing HAB 12's four quadrants, especially with Traveler's injuries, would be daunting. Every minute lost, Nan and Mollie would be more at the mercy of the pirates.

Gaddy stopped Jason with a small hand on his chest. "I no longer can leave. Things have changed here. I be a part of it."

"That's good, Gaddy. This is an important time for your people. I'm happy for you. I really am." Jason smiled and kissed her forehead. As he got up to leave, she stopped him again.

"It not much. I give ship to you. You take."

"I have no need for a ship ..." Looking outside the ship toward the hillside, something else occurred to him, "Wait, what did you say?"

"You take ship."

"Do you know how wide it is ... this ship?"

Gaddy looked perplexed.

"Ricket! How wide is this ship?" Jason yelled.

Ricket appeared at the open hatch, looked in, stood back and looked at the ship. He looked back up at Jason. "Nine feet, eight inches wide by nine feet, three inches high."

"And the dimensions of the portal window?"

"Exactly ten by ten."

"Everyone back in. We're going to try something," Jason said, a smile on his face for the first time in days.

"Gaddy, I'm going to take you up on your offer. Thank you. Thank you for everything." She smiled and said something to her three Craing friends; none seemed very happy with her generosity. "One more thing. You can never tell anyone about this portal. You understand that?"

She looked somewhat perplexed, but nodded anyway: "We not speak of this to anyone."

The Craing dissidents stood back and watched from a distance.

"You will need to pilot the vessel, Captain," Ricket said. "Time will be short and the portal access code is long and complex. You'll have sixty seconds."

"And you're certain we can't just phase-shift in?" Jason asked.

"No. Security protocols prohibit anything like that."

Rustling Leaves had carried Traveler back into the cargo area again, looking a bit worn out. Jason looked back and nodded to the faces behind him. He brought the ship up to where it was hovering less than a foot off the ground, and positioned so it was even with the lower edge of the window. Ricket was outside at the portal and entering the access codes. He had instructed Jason to maneuver the ship forward the second he heard the signal.

Beep, Beep, Beep! Jason goosed the thrusters and the ship darted forward. The left side of the hull scraped something, causing sparks and prolonged screeching sounds. Jason feathered the controls to starboard and the ship began to move forward slowly. Ricket sprinted to the rear of the ship, coming around its other side, and leapt in through the open hatch. A few more sparks and scratches, and the ship was through. They were once again at the inside cave portal of HAB 12.

The small vessel's running lights cast an amber glow to the rocky environment outside. "There's no way you'll maneuver this ship through those tunnels, Cap," Billy said.

Brian leaned forward and looked through the small hatch window. "What did we just do? Where are we?" he said to Orion, who was sitting closest to him.

"Welcome to the multiverse," she replied. Everyone seemed to enjoy Brian's confusion as he continued to peer out the window.

Jason steered the small cargo vessel over to an open area within the cave.

"There's something moving out there," Brian said, probably

a little louder than he had intended.

Dira, closest to the hatch, looked out. "Oh, that would be the six-foot-long cockroaches that inhabit this cave."

Brian smiled, not taking her seriously, then the smile was gone. "What's that sound?"

"I think that's their pincers."

"We're not getting out here, are we?" Brian asked, not even trying to hide how uncomfortable he was at the prospect.

Jason answered from the cockpit area, "No, just hold on, we're plotting our next phase-shift location." With that, they shifted again. Bright sunlight streamed through the window. Dira released the hatch and was the first to climb out. They had shifted two hundred feet from the cave entrance. Dira looked around, seeming disappointed.

"I'm afraid she's long gone, Dira," Jason said.

"Oh, I know. I was just hoping ..."

"*Birka, birka, birka, birka,*" the strange bark-like sound echoed off in the distance.

"That's her! That's Alice! Come on, girl, come on, Alice," Dira yelled into the surrounding trees. Everyone, with the exception of Traveler, stood outside the ship trying to be the first to spot the creature.

Brian, confused again, leaned over to Orion. "Who is Alice?"

"You'll see."

Alice cleared the trees and headed for them at a full run. Abruptly she stopped, retrieved something from the ground, then continued on in their direction. Dira said, "She has a toy, she's bringing us her toy!"

Brian's expression went from mild amusement to disgust as realization hit: "That's a fucking head."

* * *

He had his right fist tightly clenched around Wik-ma's neck. Jason, Billy and Ricket had phase-shifted themselves mere feet from where the Craing leader was standing. As Jason brought the little alien off the ground, Ricket asked something in their native tongue. Wik-ma squealed and gasped, and Jason released his hold. Sprawled on the ground and rubbing his throat, he croaked something to a small group of Craing males standing nearby. Several minutes passed before the little warrior returned holding an assortment of leaves in one hand and a small hollowed-out rock, a mortar and pestle, in the other. On their knees, several other warriors had joined him and were tearing the leaves into small bits, while another used the pestle to grind. Water was added. Then something that looked like salt or sugar. Within minutes they had a thick gray paste. Wik-ma took the mortar and handed it to Jason, smiling and nodding. He said something to Ricket.

"He tells me this will cure our friend. He had forgotten to give it to us earlier. What surprised him is that Traveler is still alive. They use this same poison to bring down Serapins. Traveler must be very strong."

Off the ship, Traveler now sat beneath the shade of a large tree. Rustling Leaves leaned against a nearby tree; carting Traveler's thousand-pound bulk around was taking its toll.

Jason handed the Craing paste-concoction to Dira.

"How is it applied—what do we do with this?" she asked.

"He said to smear it over the infected area several times a day," Jason replied.

Jason watched as Dira attended to Traveler's legs, wrapping them with her last supply of bandages. They needed to get going; every minute stalled here was a minute away from *The Lilly*.

"Okay, everybody, let's get back in the ship," Jason said. Rustling Leaves heaved a sigh and went to lift Traveler. He was grateful when Jason, Billy and Rizzo stepped in to assist him.

The small cargo ship needed several tries before the drive sputtered to life. Jason lifted the ship above the tree tops and headed in the direction of quadrant 3. The now-familiar HAB 12 landscape rushed by in a blur below.

"Shhhh."

Jason heard Dira shushing Alice several times. Did she really think he wouldn't notice she'd smuggled the creature on board? He hadn't decided yet if he'd allow Alice on board *The Lilly*. Unfortunately, the longer he waited to address it, the less likely he would have the heart to confront her negatively on the issue. Although Ricket assured him of the animal's safety, the simple fact was, nobody really knew for certain.

Jason spoke in a hushed tone to Ricket sitting in the copilot seat. "I need to be sure that dog, or whatever Alice is, won't cause any crewmembers to experience the same fate as Morgan."

"Alice's reproduction system is not dissimilar to those of mammals. It was a third-party organism that introduced Alice's genome into the mix. The other growths on Morgan's body were a strange collection of other organisms, including Serapins, plant life, even Craing—things indigenous to the localized area," Ricket said.

Jason felt somewhat better about it. For now, he'd pretended he had no idea Alice was on board. Right now, Brian was occupying his thoughts. Why hadn't he brought up his family? With Mollie and Nan at the forefront of his own mind, wouldn't Brian be up in arms about not seeing his wife and child again— especially now that the Loop was gone? Jason had no idea where their home planet was located, but Brian also had no idea where they were headed.

They had passed over the volcanic gorge and were nearing the cliffs of quadrant 2. Jason's mind flashed to the time he'd spent with Dira under the waterfall and he caught himself smiling. How the hell was he going to find out about courting a *Jhardian girl*. The whole idea of courting was odd at this stage in life, but intriguing nonetheless. She had alluded to the fact that he'd be able to find out more if he was interested. The only person who could possibly know would be the person who had brought her on board *The Lilly*: his father. Something he'd have to ask him about when he saw him again. Jason felt his pulse quicken as the other HAB 12 portal neared, as well as the borders of the habitat. A strange sight from this altitude—as if the world had stopped; there was nothing but white beyond the portal.

Jason brought the craft down near an outcropping of rocks. In this location, the ship would not be viewable from *The Lilly*'s Zoo portal. He wasn't sure, but keeping their now only method of reaching the Craing worlds a secret seemed like a good precaution.

Once the vessel was on the ground and powered down, Jason turned to the team. Everyone seemed anxious to get going. Traveler was sitting up and conversing with Rustling Leaves. The beneficial effects of the Craing antidote were surprising.

"Listen up, everyone. I have no idea what we'll be walking into. Comms are down. We need to assume the AI has been compromised. This is a hostage situation so at least initially this will be a reconnaissance mission—stay under the radar."

"What's radar?" Dira asked.

"Never mind that. Here's what I want each of you to do."

Chapter 28

Ricket was the first to enter the portal back into the ship. One by one the team stepped into *The Lilly*'s Zoo. Various items and trash littered the floor. Jason knelt down and picked up the remnants of a hand-rolled cigarette.

"Someone's been partying," Billy commented.

Ricket headed farther down the corridor and stopped at HAB 17. There he entered the access code. Both Traveler and Rustling Leaves disappeared into the portal.

Jason was busy hailing his crew. There was no response from his XO. Nervous, he tried Mollie. Also no response. Jason felt his pulse elevate. *Were they alive?* He tried Nan; maybe she'd undergone the nano-devices treatment before all hell broke loose. He heard the connection had been made, but then silence. Perhaps she hadn't figured out how to use her NanoCom yet? Then, slowly, a NanoText message appeared.

Receive inbound NanoText: Crew Member Nan Reynolds:
Crew Nan Reynolds:
Thank God, Jason!
Capt. Jason Reynolds:
Are you OK? I couldn't reach Mollie—where's Mollie?
Crew Nan Reynolds:
She's safe. Hiding.
Capt. Jason Reynolds:
Where are you? Are you OK?
Crew Nan Reynolds:
Jason, pirates are onboard. They've taken over. They killed Perkins!
Capt. Jason Reynolds:

Where are you now? Are you OK?

Crew Nan Reynolds:

Forced to have dinner, again, with their leader. His name is Stalls. An arrogant ass. I'm scared to say or do the wrong thing. Says if I play nice he won't kill any more crewmembers. He's leering at my chest right now. I swear, if he tries anything I'll put a fork in his eye.

Capt. Jason Reynolds:

Nan, I need to know exactly where you are.

Crew Nan Reynolds:

He's taken over the captain's suite. That's where we're having dinner. Hold on, I need to answer his question.

Crew Nan Reynolds:

OK, I'm back. Please find Mollie. She said you would know where to find her. Jason, there are a lot of them onboard. All pigs. Be careful, big guys. Stalls is huge. They're all armed."

Capt. Jason Reynolds:

I'm not worried about him or any of them. Just keep me up to date. Let me know if things get out of hand. I'll be there as soon as I can and I find Mollie.

Disconnect NanoText Command: Crew Member Nan Reynolds

Jason broke the connection. He had a good idea where Mollie would be hiding.

Ten steps down the corridor and he was standing in front of HAB 4. Sure enough, there was Mollie standing inside the portal window with her arms crossed and an impetuous expression that spoke volumes—mainly, *what took you so long?*

Jason removed his helmet while she entered the access code from the other side. Jason motioned for her to stay put, and he stepped inside. It was as if he had entered a different world, which, in fact, it was. Green and lush, the air humid.

"Dad! There are pirates all over the ship. I did what you said and hid in here with Raja and Jack." Mollie hugged her father around his legs and looked up at him.

"I'm just glad you're safe, little one. You did the exact right thing by hiding in here."

"One of them has been trying to get in."

"One of the pirates?"

"No, the one who has been helping them. He's one of the crew."

"Who?" Jason asked.

"Um, um ... Give me a minute. Bris ... No, Bristol. Yeah, Seaman Bristol with the pimply face. The pirate captain called him *brother*."

"When was the last time you saw him?"

"Not long ago. He comes by and tries to figure out the code. I make faces at him through the window. Jack tells me to stop, but I like how it gets Bristol mad."

"Where is Jack?"

"He snuck out to check on things on the ship. You didn't see him?"

"No, but we'll find him. Listen, you need to stay in here a little while longer." Jason needed to get going, reach Nan. But he couldn't be in both places at once. He turned and saw Dira in the hallway and signaled to get her attention. Mollie entered the code and Dira entered the habitat. "Dira, will you stay with her?"

Dira nodded and smiled at Mollie. When Mollie noticed Alice at her side, her eyes went big.

"What is that?"

"That's Alice, we found her in HAB 12," Dira said to Mollie.

"She's weird looking, but so cute!" Mollie was on her knees and before she had a chance to say anything else, Alice's big blue tongue was slurping her face. Mollie's giggles were contagious and Dira and even Jason laughed. Excited, Alice took off into the jungle.

"She ran off. She'll get lost!"

"Wait ..." Dira said.

Mollie stared off in the direction Alice had gone. Sure enough, they heard the distant sounds of her six oversized feet running back in their direction. Alice appeared, charging full out, ears flopping, tail wagging. First one circle, then another, and Alice was back to licking Mollie's face.

"Take care of each other in here," Jason said. "Time for me to exterminate some pests." Mollie entered the code one more time, and Jason stepped back into the Zoo. Dira and Mollie were already headed down a path into the jungle, and Alice running in circles again.

* * *

"Cap, looks like about fifty combatants onboard," Billy said. "I'm not picking up any signals from our SEAL team. Looks like it's just us against them."

The deck plates vibrated. Ricket was further down the corridor, standing at the access panel to HAB 17. Three rhino warriors had emerged and were making their way down the corridor.

"This evens the odds some," Jason said, watching as the rhinos approached. Out front, seeming no worse for wear other than bandages on his legs, was Traveler. Close behind were Rustling Leaves and their leader, Three Horns.

"Few of our kind remain," said Three Horns. "No more of our kind can die here. We will be the last to fight at your side, Captain." The three rhino warriors stood tall. Each held a heavy hammer at his side.

"Thank you, Three Horns. I won't forget your friendship and haven't forgotten my promise. We will return you, all that remain of you, to your home world."

Jason brought up his virtual tablet and a 3D representation of *The Lilly,* now hovering in the air.

"Insurgents are throughout the ship as indicated by the red icons. It seems our crew, for the most part, are at their posts, undoubtedly being held at gunpoint. We can't afford any more crew casualties. That understood?" Jason made eye contact with the team, Billy, Rizzo, Orion, Ricket, and the three rhinos. Brian stood back, away from the group, but listened as his brother spoke.

"Captain, that may be impossible," Billy interjected.

"For anyone else, I'd probably agree. But we've all fought side by side before. We can do this. These pirates have come into our home, taken our ship—what are we going to do about that?"

"What we always do; we're going to clean house, Captain," Rizzo said, enthusiastically.

"That's right, we're going to clean house," Jason said.

"Our multi-guns are fully functional again," Orion said. "Need to emphasize, we do not want to use any of our rail gun settings onboard ship."

Everyone nodded.

Jason continued, "We'll be clearing each deck one by one. These guys are seasoned fighters, accustomed to battle, it's how they live on a daily basis. We can't underestimate their capabilities. Ricket, any word on the status of the AI?"

"AI is still non-responsive, Captain, although, strangely, it seems she may want to be."

"Explain. What does that mean?"

"As you know, her core has been breeched. New or altered rule sets have been implemented. Because the AI has not been reassigned to a new command structure, such as when Admiral Reynolds transferred command of *The Lilly* to you, the AI is showing rudimentary levels of what could best be described as *loyalty* to her assigned command team."

"So she's finding ways to communicate?" Jason asked.

"Yes, I believe so, Captain."

"What do you need to take back control?"

"That is the problem, sir. Her core has been hacked and patched and hacked again—a mess. Nothing short of a wipe and reload to her previous backup will work."

"Then do that, what's the problem?" Jason asked.

"Seaman Bristol, not a total idiot, has made himself the one and only person who has access to the AI at a command level. Undoubtedly he's aware of this possibility. He's keeping tight control on her access. Not even the other pirates have clearance to interface with her."

Jason pondered that for a moment, "Okay, we need to ensure we take him alive. In fact, that needs to be our top priority. Where is he on the ship?"

"There!" Rizzo said, pointing to the Zoo entrance. Bristol, caught off guard and with a mouth full of something, stood halfway down the corridor.

"I got him," Jason said, and took off down the corridor. Seeing the lanky seaman spin on his heels and make for the exit, Jason now remembered who Bristol was. He'd seen him arguing with the chief his first day weeks ago here aboard *The Lilly*. He checked his multi-gun configuration, ensuring a non-lethal plasma pulse setting. Bristol disappeared around the corner. Jason sprinted after him, reaching the corner five seconds later. Bristol was fast and already halfway down the central Deck 2 corridor and nearing the DeckPort. *Shit, what am I doing?* Now fairly proficient at phase-shifting on the fly, Jason quickly completed the two-step process.

Bristol had no time to react to Jason suddenly appearing several feet in front of him. He ran full into Jason's fist. He'd been caught on the chin and landed on his back. The seaman was not moving and was now sprawled awkwardly on the floor; Jason peered down at his pimply face. A moment later his eyes opened, consciousness returned. Impatient, Jason firmly grasped him round his collar and pulled him to his feet. Two phase-shifts later, Jason and Bristol were back in the Zoo.

Jason watched Bristol's reaction. Seeing the three thousand pound, seven-foot-tall rhino warriors standing before him had a powerful effect. Obviously afraid, Bristol tried to pull away.

"There is nothing you can do to me. The ship is under my control. I've taken safeguards; the AI answers only to me."

"We know that."

"Good. Do you know that you will all die? My broth— Captain Stalls already knows you're here. You're all dead, you just don't know it yet."

"First thing's first, Bristol. What's the pass code for the AI. I will not ask twice," Jason said.

"Fuck you."

Jason nodded to Billy and Rizzo. Looking smaller, almost frail, Bristol started to flail. Billy held Bristol's arm out straight. Rizzo put his weight down on Bristol's chest. Traveler moved closer, towering over him. As Bristol's eyes caught sight of the massive hammer in Traveler's hand, his bowels released.

"You need a diaper, Bristol?" Billy asked, disgusted.

"Why have you become a traitor to our crew, Bristol?" Jason asked.

"I don't have to tell you anything. But I will tell you this. Your father and the Alliance murdered my parents. I want you to know your family will suffer the same fate. They will suffer just as ours has …"

"Let me guess, your parents were pirates. They went up against an allied ship, or fleet of ships, and lost."

"No. Your father murdered them with total disregard. Now you'll pay," Bristol spat and smirked. He then looked over Jason's shoulder. "Pathetic. Even your own brother sided against you. Who do you think hired us?"

"I'll deal with my brother. You need to worry about yourself right now." Jason scowled in the direction of Brian, then turned back to Bristol. "What are the modified codes to access the AI?" Jason asked.

"You said you weren't going to ask twice. So fuck you."

Jason took a breath and shrugged. "You're responsible for the death of crewmembers aboard this ship, as well as a rescue team. You deserve nothing short of a bullet to the brain. But I'm going to give you an opportunity to save your own life. I won't take your whole hand. Not at first, anyway. But I have to tell you. Losing a thumb is paramount to losing one's hand anyway. Without a thumb, you can say goodbye to picking up a bottle of beer, say goodbye to zipping up your fly, or even something as simple as unbuttoning your shirt. Thumbs are great. You'll truly miss yours." Traveler positioned the business end of the hammer directly over Bristol's thumb—eying the target. Slowly, he brought the hammer back, higher and higher, well past his shoulder and behind his head. The muscles on Traveler's shoulder tensed.

"OK! OK! I'll tell you!"

Bristol spoke too late. The rhino's heavy hammer came down on the seaman's thumb, flattening it to the thickness of a piece of paper. Billy released his arm. Rizzo and Traveler stood back. Screaming, Bristol retracted his ruined hand to his stomach while curling into a ball.

"Your next decision will dramatically impact the rest of your life, Seaman Bristol."

Bristol nodded.

"I know this hurts right now ... But having this happen to your other thumb would be even more excruciating."

"No. Please don't!"

"Perhaps I'd be willing to let you spend some time in the MediPod. Fix that thumb right up. Would you like that, Bristol?"

Tears were streaming down his face. "Yes, please. I'll give you anything you want."

"Good. I know you will," Jason said.

Jason brought his attention over to Ricket. "I think you can now get what you need from Mr. Bristol. Let me know as soon as the AI is operational and we have control of ship systems again."

"Cap, he was right; they know we're here," Orion announced, now positioned at the Zoo's entrance.

Jason was back studying the 3D representation and the multiple red icons, showing the insurgents now on the move throughout the ship. "Looks like the majority of their people are still situated on Deck 2, in the crew quarters. Some are in the mess. Billy, take two of the rhino Warriors, leave me Traveler. Orion and Rizzo, you're with me up on Deck 2."

"What do you want me to do?" Brian asked.

"Oh, you can watch over our friend here. You're with us. Since you commissioned this job, I'm sure you'll want to meet Captain Stalls face to face."

"Can I have weapon?"

"So you can shoot us in the back? I don't think so. Just stay back and keep out of the way."

"Um, Cap?"

"What is it, Rizzo?" Jason asked, anxious to move out.

"How will the rhinos go between decks, travel through the

DeckPorts?"

Jason didn't have an answer. He spun around and found Ricket.

"They'll be fine. Make sure they go in one at a time and hold up two fingers," Ricket said.

Traveler grunted and relayed the information to the others.

Jason put a hand up, "Give me a second." He initiated a NanoText hail to Nan.

* * *

Nan sat at the table directly across from Captain Stalls. He was talking about his community, what he referred to as his family. She had only picked at her dinner, and found herself watching the wax drip down the sides of a lit candle. He was talking again and she tried to look interested, even smiled at his attempts at humor. Although his intentions had been clear, she had been able to keep him at bay, so far. He seemed to respect the fact that she had a daughter on board and her safety was her priority. But it was obvious he was growing impatient. As she sat there wearing the small black dress he'd configured from the garment replicator, actually more like a negligée, his eyes continually moved over her body as he spoke.

Not knowing what it was at first, she remembered—she was being hailed for a NanoText.

Receive inbound NanoText: Captain Jason Reynolds:
Capt. Jason Reynolds:
Are you still dining with Stalls?
Crew Nan Reynolds:
He has something else on his mind right now. He does not like the word No.
Capt. Jason Reynolds:

Has he hurt you?
Crew Nan Reynolds:
No. But you better hurry.
Capt. Jason Reynolds:
Soon, on my way.

Disconnect NanoText Command: Captain Jason Reynolds

The connection was cut and she tried to relax, let her fear dissipate some.

"I don't deny that life with me, among our people, would be different," Stalls was saying. "As my wife, you would have power and influence of your own. And of course, your daughter would want for nothing," Stalls said, reaching a hand across the table and encircling hers. He scared her. She'd always been able to handle men, using her intelligence to keep them in their place. But Stalls would not be dissuaded by a flippant comment or humor. She looked down at his outstretched arm, the wide muscles of his upper shoulders and up to his thick neck. He'd tied his long black hair into a braid. Nan looked up and returned his stare. *A handsome face, but such cold cruel eyes.*

"So you're what? Like a king? King of the pirate's lair?" Nan said, not meaning for it to sound so sarcastic.

"You mock me." Stalls' face flushed. He pulled his hand away. "No, far more than a king. More like a father, or a benefactor— yes, a benefactor."

"I didn't mean anything ..." Nan withdrew, felt naked and exposed. She wrapped her arms around her chest. "Why don't you tell me more about your home. Tell me about your family. Not the other pirates, but your real family."

Stalls wiped his mouth and placed his napkin on the table. "Enough talk."

He stood and slowly walked around the table. Stood before

her, looking down.

"Up, get up," he said quietly.

"I'm not done eating—"

Stalls grabbed for her arm and pulled her to his feet. With her face inches from his, he leaned in and kissed her. As she resisted, what had begun as a gentle kiss quickly turned violent. In two steps he had her up against the bulkhead. Pressing into her, one arm around her throat and his other exploring her body. Nan's mind fought for something, some idea of how to escape this, how to avert the inevitable. She pulled at his wrist and the hand wrapped around her throat. Something was there, beneath his sleeve. The hilt of a hidden knife. She couldn't pull it free, not with him so closely pressed into her. He was pulling her hair, forcing her head back. He was kissing her neck, pulling the strap of her dress from her shoulder. Nan relaxed, stopped resisting. He stopped and looked up into her eyes. She attempted a small smile. As he pulled back, ever so little, her hands were free to move. The knife came away from it's hidden scabbard. A moment later she had the point of the slender blade pressed to his neck; a trickle of blood ran down his throat and disappeared down his chest beneath his shirt.

Stalls stopped moving. "A resourceful woman. You know, this only makes things more interesting for me," he said as the ends of his mouth curled up.

Nan continued to maintain the pressure of the blade against his neck.

"Slowly, take your hands off of me. No quick movements, or I'll shove this blade in as far as it will go."

Stalls slowly brought his hands away and stood back, away from her. Nan had no idea what to do next. How would she keep him from making a move? She wouldn't be able to maintain this position for long. And she was right. His right hand moved in a blur, catching her wrist and twisting it away from his neck. She dropped the knife. Still holding her wrist, he twisted and backhanded her across the mouth with his left hand. He'd released his grip just enough for her to pull free. She ran ...

Chapter 29

Brian was having difficulty with Bristol and his injured hand, so Jason asked Rustling Leaves to carry him. Jason felt a wave of guilt; Rustling Leaves had, again, become their de facto pack-mule.

"Get Bristol into a MediPod, then split up. Ricket, head to Deck 4B to try to re-establish communications with the AI. Rustling Leaves, you'll join Billy and Three Horns down on Deck 2. Bristol, you make one sound, and you won't live to regret it," Jason said.

They all left the Zoo at a hurried pace. Billy and Three Horns stayed to the back of the pack and would head off to the lower decks once they reached the DeckPort.

Studying his HUD, Jason counted fifteen pirates on Deck 4. Most were concentrated on the bridge; others were milling about here and there throughout the deck. There were only a handful of his fellow crewmembers—although there hadn't been that many to begin with.

Jason was the first to go through the DeckPort. The corridor was nearly unrecognizable. Trash, various types of equipment, and food trays from the mess littered the floor. They split up with Rustling Leaves and Bristol heading off toward Medical. Jason, Rizzo, Orion and Traveler moved forward toward the officer's quarters and the bridge. Jason heard noises ahead around a corner and held up a hand for his team to hold.

Jason NanoTexted Nan.

Establish outbound NanoText hail: Crew Member Nan Reynolds:

Capt. Jason Reynolds:

I'm close—can you hold out a little longer?

Nan didn't bother to NanoText, opting to use standard voice NanoCom.

"He's a lunatic! I've locked myself in the bathroom. He's trying to kick down the door; for God's sake, get your ass in here!"

"Just a couple of minutes. You should be safe in there. We need to take back the bridge first. Just try to hold on." Jason hated leaving her, knew he'd pay for this decision later. But he also knew if he didn't deal with the insurgents close by on the bridge first, all would be lost anyway.

Jason signaled his team to move forward. Still out of sight of the main corridor, Ricket and Rustling Leaves, with Bristol squirming under one arm, headed off toward Medical. Where several forward ship corridors intersected, Jason peered around the corner. Two of the biggest men he had ever seen were standing sentry outside of his cabin. Jason checked that his MultiGun configuration was set for the most powerful of the stun settings. On the count of three, they all rushed toward the bridge. Jason fired as soon as he'd turned the corner, hitting both raiders in the chest before they had time to draw their weapons. Neither went down. Both raiders wore their weapons gunslinger-style and holsters low at their hips. Their sidearms were more like shortened rifles than pistols. Both moved with practiced ease, separating away from each other, then dropping to one knee. They could be twins, long black hair worn in ponytails. Sleeveless, tattooed, muscular arms drew weapons and fired simultaneously. Jason took the brunt of the energy bolts to his upper chest, his battle suit still working enough to save his life once more. On the ground, a warning signal flashed in Jason's HUD. Battle suit integrity was at critically-low levels. He watched as the two pirates continued to take multiple plasma fire to their bodies—black craters erupted on their upper torsos. They screamed out in pain and scrambled to an adjacent corridor up farther toward the bridge. The floor shook from behind, and Jason knew Traveler was making his move. In all likelihood, they were used to being the biggest, baddest boys on the block, so when they encountered the charging thousand-pound rhino warrior barreling down on them, they hesitated. It was only a second or two, but long enough for Traveler to move ten yards closer. Traveler's hammer was already moving in a sideways swing, hitting the left raider just below his ear, caving in the side of his head. Jason, Orion, and Rizzo concentrated their fire on the other pirate. He too went down.

Jason hailed each team member at the same time: "Forget using anything less on these guys other than the highest plasma pulse setting."

Billy came back on comms, "Cap, we're at a bit of a stalemate down here. We could use some more help. Both sides are pinned down. Three Horn's not looking too good either. Think he might be down for the count."

"Hang on as long as you can, Billy. We'll get down there as soon as we take back Deck 4."

Together, Jason's team sprinted toward the bridge. Three more raiders rushed out with weapons drawn. One went down with a shot to his head. The other two dived and rolled and came up shooting. *These guys are good,* Jason thought. Again, both raiders concentrated their fire on the biggest target, Traveler, leaving their flanks exposed for Orion and Rizzo to bring them down with two shots each.

According to his HUD, there were six more raiders held up on the bridge. Obviously, the element of surprise was gone. They rushed forward with Traveler in the lead, his bulk shielding them from another barrage of plasma fire. The rhino's chest took simultaneous blasts—numerous black craters smoldered and pocked his hide. Traveler used his energy weapon and took down two of the raiders. Jason moved left while Rizzo moved right. Four raiders were left, each were within inches of fellow crewmembers. Their weapons pointed at their heads.

"Jason, stop!"

Her voice came from behind at the bridge entrance. She was wearing a short black dress, one strap hung loosely down her arm. The side of her face was pink and swollen; a trickle of blood was at the corner of her mouth. The blade of a long thin knife was at her neck. Standing behind her, with his arm wrapped around her shoulders, was a mountain of a man, easily a head taller than Jason. Smiling and confident, his eyes were leveled on Jason.

Stalls spoke slowly and calmly. "Captain Reynolds, please instruct your men to lay down their weapons. Do so now or your ex-wife loses her life."

Jason hesitated, then hailed the other teams and spoke aloud. "Stop fighting. Lay down your weapons."

"Excellent. I can see you are a man of reason." Jason noticed that Stalls, as well as the other raiders, had ear-comms devices. Jason's own NanoCom went active.

"Cap, what do you want us to do? Are we giving up?" Billy asked.

Jason had run out of ideas. "Hold, Billy. Don't do anything for now."

Nan looked terrified. Jason looked at her and nodded, tried to convey a sense of calm. He'd run out of ideas, he knew Stalls would not hesitate to kill Nan. Sounds came from behind them.

"Put me down! Put me down!"

Jason recognized the squeaky voice. It was Bristol.

Stalls moved Nan further forward onto the bridge and spun around to see what was happening. Rustling Leaves, his arm outstretched, was holding Bristol by the neck several feet in the air. Bristol kicked and flailed, his face red and angry. Jason noticed that Bristol now had all ten of his fingers fully intact.

"Put me down!"

Stalls' irritation was evident as he watched his brother pulling at Rustling Leave's fingers.

"There is a way out of this, Stalls," Jason said.

Stalls didn't say anything but looked over toward Jason.

"Let's make this about you and me. You release her, and your brother's neck stays in one piece. You and I handle this one on one. That is, unless you prefer fighting defenseless women?"

Stalls smiled, then looked over at Bristol again.

"The lengths we go to for family." Stalls shook his head and frowned at his brother. "All right, Captain. It's to the same end, anyway. Killing you with my bare hands makes this all the better."

Chapter 30

The Deck 2 mess had been decided upon as being open and large enough. Both men relinquished their weapons; both were shirtless. Jason watched as Captain Stalls removed the small knife sheath from his arm. Jason had left his boots on, while Stalls had opted to go barefoot. His pirates stood right along side *The Lilly*'s crewmembers around the perimeter of the mess. Nan was back wearing a spacer's jumpsuit.

"This is juvenile, Jason. What ... are you back in high school?" Nan said, irritated.

Jason eyed his opponent. He was a big fella. Broad muscular chest, arms twice the size of his own. Easily a seven or eight inch height advantage. Jason saw Billy out of the corner of his eye and looked over at him for moral support. The best Billy could offer was a shrug and half smile. *Great.*

Jason didn't wait on formalities. He charged the bigger man, feigned a punch, then spun low with a sweeping motion to the back of Stalls' legs. He went down hard. Jason followed with a kick low to his head. Stalls dodged, rolled to his right, and got to his feet. He moved fast and came directly at Jason, both fists clenched. Stalls punched, a wide roundhouse swing that glanced off Jason's ear, which was immediately followed up with an upper cut to Jason's chin, sending him onto his backside. Dazed, Jason stood and stayed low, hands out—he moved back and forth, ready to anticipate Stalls' next move.

"Come on, Captain, you're not giving up so soon, are you?"

Jason didn't like Stalls' heavily accented voice. He didn't like anything about Stalls.

"Are you here to talk or fight?"

Jason didn't wait for an answer. He took two quick steps, a jump and spin in the air that ended with a sidekick that connected his right foot to the bridge of Stalls' nose. Blood spurted and continued to flow down into his mouth. Stalls spat, then smiled a bloody, toothy grin. Now, also staying low, he came at Jason. Feigning a jab, he punched out with his right and caught Jason's left cheek, tearing flesh from bone and causing his own blood to flow down his face. Stalls' men cheered—Nan screamed. Jason was seeing stars. He couldn't remember ever being hit that hard. He staggered and fought to stay on his feet.

Stalls was on the move again. He swung and Jason ducked. Stalls swung again and Jason blocked and countered with a jab to Stalls' already broken nose. The bigger man staggered backward, then regained his footing. Jason came at him, swung and missed. Stalls surprised Jason with his speed. He moved in close, then angled in behind Jason and placed his forearm firmly over his throat. Jason fought against Stalls' hold, making him work for control. Stalls quickly glanced over his shoulder to Nan, and smiled.

Jason moved, bringing his right knee up, then forcing his boot down with all his strength. Comprised of a hardened composite material, the back ridge of his boot heel came down directly on Stalls' right foot—right where his toes intersected. Although Stalls' big toe held on, his second and third toes tore away with a relatively clean separation. The move wasn't pretty, but highly effective. Stalls released his grip and reflexively reached for his damaged foot. Jason knew he was still in trouble and had no more than a second, maybe two, before Stalls composed himself. With Stalls doubled over, again Jason targeted his broken nose—this time with his knee. Stalls went down and stayed down.

Jason turned and saw that Billy was smiling. Nan, on the other hand, had a furrowed brow and was shaking her head.

Then her eyes went wide.

How Stalls had recovered so quickly and had found his knife, Jason had no idea. Again, Nan was held at knifepoint.

"Seriously, Captain, you trust a pirate to play fair?" Stalls said, grinning.

"Stalls, you've lost control of this ship. Why go through this?"

"Where is my brother? I need to know he is still alive."

There was no need for Jason to answer. Rustling Leaves moved forward and came to a stop several paces behind Stalls. Seeing movement, he quickly glanced backward over his shoulder. Bristol was still secured under one of the rhino's arms.

"What have you done to him?"

"He's fine. Well, a little scratch to his thumb, earlier," Jason replied. "It's been attended to."

"Scratch!" Bristol whined.

"Quiet, little brother," Stalls said, with irritation.

Nan started to shake. Tears ran down her cheeks. Jason felt his rage building; his fists clenched, knuckles white.

"I'll be taking her with me, insurance of safe passage."

"Yeah, that's not going to happen. Listen, you have my word. If you release her now, you'll have safe transport back to your ship."

Stalls' men had their weapons pointing at Jason. Billy, Orion and Rizzo had their weapons pointed at the raiders. At a stalemate again, Stalls looked to be weighing his options.

"Let go of my brother."

Jason nodded to Rustling Leaves. Bristol fell to the floor.

Stalls released Nan and pushed her toward Jason. She staggered and moved behind him. He heard her whisper something—then she said it again, louder.

"Don't trust that animal, Jason."

Stalls moved in closer toward one of his men, grabbed for his sidearm and leveled it in Jason's direction. Walking backward, he helped Bristol to his feet, and they continued backward into the Deck 2 corridor. His men followed, guns raised high.

Bristol fished in his pocket for something and came out with the little handheld device. In a flash, a large section of the Lilly disappeared, phase-shifted to the multiverse. Jason flinched, expecting to see and feel the vacuum of open space. Before them was another ship, also with a large section missing. Apparently, both ships were butt-up against each other. Not a perfect fit, the vacuum of space was sucking the oxygen out of *The Lilly* from around the edges where the two ships' hulls made loose contact. One by one, the remaining raiders jumped across the open void into the other vessel. Bristol made a sneering glance in Jason's direction and was the next to jump across.

Jason was surprised to see Brian rush by. "Sorry, I have some unfinished business with these people, Jason. To be honest, the prospect of sitting in a brig back on Earth doesn't really work for me. You understand. Say hello to dad for me." Brian smiled, and he too jumped across the void into the pirate ship.

With a smile, Captain Stalls turned, limped to the edge of the void and jumped. Five seconds later there was another flash and the corridor phase-shifted back to normal.

* * *

Later, Jason found Nan back in her suite, toweling dry her hair. Every muscle in his body ached and his head throbbed. He slowly sat next to her on the bed.

"That's three, Jason."

He looked at her, not knowing what to say.

"Twice thrown into Craing cages and now almost raped by

a crazed pirate."

Jason nodded, but still held his tongue.

"I think you know what I'm going to say next."

He stared at her.

"I want a weapon. And I want to know how to use it."

"That was not what I expected you to say," Jason replied.

"I'm tougher than you think. But I'm through being a victim. So if you want me and Mollie onboard this ship, we're learning self-defense and how to use weapons."

"Mollie too?"

"Yes, most importantly Mollie."

"Deal. And I know just the person to teach you."

"Who?"

"Gunny Orion."

"She scares me," Nan said, sounding less sure of things.

"I'll set it up. Starting first thing tomorrow."

Jason was being hailed.

Go for Cap.

"I think you should see this, Captain," Ricket said.

"I'm on my way."

Jason turned to Nan. "I have to go. Your daughter is still hiding in HAB 4. Oh, I need to warn you about something."

"Oh God, what now?"

"It's about Alice."

"Who is Alice?" she asked.

"Not sure if it's so much of a *who* as a *what*. She's a dog-like creature we found in HAB 12. It's my guess Mollie's going to want to keep her. Don't let her pressure you. We can build her a kennel in the hold. I'm just warning you ahead of time."

"Well, it might be good for her to have a dog. I don't know."

* * *

Coming out of Nan's quarters, Jason nearly walked into Chief Horris.

"Cap, I was just on my way to see you."

The chief fell into step with Jason. "I wanted to talk to you about the XO."

"I hear you kept them from throwing his body out an airlock. I appreciate that. His family will as well," Jason said.

"That's fine, sir. Thank you. The thing is, Lieutenant Commander Perkins wasn't taken to the morgue."

"Where did you put him?"

As they approached Medical, the chief gestured for Jason to turn. "Sir, I did my best to get Perkins into a MediPod, and perhaps save his life."

"That's wonderful, Chief. Quick thinking on your part. In here?"

"But Sir ... I'd never been trained how to use any of the medical equipment, including those MediPods."

"Oh, I see; he didn't survive," Jason said, his shoulders sagging a bit.

"I didn't say that either, sir. Best if I show you." Chief Horris took several steps into the room, went to the control panel for the second MediPod, and a moment later the clamshell began to separate. Jason looked at the dimly lit face through the small window at the top of the pod. Something was definitely wrong. The rest of Perkins' body came into view.

"I've kept him sedated until someone who knows more than I do can address the problem. Perhaps Ricket can help?" the chief asked, concern on his face.

"Good decision, Chief. Yes, best if Perkins is not aware of his condition. At least for the time being."

Both Jason and the chief continued to stare down at the

XO. "And, as I was saying, sir, he seems to be in perfect health otherwise."

* * *

"Sorry for the delay. Putting out fires," Jason said, entering Ricket's domain on Deck 4B. "I need to contact the outpost and we need to get back to Earth. For all we know, the Emperor's Guard is already there. So we need *The Lilly* back to her old self as soon as possible."

"The information Bristol provided did, in fact, allow me to re-access the Lilly AI. We do need to do a cold-start and refresh her back to the previous core version."

"You mentioned you would have to do that. Is there a problem?" Jason asked, looking at the cluttered bench top and array of strange devices. Ricket was impeccably organized, and this mess seemed out of the norm.

"No, and with your permission, I'll begin the cold-start within the hour. But that's actually not what I wanted to talk to you about. It seems Bristol was an inventor. In addition to in his own cabin, he had been working here as well. This is his mess. He was building upon some of the technology I had used for the phase-shift belts."

"Like the devices he made for the raiders to access the ship?"

"Yes, exactly. But there are other items here. Things based on Caldurian technology that I had not thought of," Ricket said.

Jason picked up the largest of the devices. "What's this one do?" he asked.

"That one, I believe, is a phase-duplicator."

Jason's face went blank.

"As you know, when we utilize any of our phase-shift devices, things are instantly shifted to a designated plane within the multiverse, yes?"

Jason nodded for Ricket to continue.

"I believe this unit functions identically to any other phase-shift device we have, with one significant exception. Mid-way through the phase-shift process, the originating item is phase-shifted again, perhaps over and over. This happens in virtual space—each residing in subsequent, other, slightly out-of-phase layers. Then, as a batch, they are returned back to the originating time-location continuum."

Jason let that sink in. "So, for example, if *The Lilly* phase-shifts to the multiverse, it could return as multiple versions of itself?"

"Basically, yes. What I've been able to piece together from the AI database, and Bristol's own notes, is he had a problem setting numerical values. For this device to play nicely with physics, and be effective, it would need to be one hundred percent configurable for the quantity and the timeframe. Imagine an infinite number of *The Lilly*s phase-shifting back into one's own particular time and space. Or producing multiples of herself that never leave your timeframe."

"Would you be able to design-in those parameters? That would align to the laws of physics?" Jason asked.

"Already have. The answers were there, he just hadn't discovered them yet."

"Would it be possible for the duplicated items to interact with each other?" Jason asked, now getting excited.

"Yes, and that's where things get interesting," Ricket replied.

Chapter 31

The Lilly was dead in space and only minimal ship systems had been operational, so the cold-start reset had no real effect on anyone. Within an hour, the ship was back to normal. Jason's first order of business was to send the necessary FTL markers to the outpost that would allow for bidirectional communications. He was expecting a reply any minute.

Ricket stood with Dira in front of Perkins' sealed MediPod. Jason found a countertop, grimaced, and carefully leaned against it.

"I don't understand," Jason said. "You can save a life, rebuild a heart, for God's sake. What's the big deal with simply changing him back?"

"At this point, the MediPod software does not recognize there is a problem. It will take me some time to reconfigure the software parameters," Ricket said.

"Seems strange this could even happen," Jason said, looking at Perkins through the window.

"MediPods typically can distinguish the species of the patient. But commands were input improperly. The chief confused the device to the point it defaulted to its default species condition, Caldurian."

"The issue is, do we keep the XO in stasis while I figure this out, or bring him back now—for the interim?"

Dira continued, "Physically, Perkins will be fine; it's more a question of how he'll react to the physical anomaly."

Jason took it all in. "So how much time are we talking about? Before you figure this out?"

"It could be as long as a week," Ricket replied.

"What do you need from me?" Jason asked.

"The decision to wake him up or not," Dira said.

"Okay, I still don't understand why I'm involved. This is a medical issue, and you are the doctor, right?"

"Captain, the question is, do we need him back on the bridge? He'll be an able-bodied officer," Dira said. "If so, we'd like you to be here. Help explain things."

"So we'll bring him back while he has the body of a—" Jason stopped and looked through the MediPod's window—"a Caldurian."

"That's right," both Dira and Ricket said at the same time.

"Fine, wake him up. I'll tell him about it. You can talk to him about his options, which don't sound like there are any."

Dira was at the control panel. In less than a minute, the MediPod was opening. Perkins' eyes fluttered, then opened wide. Startled, he sat up.

"I've been stabbed!"

Jason stepped in closer and knelt down. "Easy, XO, you're fine. Everything's fine. Pirates are gone ... you've been pretty much all patched up."

Perkins looked somewhat relieved and laid back down. "That pirate, Stalls. He stabbed me in the heart." Dira, Ricket and Jason watched as he crossed his arms over his chest.

"You can thank the chief for getting you here in time," Jason said. "From what I understand, it was a close call."

Perkins nodded. "I'm surprised the old coot knew how to operate one of these things. They're a bit tricky. Don't need to tell you that, huh, Dira?"

Perkins' arms were moving now, fingers opening and closing. Jason and Dira exchanged quick glances.

"Hey, listen. There's something we need to speak with you about," Jason said, kneeling down again. "You said it yourself, these devices are tricky. And the truth is, they're very tricky."

Perkins wasn't listening. All of his attention was focused forward. Holding up his two hands in front of his face, and the long, tapered fingers of a Caldurian. "Now that's weird ..."

* * *

The FTL connection was established as soon as Jason entered the bridge. Once situated in the command chair, one of the Gordon twins, Jason wasn't sure which one it was, opened the channel. Admiral Reynolds, hair somewhat tussled, acknowledged his son with a brief smile.

"Good to see you made it back, Jason. I'm looking forward to hearing about it all. But that will have to wait. Earth is under attack. Right now I'm sitting in the shuttle you left behind. We phase-shifted to the second underground location. In fact, we've shuttled more than one hundred and fifty people down here."

"I didn't think there was enough space for that many people," Jason said.

"Well, there is, and there's something else. It's inhabited."

"Say again?"

"You heard me."

"Fine. First tell me about the attack. Who's attacking?"

"Three ships. Small—each about a quarter of the size of *The Lilly*," the admiral said.

"That would be the Emperor's Guard. From what I understand, those ships, like *The Lilly*, are actually Caldurian technology. The may be more advanced than *The Lilly* by as much as a hundred years. But make no mistake about it, it's the Craing behind the wheel, not the Caldurians," Jason said.

"Seems the ships are being selective about their targets. They're not going after government seats of power, or even military instillations or assets," the admiral remarked, looking confused.

"Maybe they're looking for *The Lilly*."

"I thought that too, but that doesn't add up either. The ships are situated here in Earth's outer orbit, where they're scanning as deep as ten miles below the surface. Every so often one of the ships comes down to ground level and phase-shifts somewhere subterranean."

"Still, they could be looking for *The Lilly*. But you're right, that does sound strange. You said Earth was under attack, what have they attacked?" Jason asked.

"Anything that leaves the ground—commercial planes, helicopters, that sort of thing, as well as orbital satellites. They're taking those out, one by one, any time they come close to their position in orbit. Needless to say, communications are a mess."

"What about the Allied Craing fleet?" Jason asked.

"Three battle cruisers and one light cruiser in high orbit were destroyed before anything else. The ones on the ground have been left alone. Strange."

"What does Washington have to say?" Jason asked.

"Well, they wanted to deploy the rest of the Craing Allied fleet until one, they saw how quickly the four in orbit went down, and two, they discovered we don't have trained pilots for them anyway. They're waiting to see what demands are coming; so far there haven't been any. They've been checking in on an hourly basis about *The Lilly's* whereabouts. As far as they're concerned, she may be the planet's only hope of defeating those ships."

Jason noticed Ricket standing at his side and looking at the display, his little wheels turning, *literally*.

The admiral continued, "What's the status of the Loop? How did it go on the Craing worlds?"

"Loop's destroyed. And, subsequently, there appears to be an uprising, so I don't think we'll need to worry about the Craing bothering us again. At least not for the near term, other than the three Emperor's Guard vessels there in orbit."

"We need you back here now, Jason. I can't emphasize enough what's at stake. Perhaps planet Earth itself. What's your ETA?" the admiral asked, looking impatient.

"Tomorrow afternoon at the latest. We'll see if we can come up with a plan of attack en route," Jason replied, looking over at Ricket.

Ricket took a step forward. "Admiral, those Caldurian ships. They were built for battle, whereas *The Lilly* was primarily built as a natural sciences and exploration vessel."

"I don't know, *The Lilly* seems pretty capable to me," the admiral replied.

"From what I've discovered, as hostilities between Caldurian and the Craing worlds grew hundreds of years ago, defenses and weaponry were added as needed. How *The Lilly* compares now, I don't know. Our only advantage may be the Craing's unfamiliarity with these ships' technology and capabilities," Ricket said.

"Dad, we know we have to get back there as soon as possible." Jason was still curious about something. "Before we sign off, who exactly is inhabiting the underground cavern?"

The admiral looked amused. "They are a skittish bunch and keep their distance. From what we've discovered, there are many more caverns down here, most much lower—maybe as deep as five miles. These subterranean caverns are interconnected throughout much of Texas and a good portion of Mexico."

"And you've seen them?"

"Oh, yes, now that we know what to look for; they show up on the shuttle's short and long range scans. There seem to be multiple tribes."

"You've seen them? What do they look like?" Jason asked again.

"We've done some exploring. As I said, they're skittish and typically move to deeper caverns whenever we approach. One time we caught several off-guard. Saw them up close before they ran off. Truth is, they look a little like Craing. But tall, like a human," the admiral replied.

Chapter 32

Perkins insisted he was fit for duty, which would make Jason's life easier. Double shifts, prolonged hours sitting in the command chair, had started taking their toll. Earlier, Jason had gathered the remaining crew together in the mess as a way to convey information and address any ship-wide issues. It was more apparent than ever how understaffed they currently were. Their skeleton crew was down-right anemic. Once they were back at the outpost, finding able-bodied applicants would be no problem. Serving aboard *The Lilly* was in high-demand. For now, Jason needed to bolster morale and reestablish discipline. Ship life had become lax and overly casual. He also needed to address the rumor mill.

"Yes, Lieutenant Commander Perkins is alive. Yes, he is fine and will return to duty shortly. And yes, he has undergone some minor physical changes. It's temporary."

The crew immediately started to speak amongst themselves in hushed murmurs.

"This is not for open discussion, people," Jason said, reprimanding them again for their lax conduct. "When the XO returns to duty, you will not bring attention to his—" Jason had absolutely no idea how to talk about this. At the back of the room, Nan and Dira were standing together, both smirking. Jason continued, "When he returns to duty, just ignore his differences. Don't gossip or talk behind his back—give him a break, OK?"

Chief Horris raised his hand.

"Chief?"

"Captain, what's our destination? You know, now with the

overlords dead."

"There's really no point in continuing on. We're headed back to Earth. Anything else? Anyone? Then you're dismissed."

Now, Perkins stood at the entrance to the bridge. Jason turned in his seat and nodded to his XO. He looked fine, Jason thought. Apparently his garment replicator had no problem with his physical alterations.

"I am ready to relieve you, sir," Lieutenant Commander Perkins said.

"I am ready to be relieved," Jason replied and relinquished the command chair.

* * *

Jason entered Orion's domain. Other crewmembers on board also utilized the gym, but there was no mistaking that it was Orion who was in charge. A sectioned-off area of the forward hold, the gym was comprised of different sections one would find at any well-appointed facility, including aerobic, endurance, conditioning and strength-building. The similarities stopped there. Orion, from what Jason had gleaned since being on board, was a well-known sports figure on her home planet of Tarkin. He'd learned that on her planet the women were the larger, stronger of the sexes. The only similarity between females from Earth and Tarkin is they were both the bearer of offspring.

Orion's acclaim as a sports figure came from the team sport of *Bend*. Two teams on an elevated field, of sorts, and something they call the *Lorm*. Jason had assumed the *Lorm* was equivalent to some kind of ball. Orion had scoffed at that. Turns out, the *Lorm* was a four-sided open square, with only metal struts connecting the sides together. Easy to grab, get your fingers around. That is, if you could heft it. At nearly three hundred pounds, only the strongest, most agile females competed at the national or international level. Few athletes competed beyond their twenty-fifth birthday. The toll on one's body was cumulative, causing tendons and joints to wear down quickly. Jason found out Orion didn't like talking about her life on Tarkin, but she did mention she had retired as some kind of superstar athlete and was undefeated.

Now, looking around the ship's gym, Jason assumed that much of what was in evidence here was reflective of what Tarkin *Bend* athletes would have utilized for their training. The other sections of the gym, uniquely configured to Orion's predisposition for weapons and self-defense, were the dojo, where he stood now, and the weapons practice range next door.

Nan and Mollie were on mats. Both wore a modified version of their spacer's jumpsuits—but looser. Orion was wearing sweats and a snug tank top. Seeing her here, with her tattooed skin and enlarged musculature, Jason was confronted by her beauty, femininity, yet overt masculinity. Billy, a cigar-smoking, macho SEAL, having such attraction to Orion, reminded Jason that there was someone special for everyone and, if nothing else, Billy and Orion were the most quintessential power couple.

Orion was talking in low tones to her two students. Another woman entered the gym. Like Orion, she wore sweats and a tight-tank top as well. Dira rushed over and joined Nan and Mollie on the mats, both greeting her with excited smiles.

Orion looked over at Jason and gestured for him to come closer. He removed his shoes and stepped onto a mat.

"Thank you for coming, Captain," Orion said.

"My pleasure, but I'm not real sure why I'm here."

"I just want you to be clear on what I'll be teaching these three. I have a rough idea from what Nan has told me, as well as Dira, but I'd like your input, too, especially from a Navy SEAL standpoint."

"As both Nan and Dira, and even Mollie, have discovered, life in space can be dangerous: Craing mutants, rhino warriors, Serapin-Terplins, man-sized insects, pirate raiders ... there's no one size that'll fit all combatants when it comes to self-defense. Weapons training will be just as important as hand-to-hand drill, what we call close quarters combat training. Being able to think strategically, intuitively and even in new or abstract ways, may save their lives. So I'd concentrate on those areas, as well. Does that help?" Jason asked.

"Yes, sir. I think I have the perfect training regimen for them."

"Good. Don't go easy on them."

"Little chance of that, sir," Orion said with a smile.

Jason noticed all three students were watching him. They were excited, having fun. If Orion did her job right, they wouldn't feel that way in an hour or so. Jason was hailed.

"Go for Captain."

"Cap, we had changed course back to Earth, were about to transition FTL, when we detected an anomaly. Showed up on our long-range sensors."

"What do you have, McBride?"

"A fluctuating wormhole. It's there one second, gone the next. It's as if it's in transition."

"Just stay clear of it. We've got bigger issues to contend with, Ensign," Jason said.

"That's just it, sir. There's a ship at its mouth and the fluctuation is changing—becoming more stable. We estimate the wormhole will stabilize enough in the next hour for the ship to pass through."

"And you have determined it's a Craing vessel?" Jason asked.

"Definitely, Cap. It's a Dreadnaught-class warship."

"I'm on my way. Hail Ricket."

* * *

"Captain on deck" was announced as Jason entered the bridge. Ricket was already there. Perkins relinquished the command chair and stood at his side.

"How are you doing, XO—with everything?"

"Fine, sir. To be honest, I barely notice the difference. Although it does seem to cause a bit of uneasiness with the crew. Sir, as I mention on comms, we have something of an anomaly occurring."

"Captain, the wormhole fluctuations are down to four-minute intervals. We've noticed the ship consistently moving forward—it should breech the mouth during the next fluctuation," McBride said at the helm.

All eyes were on the display. There was nothing but open space, countless stars.

"Here it comes again, Captain," McBride said.

A section of space seemed to move in and out of focus. The contours of the wormhole were fluctuating rapidly. A massive shape, blurry at first, then came more in focus. As if breaking free from a gravitational pull, the ship shot forward then stopped.

"That's not a Craing Dreadnaught," Jason exclaimed.

Jason was more than a little familiar with Craing Dreadnaught vessels. He'd recently fought against one on the outskirts of the solar system. Propulsion systems destroyed, along with most of her weapons, the remaining remnants of that ship were now in high-orbit around the moon—a space station, of sorts, used for their fleet of Allied Craing vessels. But this ship was nothing like that. In contrast to the boxy, angular shape they were used to, this vessel was rounded and was comprised of multiple nearly-transparent rotating spheres.

Ricket took several steps closer to the display. "Captain, this is not a Craing Dreadnaught. *The Lilly's* sensors, as well as my own, confirm that much. More advanced technology here. Approximately thirteen miles in circumference."

"Captain, I'm not detecting any major life forms—not much is moving around on that vessel," McBride reported.

"Maybe it's some kind of drone ship?"

"No, sir, at least not entirely. The ship's shields are down, as you can see from our scans. I'm seeing clearly-defined living spaces. It's huge."

Jason took in the 3D representation of the vessel. "Is it operational?"

Ricket said, "Yes, sir. Multiple background systems are running. It's as if those on board were there one minute and gone the next."

"Could this have something to do with our shutting down the Loop?" Jason asked.

"Possibly," Ricket replied. "And since wormholes do not necessarily conform to any prerequisite time continuum—we may have altered the course of a ship in transit from years in the future. One other thing: although there are no life signs, there are organic remains. There's also an abundance of other, smaller life forms."

Jason knew he needed to make a decision. Any delay now could impact saving lives on Earth. He wasn't sure if *The Lilly* should go up against those three Caldurian technology vessels—vessels potentially more advanced than *The Lilly* herself. Jason continued to look at the strange ship. Perhaps, somehow, that ship could level the playing field.

"Does that vessel have armaments, weapons?"

"Definitely Cap, but nothing like I've seen before," McBride replied.

"What's that?" Jason asked, pointing to a large section near what he assumed was the forward end of the vessel. "It looks like some kind of courtyard."

"Whatever it is, it's close to a half-mile long, not quite as wide," McBride said.

"Sound general quarters. Prepare to phase-shift into that area. Hail Orion; we're going to need some new battle suits. I'll need Billy and Rizzo, and you too, Ricket; we're taking that ship."

* * *

They'd converged at the armory on Deck 2. Orion helped Jason and his team make final adjustments with their battle suits. Each wore a phase-shift belt and carried a multi-gun.

"Sure you don't need me along on this one, Cap?" Orion asked.

"Not this time, Gunny. I want you here on tactical. We may need to blow something up, which seems to be a unique talent of yours."

"Yes, sir."

Jason saw her give Billy a quick glance; she obviously did not like being separated or, more likely, not having his back.

"I'll take good care of him, Gunny."

Jason, Billy, Rizzo, and Ricket filed out of the armory and headed toward the DeckPort. Jason was being hailed.

"Go for Captain, XO."

"Captain, we're ready to phase-shift," Perkins said.

"I want to phase-shift in with rail-guns charged and ready. As soon as Gunny is at her post, go ahead and phase-shift."

At the aft airlock, Jason watched his HUD display until the

readings changed. They'd just phase-shifted. Once *The Lilly*'s forward ramp deployed, Jason led his team off the ship.

The courtyard was not what Jason had expected. As if walking into Central Park, they were surrounded by large trees and rolling green hills. There were beds of flowers with strange shapes and colors. A slight breeze rustled branches and leaves above. A lake shimmered a short distance from where *The Lilly* sat. Jason spotted a waterfall—one where the water rushed upward into the air—seemingly ignoring the laws of physics. A small island hovered, weightless. In the distance he saw the reflective outside perimeter of the ship itself. Thousands of buildings of various heights occupied long, quiet mezzanines and green belts. The structures were nearly transparent. He felt as if they were surrounded by a glass city. A city with thousands of windows looking down on them. Jason figured this vessel, this city, was easily the size of Manhattan. The familiar blue glow of a phase-shift portal hovered nearby. Then he noticed more portals, hundreds of them, throughout the city.

Although there wasn't an actual track, far in the distance a tram was winding its way in their direction, toward the central courtyard. Soundlessly it approached and hovered several inches above the ground. Like the buildings, and everything else here, the four-car tram was almost completely transparent. Doors opened at the mid-point of each of the four cars. Jason glanced inside. Empty. The doors closed and the tram continued on its way without making a sound.

Jason felt he could spend weeks, months, exploring this place. He heard his NanoCom chime.

"Go for Captain."

"Captain, a fleet, maybe two hundred ships, is approaching. Looks to be our pirate friends again," Perkins said.

"Hail them. Inform them they are too late to the party.

We've claimed this vessel for the Alliance. Let Stalls know we're aware of their presence and we won't hesitate to fire on his fleet. Starting with his ship. You may need to phase-shift back to open space to further convince them. Keep me abreast of the situation, XO."

"Aye, sir," Perkins replied.

Billy pointed toward the air above. A small flock of birds with bright red feathers flew overhead and disappeared into the trees.

Jason brought the ship's layout onto his HUD. Four blue icons indicated their current location within the courtyard.

"This way," Jason said, heading out of the courtyard toward the city ahead. The further they went, the more apparent it became that the ship had been left unattended for weeks, perhaps months. Eerie, like walking down the streets of a modern-day ghost town, trash and leaves from the nearby park skittered across the wide thoroughfare. Jason noticed the buildings, although transparent, were actually various shades and muted colors.

The first corpse found was sprawled awkwardly on a bench. As if waiting for a bus. A bus that would never arrive. Ricket knelt down next to the body and proceeded to poke and prod at the remains. Partially decomposed, it seemed obvious to Jason by the large eyes and somewhat triangular-shape of its head.

"Looks like Perkins. Is he Caldurian?"

"Yes, I believe so, Captain. This is interesting," Ricket said and continued to probe the body. "The DNA of this individual is similar, almost identical to that of human. In fact, it is human."

"I thought our scans showed this to be a Craing vessel," Jason said.

"Mistaken; this vessel is like nothing I've come across before. Highly-advanced, and this is a far more cultured civilization than any you'd find on a Craing vessel." Ricket stood and looked up at Jason.

"Any idea what killed him?"

"I know exactly what killed him."

"What?"

"An implant. Interesting, it's not dissimilar to the nano-devices aboard *The Lilly*."

"The ones in our own heads?"

"Yes."

"The one in my daughter's head?"

"Yes."

"Can our nano-devices be triggered to do that? To snuff the life out of someone?"

"I believe so. I may be able to disable that feature."

"Feature? Let's make that a priority," Jason said, scowling down at Ricket.

Jason stood back and hailed *The Lilly*.

"Go for XO."

"What's the status on our pirate friends?" Jason asked.

"I was just about to hail you, sir." Perkins said. "They say we are free to leave, but if we try to take this ship, take it out of *their space*, they'll fire every missile they have. Our scans indicate they have conventional missiles, as well as nuke and fusion-tipped missiles. If they fire a barrage, which is likely, *The Lilly* won't be able to fend that off."

"Then we need you to stall them somehow," Jason said. "We're going to try to get this ship moving, perhaps jump it to FTL. I take it you're speaking with Stalls? Tell him you need to retrieve an away party ... thirty, forty minutes max. Tell him we're not interested in this old bucket, it's been gutted. Dead in space. Maybe they can tow it and sell it for scrap—whatever, make something up."

"Aye, sir, I'll get you some time. Oh and Captain, at this

point Captain Stalls believes I'm dead. So Ensign McBride is handling communications with them."

"Understood," Jason said.

"One other thing, Cap. And this is really strange; *The Lilly*'s bridge has completely reconfigured itself. Multiple virtual consoles have been added, and three more actual consoles in the open area, toward the front of the bridge. They emerged from beneath the deck plates. Truth is, without Ricket here, we have no idea what's going on."

Jason listened to the XO and watched Ricket moving about, investigating the local area. "That makes certain kind of sense, XO. Don't touch anything. I'm cutting this expedition short; we'll be on our way back shortly. Oh, and have McBride tell Stalls we're leaving in fifteen minutes. That should be believable."

"Aye, sir."

Jason brought his attention back to his team. "Ricket, *The Lilly* has undergone a reconfiguration. New virtual and actual consoles."

Ricket listened, then nodded. "And that is why we will not find a bridge on this vessel. Like most things with Caldurian design, the bridge is virtual. At least for now, *The Lilly* is the bridge. I need to get back to the ship, Captain."

"Head on back. See if you can establish control, and fire up the propulsion system." With the advanced level of anything Caldurian, Jason felt fairly confident that as long as *The Lilly* was still within the confines of this vessel, no harm could come to her or the crew. "Go ahead, we'll continue on here for a few more minutes."

"Yes, sir." Ricket ran off in the direction of *The Lilly*.

Jason, Billy and Rizzo continued on. As they moved further into the glass city, it was evident the vessel's systems were coming back on. Hover drones, hundreds of them, were moving about.

Jason and his team brought their weapons to bear, then relaxed as they realized they were fairly innocuous. Each drones, robot-like, had two arms with multiple-fingered hands. No head and no legs, the upper front section of each drone had several clear indentations. Jason thought it gave the drones somewhat the look of a face. As the team continued on, they found more bodies.

"Cap," Billy said, "over here."

Billy had turned down a smaller side street and was now waving Jason over. This block of structures was distinctly different from the others. Through its glass walls there were row after row of MediPod-type devices, as well as a variety of others. Here there were more bodies. Too many to count.

"This is their hospital," Billy said.

"And from the looks of things, the populous knew the end was coming. They converged at the one place they thought could help them," Jason replied. "Who would do this? Who would instigate mass genocide?"

"Yeah, and if we had been around, we'd be dead too," Billy added. "Maybe we should get as far away from this place as possible."

Jason watched as the drones systematically picked up the remains of the dead and transported them off to somewhere else.

The three watched in silence for a few more minutes as the drones continued to transport bodies through portal windows. The hover tram had made it into the city and was making stops every few hundred feet.

Rizzo shook his head. "Cap, can you imagine the pirates getting hold of the technology here in this place? Or worse, the Craing?"

"No, and that can't happen. If we can't get this vessel moving at FTL, we'll need to destroy it," Jason said.

Their conversation was cut short by a new sound, more like a vibration beneath their feet.

"Looks like Ricket's made some progress. Let's get back to the ship."

Chapter 33

Jason reached the bridge to find it had indeed undergone a radical transformation. It was larger, somehow, with the forward bulkhead extending ten feet further toward the bow. It seemed wider as well. Not only were there additional workstations, the existing ones contained numerous new virtual displays and more controls than Jason thought possible.

Ricket sat at one of the new consoles, his mechanical hands moving fast across virtual keys.

"Captain Stalls has given us an ultimatum. We have three minutes before they fire on us, actually, on this vessel. I don't think they're bluffing. Sensors show they're powering weapons."

Jason took in a deep breath. "I'm getting really tired of this guy." He held up a hand to put Perkins on hold for a second. "Ricket, what's your timeframe for moving this thing, getting it into FTL?"

Ricket didn't turn around and spoke while he worked. "Propulsion systems on the vessel are coming online now. I need five minutes."

Jason took the command chair. "Open a channel to Captain Stalls."

"Good to see you again, Captain," Stalls said with his typical superior tone. His face was bruised and his nose bandaged. "Needless to remind you, I'm sure. You are still in within the limits of our territorial space. As you have undoubtedly noticed, we are fully prepared to destroy that vessel, or what ever the hell it is, if you attempt to move it or jump to FTL."

"No need. It's all yours, Stalls. Just give us a minute or two to get my people back on board and clear out of your space," Jason replied.

"Unfortunately, I don't think you have any intention of abandoning that vessel, Captain. Several moments ago we detected its propulsion systems coming online."

Jason looked confused, as if this was all news to him. "Well, our ship just came back online; you must be detecting our drives."

"Shut it down. Right now, Captain Reynolds. You have ten seconds."

Jason's eyes went to Ricket, who quickly turned in his seat shaking his head. "We still need two minutes."

Annoyed, Stalls' dark eyes glared back at Jason. "It will be a shame to destroy such an amazing vessel, Captain. You and I both know the technology aboard that ship is far beyond anything—"

Jason cut him off; he had an idea. "Listen to me, Stalls: you said it yourself. This vessel, or whatever it is, is far more advanced than anything you've come across. Do you really think it would be sitting out here defenseless ... out here in open space? You've already lost hundreds of your crew to our defenses, are you prepared to lose more? This ship has the capability to vaporize your entire fleet in seconds." Jason glanced over to Orion, who had been working at the new tactical console. As if knowing she was being watched, she nodded her head and held up two fingers. *What is it with everybody needing two minutes?*

"Just shut down now, Captain. No more stalling."

Jason shrugged, "You're making a mistake. What's two more minutes?"

Jason watched as Stalls looked away and nodded to someone off screen.

"Incoming!" Orion yelled. "And it's a whole lot of missiles. Over one thousand and counting. Captain, looks like a variety of conventional, nukes and fusion-tipped."

"Break the connection," Jason barked. Captain Stalls' face

disappeared from the display.

"ETA, Gunny?"

"Less than a minute, sir."

"Ricket?"

"We're moving, sir, but it won't be fast enough," he replied.

"Orion, what have you discovered? Do we have shields? Weapons?"

"Both, sir. Think I almost have it figured out."

"Thirty seconds to impact," Perkins yelled from the adjoining station next to Gunny's.

McBride at the helm spun in his seat, "Captain, I think *The Lilly* can—"

"Just do it, Helm—whatever the hell it is, we're out of time."

"Eight seconds to impact," Perkins yelled.

The display flashed white.

"We're right smack in the middle of their fleet, sir," Perkins yelled.

Jason spun in his seat, looking up at the 360 degree display. Sure enough, pirate warships encircled them on all sides. Hundreds of them.

"What the hell did you do, McBride?" Jason barked.

"Sorry, sir, I realized we still had the capability to phase-shift *The Lilly*, along with the Caldurian vessel. Not far but ... I didn't have time to set the coordinates. I guessed."

"Cap, Caldurian ship's shields are up," Orion said, smiling. "Oh, and we destroyed eighteen pirate vessels when we shifted along with the Crystal City into the middle of their fleet."

"Open a channel to Captain Stalls," Jason ordered.

"Channel open, sir."

Stalls' cocky bravado was replaced with seething hatred. "Mark my words, Reynolds, I'm going to kill you. But before I do, I'm going to take your wife as my personal whore and sell your daughter off to space slavers. This isn't over. Don't forget to look over your shoulder, Reynolds. I'm coming for you."

With that, the display went black. One by one, the remaining raider ships headed off into deep space. They'd won the moment, but Jason knew his troubles with Captain Stalls had only just begun.

* * *

Two hours later, Jason was seated alone at his desk in the captain's ready room. It had taken that long to establish an FTL link with the outpost back on Earth. It had been a while since he'd last checked in, and there was a lot to cover. When his father's face appeared, it was evident he was sitting in the cramped confines of the shuttle.

"We're not back yet because we've been delayed—several times now. A group of raiders—pirates—infiltrated *The Lilly* while we were moving through HAB 12. Recognize the name Captain Stalls?"

"Oh yeah, know the name well. A constant thorn in the side of the Allied forces. How the hell did they get on board?"

"Turns out it was our illusive mole, Seaman Perkins from Engineering. Not sure what his real name is, but apparently he's Captain Stalls' little brother."

"That's a bad bunch, Jason, not the kind of enemy you want to go up against," the admiral said.

"So where are you—are you underground right now?"

"Yes. Each branch of the military has poured into the outpost. You wouldn't recognize the place. Thought it best to keep any phase-shift technology away from them."

"What about the three vessels, the Emperor's Guard, in orbit?" Jason asked.

"Still there, and they've increased the number of subterranean phase-shifts by the hour. They've also concentrated their search now to the Americas."

"Have they phase-shifted anywhere near the outpost?"

"No, the lower United States and upper Mexico have yet to be touched. One ship has been moving across Canada; the other two are making their way up South America."

"The last time we talked, you described the inhabitants as looking similar to Craing, but tall, like humans. Is that correct?"

"That's right. Why?"

"It's just that what you described is similar to beings we've discovered on what we believe to be another Caldurian vessel. It's actually more a city than a vessel. "

"You've discovered a Caldurian city in open space?"

"More like it discovered us. Dad, it's amazing. Beautiful. Highly advanced. It emerged from a wormhole not far from where we were located. At first we thought it could be a random result from us closing down the Craing Loop, but Ricket now believes it, what we're calling the Crystal City, moves through space by generating its own wormhole. It would be too much of a coincidence for it to have shown up right where we were, where *The Lilly* was located in open space."

"Have you contacted them? Who are they?" the admiral asked.

"We've shifted *The Lilly* onto the Crystal City itself. Unfortunately, the populace is dead, many thousands dead. Subsequently, *The Lilly*'s bridge has been reconfigured. It's now taken over as the ship's de facto control center. We're thinking it may be the Crystal City's default. Something that happens when reunited with another Caldurian vessel such as *The Lilly*."

The admiral furrowed his brow. "But you're still on your way back to Earth?"

"Yes, but there's one more thing. These Caldurians had

nano-tech devices in their heads. It's what killed them all. It's virtually the same tech we have in our own heads, Dad.

"Personally, I believe we need to get as far away from this vessel as possible. Ricket warns that if he is unable to further investigate, you, me and the rest of *The Lilly* crew may eventually be facing the same fate."

Jason wondered why he hadn't made the connection before. Those three Caldurian ships in orbit around Earth had first been discovered underground, lying dormant. Just as *The Lilly* had been. *Was there a link?*

"Dad, fifteen years ago when you and Granddad first discovered *The Lilly*, you mentioned both the AI and Ricket's memory had been wiped."

"That's right. We had no idea what we were doing. Once we cleared away the rubble, we were allowed access to the ship, didn't have to break in or anything. Once inside, it was dark as a tomb—seemed to be dead. Apparently, though, minimum ship functions were still running, because when we started moving about the ship, more and more systems came back online. All of a sudden a repeating voice sounded." The admiral paused, as if searching his memories. "It said something like, *Bio-form 'human' detected, prior function complete, you may enter a new start access code* ... something along those lines. It repeated that over and over again, really annoying. As if the AI had been waiting for us, or someone, to enter a new code. When we entered the bridge, it came alive. The big overhead wrap-around display came on. At the nearest console that same message appeared—"

"Like a sentence written in English?" Jason butted in, looking skeptical.

"Yes, in English. I wouldn't be able to read Caldurian, now would I?" the admiral replied, irritated by Jason's interruption.

Jason nodded; stupid question—*The Lilly* AI was incredibly

intelligent. It would have detected his father's and grandfather's speech and language patterns.

"So what did you do?"

"I didn't know what the hell to do. Grandpa Gus suggested I enter a number I'd remember later, so I entered my social security number."

"So that brought the ship alive?"

"No, another annoying message started to repeat. Something to the effect: *initiate biomechanical sub-routines.* Over and over again ... we wanted to kill the fucking thing. We didn't find Ricket for several days."

"Where was he?"

"That's the strange part. Ricket wasn't inside the ship. Ol' Gus couldn't take that repeating voice anymore and was outside clearing dirt and rocks from the front of the ship. He found Ricket buried. Your grandfather fetched me from the ship, and together we pulled Ricket free."

"Why was Ricket outside the ship?" Jason asked, confused.

The admiral simply stared back at Jason.

"Sorry, go on."

"Ricket was lifeless. Then all of a sudden, his little gears and actuators started to move, and then he too started repeating the same phrase, only this time he added something else—something like: *enter command authorization code for Reechet biomechanical sub-routines.* Obviously, there wasn't a keypad to enter anything, so I just said my social security number aloud."

"Wait, so how did you get the name Ricket from Reechet?"

"What? Oh, your grandfather's hearing was terrible. He heard it as Ricket. I corrected him numerous times, but Ricket seemed to stick. He's been Ricket ever since." The admiral smiled as he recalled the memory of his father.

"Anyway, we were able to converse with Ricket. He seemed

to be confused at first, had no idea who he was, or why he was lying beneath a mound of dirt next to a space ship. But his deductive powers, as you've discovered, were quick to put things together. Apparently, the ship, *The Lilly* AI, had reconfigured Ricket's internal software. I haven't been able to connect the dots with that aspect yet."

"Dad, suppose those Caldurian vessels in orbit were mothballed underground, same as *The Lilly* had been. But just because The Lilly AI and Ricket's memory were wiped doesn't mean the other ships' memories were wiped." Jason was figuring things out as he spoke.

"I don't get the correlation, Jason."

"To be honest, I'm not sure I do, either. But suppose *The Lilly*, or whoever was controlling her, was after the same thing those Craing are after now? Maybe they are searching for something— something down there in that subterranean world?"

"You're thinking it has something to do with the inhabitants beneath North America, in this area?" the admiral asked.

"Well, it's not a big leap, Dad. From how you've described them, they look exactly like the Caldurians on the Crystal City— right? Maybe they are early Caldurians."

"So what are you thinking? That this is some sort of return to mecca or their homeland?"

"No, well, actually that kinda works too," Jason said, sensing that the puzzle pieces were starting to come together, but not quite.

"Jason, I have to be honest with you; the inhabitants down here look fairly primitive. They're running around in animal furs. They're cave men. There's certainly no advanced technology going on down here," the admiral added, looking like he was going to say something more.

"What?"

"You say that ship, that Crystal City, can generate its own wormhole to move about the universe?" the admiral asked.

"That's what Ricket concludes ... makes sense, though."

"Having the ability to move about the universe with that kind of ease—" Jason's father stopped mid-sentence, then continued: "Jason, as powerful as the Loop was for the Craing, it would be nothing compared to this technology. With the Loop they needed to map the various end-points across the universe, which they had no control over. Here, they could traverse anywhere at any time. We're talking about the secret to totally unrestricted, near instantaneous space travel."

Jason nodded. "Perhaps when those three Caldurian ships came alive, something else happened. Perhaps the Craing learned some sort of Caldurian wormhole travel secrets. Secrets that could only be fully-uncovered in one place."

"Earth," they both said at the same time.

"Anyway, we estimate the three vessels in orbit will discover our location here beneath the Chihuahuan desert within the next twenty-four hours. If what you're saying is correct, and they're looking for clues to unlock the secret of Caldurian wormhole travel, we need to stop them. As important as it was to bring down the Craing Loop, and it certainly was, we have to stop the Craing again and those three ships."

"Dad, one more thing. Off subject. How well did you know Dira, when you first assembled the crew for *The Lilly*?"

Chapter 34

Jason was back on the bridge, Ricket still busy at the forward-most console. His fingers stopped moving and he turned toward Jason.

"Captain. I've been studying their wormhole travel technology. It is far more advanced than anything I've come across on *The Lilly*. It's actually not a technology specifically located aboard the Caldurian ship," Ricket explained.

"Then how does it work?"

"I have been trying to decipher that for several hours now, sir. From the little I've been able to unravel, it's more like an interstellar communications transmission." Ricket retrieved his baseball cap from the console, climbed down from his seat, and walked back to Jason. "Captain, prior to this vessel moving through space, actually bending space via a wormhole, it sends out a massive amount of information. It uses a communications protocol I'm unfamiliar with, and the corresponding response *is* the generation of the wormhole."

"Why can't we simply send the same communications request they do?" Jason asked.

"That's the beauty of this. Every time a new communication—a new request—is sent, it's totally unique. As if it's a code issued to the universe—one that is atypical and ultimately undecipherable."

"If you're talking about some kind of God code, I don't buy it," Jason said.

"I don't believe spirituality has anything to do with this. With that said, someone has figured out a formula. If it were strictly mathematical, that would be one thing, but this is based on something else, as well."

"So you're talking about what? Some kind of secret formula, a way to speak directly to the universe in a way that can alter the nature of physics itself?"

"It may be something far simpler, as well as far more complex, than that. I don't know."

Jason nodded, realizing whatever it was, right now the Craing were searching miles beneath the surface of Earth for the answer.

It was becoming more and more evident the Caldurian's home world was in fact Earth, and not some far-off planet thousands of light-years away. Perhaps these cave people beneath the Chihuahuan desert were in fact original Caldurians descendants? Descendants that still hold ancient secrets to communicate directly with the universe?

"Unfortunately, the Caldurian vessel, this Crystal City, is not capable of FTL travel. We will not get to Earth within twenty-four hours as long as we are moored here."

"Can you secure this vessel against intrusion? Leave the shields up?" Jason asked.

"Yes, the raiders, or anyone else for that matter, will not be able to board this vessel. In fact, only another Caldurian vessel would be able to land here, such as we have."

"Good, then the decision's made. We'll come back here after we've dealt with the Emperor's Guard."

* * *

Jason was tired, not having had a break since before Admiral Cramer's militia took control of the outpost, then the arduous trek across HAB 12, destroying the Loop on Halimar, the pirates, and most recently the discovery of the Crystal City with its populace all found dead. They'd lifted off from the courtyard and were heading out into open space. Almost immediately, *The Lilly* reconfigured its bridge back to normal. They needed to reach Earth, fast. Even at FTL, it would take them almost twenty-four hours. Now, with Perkins back in the command chair, Jason left the bridge.

He had received a NanoText from Mollie several hours earlier. *Kids and texting.* She had requested he drop by the Zoo; she had something she wanted to show him.

Jason found the Zoo empty, at least of people. He walked to the first habitat across the isle and waited for his favorite creature, the Drapple, to appear. A moment later there it was, seemingly inches from his face, big and powerful, yet agile, as it positioned itself through the water in front of Jason. Jason wondered what was it about this strange creature that evoked such a strong kinship. Being worm-like and not actually having a head made finding the Drapple's face sometimes a challenge. Then he noticed his smile and then the warm, kind eyes looking back at him. He reached his hand out and placed it on the habitat's window. The Drapple turned slightly in the water and let his bulk press against the same spot. An unspoken connection.

"Dad! I'm waiting for you. What are you doing?"

Jason turned to see Mollie standing in front of HAB 4. When he turned back, the Drapple was gone.

"I'm just reconnecting with a friend. Where were you?" Jason asked.

"In here, come on before the window times out and I have to get Jack again. I want to show you something," she said.

Jason jogged over, and he and Mollie entered Habitat 4. The first thing that struck Jason was the humidity. Green and lush, the jungle was alive with sounds and movement. Mollie pulled Jason's arm towards a makeshift wooden fence. Raja and three other large Indian elephants stood together. Raja's trunk curled and rose high above its head, as if trumpeting Jason's arrival. Up close, Jason gave each of the elephants a pat. Jack was nearby, scattering branches with thick green leaves at their feet. Off in the distance, sitting on the fence with her nose in a paperback, was Nan. She looked up and waved, then was back engrossed in her book.

"We're not here to play with the elephants, Dad. Stand there. This is what I wanted to show you," Mollie said, then scurried ten yards down the dirt path.

"Alice. Command five. Alice, command five." Mollie smiled over at her father and then became serious again.

There was rustling off in the distance, deep in the overgrown foliage. Closer now, Jason recognized the sound, the odd gait of the running dog-like creature with its six legs. It broke from the trees, big blue tongue hanging from its mouth. Excited, it headed right for Jason.

"Command five, Alice, Command Five."

Alice changed course and veered toward Mollie. Once close, she slowed to a walk and then stopped in front of her. She gathered her feet beneath her, crouched low, then sprang into the air and over Mollie's head. She landed, turned, crouched and sprang again. Once seated in front of Mollie, Alice waited patiently, her eyes never leaving Mollie's. Mollie waited a moment, then knelt down.

"Good girl, Alice, good girl." Mollie kissed the creature's head, then enfolded her in her arms—Alice's tail wagged and her big tongue licked at Mollie's face.

"Pretty cool, huh, Dad?"

"Very cool!" Jason replied, excitedly. "How did you do that? Teach her how to do that?"

"She's really smart. I've taught her other things, too. Each trick has a different command number. She's really good at fetching things. Watch this! Alice, command eight, shoe. Command eight, shoe."

Alice ran off and disappeared into the trees again, only to return moments later with something in her mouth. She ran until she reached Mollie and dropped an old shoe at her feet. Again, Mollie praised and hugged the animal.

"I'm impressed. And it looks like you've made a friend," Jason said.

"She's the best friend in the world. I just feel sorry that she doesn't have other drogs to play with."

"Drogs?"

"Yeah, that's what I've named her species. Do you like it?" Mollie asked, looking up at her father.

The parallel wasn't lost on Jason. Mollie too needed to be with other kids. Have a more normal life.

"Alice is a fine drog. I'm going to say hi to your mom. I'll watch you from over there."

Mollie was off and running with Alice before Jason finished talking.

As he approach, Nan laid the book down on the wooden fence and looked up at Jason. The sun was low and amber in the sky, and her long chestnut hair fell free around her shoulders. She was wearing jeans and a white button down shirt, and as always, her cleavage caught his eye.

"Sit down next to me for a minute," she said, smiling.

"You know, I've never been in here. It's nice. Relaxing."

"It's one of the few Earth habitats. Whenever I'm homesick, I come sit here on this fence for a while."

She looked at him, as if studying his face. "What are we doing, Jason?"

He didn't know how to answer. Things had gotten

complicated. After being pushed away for so long, he didn't know if he could put his heart out there again. And then there was Dira.

"You look beautiful. More beautiful than the day I met you."

"I bet you say that to all—" She stopped mid sentence. Tears welled up in her eyes and she looked away.

Jason touched her face and gently turned her to look at him. He kissed her softly. Her arms came up and encircled his neck. She kissed him back, just as softly, her eyes open and locked on his.

"I've made so many mistakes. I don't blame you, you know."

"Blame me for what?" he asked.

"For giving up on me. And for finding someone else. Dira."

Jason didn't know how to respond. His feelings for Dira were so new, so undefined. What he had with Nan was the real thing. But he'd been hurt. Numerous times.

"I want to make you a proposition," she said, leaning away from him, serious and still looking in his eyes.

"A proposition, huh? What kind of proposition?" he asked, equally as serious.

"If you can make me a promise. A very simple one. I propose that you keep on doing what you're doing. Continue to explore things with Dira. She's amazing, young, beautiful—"

"Which you are all the above yourself, I might add," Jason interjected.

"Let me finish. See where it goes. But don't give up on us either. On me. Maybe it took the cataclysmic events of the last few months, or maybe being chased around the captain's suite by that pirate thug, but I know you're the only man I want in my life. But I want you to return to me only after you know for sure what you want. As I now do. I love you, Jason. I'm so sorry I've waited so long to do this." The tears now ran freely down her cheeks, her eyes still locked on his. Jason pulled her in close and wrapped his arms around her.

Chapter 35

The pain struck without warning. Intense and relentless. Jason had caught a few hours of sleep before, as if being hit by a bolt of lightning, he sat up grabbing for his head. It only began to subside once he had showered and dressed. Making his way to Medical, he noticed more and more people in the corridor—all headed in the same direction.

Tired looking, Dira was already there, attending to others. Mollie was crying, Nan holding her tight. Ricket entered Medical several seconds after Jason.

"What is this? What's going on with everyone?"

Ricket was moving fast. Someone was in a MediPod and he checked its readings. "Nano-devices."

Jason stopped and stared, paralyzed by the implications. He looked over to Mollie, still crying.

"You're talking about—"

"Yes," he said, "same as the Crystal City. They are counting down."

"How long?"

"Fourteen days, three hours, eight minutes."

"Can you do something? Turn them off?"

"I've turned them off. They turn back on. They are being controlled externally."

"Can you remove them—maybe the MediPod can remove them?"

"They are permanent—integrated into the bio-structure of the brain. Removing them would be fatal," Ricket said, still taking readings.

"So what do we do?"

"We need to stop them at the source. I've discovered where all Caldurian signals emanate from, including the instructions for wormhole transport—such as what the Crystal City uses.

"Where? We need to change course. Get there and turn these things off!"

"We are already on the right course, Captain." Ricket said.

"You're saying it's Earth?"

"Yes."

Jason found it nearly impossible to think around the pain. He knelt down next to Mollie. Her eyes were red and puffy.

"Can you make it stop, Dad?"

"We're going back to Earth, sweetie. Once there, we'll figure this out." Jason hugged her then stood and hugged Nan.

"Can you give everyone something for the pain?" Jason asked, looking to Ricket and then to Dira.

Ricket nodded, "Yes. It won't stop the pain completely, but it will help."

* * *

From the bridge, Jason sat and watched the overhead display, mesmerized as stars continuously streamed by. He kept coming back to the same conclusion. The reason Earth was generating Caldurian signals was simple: Earth and Calduria were one and the same. It was Earth that had been attacked by the Craing thousands of years earlier. What few remained alive, like those in the Crystal City, now moved about the universe. *How many other crystal cities were there?* He then thought about the Craing and the three Caldurian vessels in Earth orbit.

"That's why they haven't been attacking!" he blurted out loud.

Orion looked back at him from her station. "You all right, Cap?"

Jason was still deep in thought, "Oh, yeah. I'm alright, Gunny."

He needed to contact them. He looked over to the communications station. "Gordon, I want to open a channel."

"Yes, sir," came two voices. Both of the red-headed Gordons were on duty. Jason couldn't remember if it was Jeffery or Michael he was looking at.

"Which one are you?" he asked, irritated.

"Jeffery, sir."

"I don't want to see either of you on this bridge again unless you have full name tags, understood?"

"Yes, sir," the two Gordons replied.

"You, Jeffery, can you open a channel to the shuttle?"

"Yes, sir."

As Jason waited, he ran through what he had figured out, or at least thought he had figured out. Somewhere on Earth, a Caldurian signal was being generated. It wasn't a coincidence that the Craing were also searching Earth with those three Caldurian vessels. Where Jason and *The Lilly*'s crew needed to turn off the signals for their nano-devices, the Craing's search was for something else. What's the most important thing to the Craing, especially now that the Loop had been destroyed? It was the ability to move about the universe uninhibited. This Caldurian signal—it was universal and powerful. Jason wondered what else it was.

"Channel open, sir," Jeffery Gordon said.

Admiral Reynolds looked terrible. Annoyed, he spoke first. "I was sleeping. Something that does not come easily lately."

"Hello to you too, Admiral," Jason replied. "Let me guess, a blinding headache. You're ready to jump in front of a bus or dive off a cliff?" Jason asked.

"Exactly, how'd you know?"

"It's your nano-devices. Dad, like the rest of us, you will be dead in two weeks, actually less now. Sorry for putting it so bluntly."

"All of us?" the admiral asked.

"Yes, anyone that has these devices in their heads."

"What can we do to stop this from happening?"

"I believe the answer lies with the cave people you've discovered. As we talked about, I'm sure they are descendants of the Caldurians. There's a universal signal being generated. Multi-functional, it controls things such as wormhole generation, offering Caldurian ships the ability to move about the universe with ease. Apparently it also signals things like our nano-devices to shut down. I'm sure it does far more, but for now finding its source is what's paramount."

"Ricket, can you locate this signal?" the admiral asked.

Jason had not noticed the mechanical alien was standing at his side.

"This is not a signal generation in the same sense of a radio frequency or light waves. This would be closer to trying to find the origins of thought or consciousness, nearly impossible," Ricket said.

"So we need to find this before the Craing do."

"Yes," Jason replied. "We have the advantage of knowing where their tribe is located, or at least where one of their tribes is located," Jason said.

"What do you want me to do? They're not exactly friendly—it's not like I can invite them to tea."

"Who's there with you in the shuttle?"

"It's me and two SEALs, that's it," the admiral replied.

"If we can get past those three Caldurian vessels, I know exactly who we can send to talk to them," Jason said.

* * *

"Why me?" Perkins asked, defensively.

"Because you look just like them. Think about it. You won't be nearly as intimidating as we would be," Jason replied.

Jason had wanted to talk to Perkins away from everyone else. It was bad enough he looked so peculiar. This was a sensitive conversation. One that only compounded the issue that he was *different* than everyone else.

"I don't speak their language—oh, wait, I guess Lilly will help translate," Perkins said.

"That's right." Jason hesitated, then continued, "Right now, we all have a death sentence hanging over our heads. In less than two weeks, we'll all be dead, including my ex-wife and daughter, who aren't even crewmembers. We need you to do this. Our very survival hinges on you being able to do this."

"Yes, sir. I won't let you down, Captain," Perkins said.

Jason was being hailed.

"Go for Captain."

"Captain, we'll be entering Earth orbit within five minutes," McBride said.

"On my way. Sound general quarters, battle stations."

* * *

Jason and Perkins entered the bridge together. Ricket was there, as well as Orion on tactical.

A view of Earth filled the wrap-around display above. It change to a segmented view, with close ups of each of the three Caldurian ships at their various orbital coordinates.

"They certainly don't look anything like *The Lilly*," Jason commented. Smaller, the three vessels were stark white, and squatty looking like pugged-nosed bulldogs.

"They see us, Cap," Orion said from tactical. "Their shields are up."

"Distance?"

In a flash, one of the segmented displays changed, the Caldurian vessel gone.

"They've shifted away, sir."

With the vessel reacquired, the same ship filled the display again. "Closest one is right on top of us at sixty-five miles out, sir."

Jason put Lieutenant Miller and his fighter crew on standby. Figuring this was as good a place to make a stand as any, he was about to deploy.

"Incoming!" Orion shouted. "Six missiles—fusion-tipped, Cap. Ten seconds to contact."

"Select and load fusion-tipped missiles, Gunny. Helm, shift us in three miles closer to their starboard side, do it now," Jason commanded.

The Lilly phase-shifted. "Fire missiles."

"Missiles away, sir."

"The two other vessels have shifted as well sir," McBride said. "They're now right along side the other one."

Ricket said, "Obviously, they don't have our three-mile phase-shift limitation or the need for prolonged recharging, Captain."

The display changed; the Caldurian vessels all shifted at the same time and had surrounded *The Lilly* at less than ten miles out.

"Taking heavy plasma fire, Captain," Orion yelled.

"Shields already down to fifty percent!" Perkins added.

The Lilly was being thrown about. Those standing reached for something to grasp on to. Ricket fell to the floor, then Perkins.

"Deploy rail guns," Jason commanded.

"Already on it, sir"

Jason felt the familiar vibration of *The Lilly*'s rail guns snapping into place beneath the hull.

"They're shifting every second or two now, can't get a lock on them. *The Lilly*'s taken over defenses."

"Shields are completely gone!"

"We're taking direct hits to our outer hull. They're targeting our drives, Captain," Orion said.

"Breech on Deck 1, we're venting to space!" Perkins said, back on his feet and at his post.

Jason felt three plasma pulses hit the outer hull at the same time.

"Primary drive one is now offline. One more hit like that and we're dead in space, Captain," Perkins said, trying to stay calm.

Jason watched the display. *The Lilly*'s ability for continuous fire of their rail munitions was driving the enemy to shift back.

"Hull breech on one of the enemy ships! They're starting to take damage."

"They're now four hundred miles to our starboard, sir. And the missile original salvo has re-acquired our location. Ten seconds to contact."

"Shift us out of here, Helm!"

"Still waiting to recharge, sir."

"Gunny, blow those missiles away," Jason commanded.

"Aye, sir."

The munitions made quick work of the incoming missiles.

"All incoming missiles destroyed, Captain," Orion said.

"Why fire only six missiles?" Jason said, thinking aloud. "Either those ships don't have the same JIT munitions as we do, or the Craing crew hasn't figured out their ship's capabilities yet."

"They've phase-shifted again, sir. Two hundred miles from

us and they've separated one hundred miles from each other. Incoming! Salvo of eighteen missiles. Six fusion-tipped missiles from each."

Jason smiled. "Gunny, not including Earth, please, and with a ten percent margin either side, I want continuous deployment of rail munitions, all directions incremental at a five percent spread. Do the same with JIT fusion-tipped missiles—again, all directions, incremental at a five percent spread."

Orion hesitated, then smiled, "Aye, sir." The display came alive; blue targeting vectors filled space in all directions. Jason felt the vibration increase through the deck plating.

"The incoming eighteen missile salvo has been destroyed, sir. Our rail munitions are now connecting with the enemy; their shields are holding. Five seconds to missile contact."

"Captain, they've phase-shifted away," McBride said. "There they are, they're three thousand miles out. Now they've phase-shifted again, looks like they're hiding behind the Earth."

"I figured they'd do that," Jason said. "Orion, without interrupting our current deployment, I want three tracking fusion tips with phase-shift capabilities. You remember those, right?" Jason asked. "Allow only these three to deviate and cross over to the area behind Earth. Try not to blow up our planet in the process. Got that?"

"Aye, captain." Orion turned and made the necessary entry selections at her console. "Firing three missiles."

The virtual battle logistics came up on the display. Three red icons moved across space toward Earth, each staying just outside of the ten percent margin. The display changed perspective to show the three Caldurian vessels hiding behind the planet.

"They're firing at the missiles, sir. Our missiles just phase-shifted," Orion said.

Jason waited. First one, and then another of the Caldurian

ships disappeared from view.

"Captain, two the Caldurian ships have been destroyed. The third has taken significant damage to their drives. And all are adrift in space."

With fist pumping and high fives, the bridge exploded with cheers.

"Cease firing, Gunny," Jason commanded.

"Helm, move us to within five hundred miles of that ship. Let's see if they want some help. Open a channel to the Craing commander on board that ship."

"Aye, sir. Channel open," McBride said.

A Craing officer appeared. He was a captain, Jason surmised, evident by the gold medallion worn around his neck.

"I am Captain Reynolds of the Alliance vessel *The Lilly*. Who am I addressing?"

The small alien looked young and unprepared for this. "I am Captain Dolom."

"Prepare to be boarded, Captain. If you comply with our directives, there will be no need for us to destroy your vessel."

"I understand, Captain."

Chapter 36

The Lilly phase-shifted to the Chihuahuan desert, a little more than two miles from the United Planetary Alliance Outpost. Within moments, the shuttle phase-shifted from a mile below the surface into *The Lilly's* flight deck.

Admiral Reynolds had made his way to the bridge. He was eager to speak with Jason; he wanted to discuss this countdown with the nano-tech devices. He could handle the prospect of dying for himself, but not his eight-year-old granddaughter. Orion smiled and welcomed the admiral onboard. The admiral nodded and stood beside the command chair. He hadn't noticed the man sitting in it wasn't Jason. In fact, it didn't appear to be human.

"Welcome aboard, Admiral," Perkins said.

Admiral Reynolds hesitated. The anemic bridge crew was obviously enjoying the surprise exhibited on his face.

"It's me, Admiral. I'm Perkins."

"Perkins?"

"Yes. It was a mishap with the MediPod."

"Perkins, if I came out of the MediPod looking like—"

"Dad!" Jason entered the bridge, brow furrowed. He looked at Perkins, "Perkins, you're relieved. Why don't you grab some chow. Ignore the Admiral's total lack of tact."

"Aye, sir," Perkins said with a forced smile, and left the bridge.

"Damn it! You couldn't warn me?" the admiral asked.

That brought more chuckles. Jason, irritated, signaled his father to follow him. "Ricket is waiting for us in my ready room."

* * *

Jason and the admiral entered the captain's ready room. Ricket, along with Captain Dolom, was seated on the other side of the conference table.

Jason was still speaking to Billy via NanoCom, getting an update on securing the last remaining Caldurian ship.

"Cap, the ship's a mess, drives section is gone and the stern is open to space. We're moving the remaining crew into the shuttle."

"Keep me up to date, Billy."

Still standing, Jason brought his attention back to matters at hand. Looking across at the small alien, he removed his sidearm, sat and slammed the weapon down with far more force than even he had anticipated. "I need to know what, specifically, you were looking for below the surface of our planet. Tell me one lie and I'll shoot you, right now, between the eyes. Do you understand?"

The Craing officer squirmed in his seat. He looked surprised by Jason's fury.

"I will tell you the truth," the Craing officer said. The Lilly A.I. translated as he spoke. "Our directive was simple, to find the *Source*." Seeing Jason's irritation rise, the Craing officer continued. "Recently on my home planet of Terplin, all three of the vessels, the ones you call Caldurian, became active. This caused a great commotion. The hulls of these ships had never been breached. Made of a strange and exotic substance, it was considered impregnable. Over time, the Craing lost interest in them. The ships were secured in an underground vault. Only recently, the ships came alive. Hatchways were released. Access was permitted. The artificial intelligence was fully functional. Over the course of several weeks, we learned of the ship's unique and highly advanced capabilities, many of which were in line with the stories we'd heard of your vessel—this one." Captain Dolom nervously looked around the table, looking for an indication to continue.

"I'll tell you when to stop. Keep going," Jason said.

"Advanced capabilities continued to be found. Medical devices with the ability to heal, even bring individuals back to life. Eventually, we learned of Caldurians using wormholes to traverse the universe. There is nothing more important to the Craing than this capability."

"Probably even more, now that your Loop has been destroyed," the admiral said.

Captain Dolom looked somewhat perplexed at that, but continued, "Specifics to how this capability worked were vague. Wormholes and the bending of space was not new to us. But wormholes that could materialize on demand, take us anywhere, at any time ... that was unimaginable. We learned that it wasn't a function of the Caldurian vessels themselves, so much as an external power emanating from one specific location within the universe. The information was not self-evident and was hard to decipher. But we learned the *Source* would be found here on your planet, four miles below ground. It would be protected by an indigenous people. We learned utilizing the *Source* without compliance or interaction with the indigenous ones would be futile."

Jason had been watching the Craing alien. He had started to slur his words. His hands were shaking.

"What's wrong with you?" Jason asked. "Do you need some water?"

Captain Dolom shook his head.

Ricket looked closer at the Craing sitting next to him. "Did you use medical devices aboard the ship? Did you have devices implanted in your head?"

He nodded. Then swayed in his seat. Tears filled the young

officer's eyes. He looked to Ricket as a child would a parent.

"Help me, please."

He died in his seat. Ricket leaned over and felt for a pulse. Then prodded and probed his limp body.

"Evidently, his nano-device just extinguished itself."

The room went quiet. Jason was being hailed.

"Go for Captain."

Billy was out of breath, and something else. He sounded scared. "Captain, the remaining Craing prisoners from the Caldurian ship—they've all keeled over dead. Strangest thing I've ever seen. They're all dead."

Jason sat back in his chair and looked at the lifeless body of the Craing officer.

To be continued...

Thank you for reading HAB 12. If you enjoyed this book and would like to see the series continue, please leave a review on Amazon. com. To be notified of the soon to be released next Scrapyard Ship book, **Space Vengeance***, contact markwaynemcginnis@gmail.com, Subject Line:* **Space Vengeance List***.*

Acknowledgments

I'd like to thank my wonderful wife, Kim, for (again) providing the loving and supportive space for me to write this book. Thank you to my amazing editors, Lura Lee Genz , Rachel Weaver and Mia Manns-the many hours invested are so very much appreciated. A big thank you also goes to Ryan Knope, for the cool CAD designs of The Lilly, and to Lura Fischer and Drusilla Tieben for their continued support; it really means a lot to me. I'd also like to thank the book's subject matter experts, and others who supported, contributed, and reviewed this book, including James Fischer, Sue Parr, Eric Sundius, and David Brock. They selflessly gave their time to this project. I'd also like to thank the fans of this ongoing saga. I read every one of your many encouraging emails.